the red pill

A NOVEL

Blake Nelson

Post Hill
PRESS

A BOMBARDIER BOOKS BOOK
An Imprint of Post Hill Press
ISBN: 978-1-64293-189-1
ISBN (eBook): 978-1-64293-190-7

The Red Pill:A Novel
© 2019 by Blake Nelson
All Rights Reserved

Cover Design by Cody Corcoran
Author photo by Marne Lucas Photography

Post Hill Press
New York • Nashville
posthillpress.com

Published in the United States of America

PART ONE

April 2016

"Yeah, she's perfect. Now all you gotta do is walk over there and say hi," Rob said to his brother-in-law Martin.

The two men—Rob, 38, Martin, 41—had settled at a table at Café Avignon. Martin sipped his mint tea and frowned. As they'd walked in, he'd made the mistake of mentioning to Rob that a woman seated near the window with her friend was "exactly his type." Now he was screwed. Rob was going to pester him until he talked to her. Martin quietly swore to himself to never again reveal anything to Rob. Or anyone else.

It was dark outside, a damp, rainy evening in Portland, Oregon. The mostly empty café would close soon. Both men sipped their drinks. The two women by the window looked to be in their mid-to-late thirties. The one Martin liked had thick, wavy black hair, pale white skin. Both were typical of this part of downtown: affluent, well-coiffed, though Martin's woman had a definite bookish, bohemian vibe going as well. She wore black TOMS slippers and a cute beige raincoat that looked French, though it was probably J. Crew. On the floor beside her was a Powell's Books tote bag, which was common enough in Portland, but which Martin found encouraging.

Rob pressed Martin: "Hey, you said it yourself, she's exactly what you're looking for."

"Yeah, but I'm not going to walk over there and interrupt their conversation," said Martin.

"Why not? How else are you going to meet her?"

Martin sighed.

"I'm serious," said Rob. "She's right there. This is your chance."

"She's *busy*," grumbled Martin, watching her again. "She's talking to her friend."

"She's in *a café*," said Rob. "They're talking *in a café*. Why do women hang out in cafés? So that men will talk to them."

Martin wasn't so sure about that. He recalled a recent flurry of "unwanted male attention" posts on his Facebook wall. Women pissed off about being catcalled, harassed, spoken to in inappropriate environments. Women did seem to hate being hit on. Women his age did. Or at least they said they did. But that was one of Rob's main selling points for his "be aggressive" strategy with women. Just because a woman says she wants or doesn't want something doesn't mean that is actually the case. It was all part of some vague gender conspiracy Rob claimed to understand and have an insider knowledge of. This being the same Rob who had made it through one year of community college and thought presidential candidate Donald Trump had some "good ideas."

"The longer you wait, the harder it gets," said Rob.

"Yes, I understand that," said Martin.

"What are you going to say?"

"I don't know what I'm going to say," said Martin, tightly. "That's why I'm still sitting here. I'm thinking about it."

"Here's what I would do," Rob told Martin, scooting closer and lowering his voice. "I'd walk over and say, Listen, I'm sorry to bother you, but I told my brother-in-law that you're the exact type of person I'd like to date. And now he won't leave me alone until I ask you for your number."

Martin thought about this.

"That's easy enough, right?" said Rob. "And the best part is, *it's the truth*. Right? Isn't it the truth?"

Martin was forced to nod his head. Yes, it was the truth.

"So that's it," said Rob, sitting back. "That's your opener."

Martin did want to meet the woman. But could he really just walk over there and start talking to her? His whole body roiled with anxiety, fear, panic. This arrangement he'd agreed to, having Rob help him with his dating life, it had been a terrible mistake.

"That's okay," said Rob, leaning back. "Take your time." Rob took a sip of his decaf latte. "You can always go back to the dating sites. Chicks with club feet. Or brain injuries. Or slight mental issues, like they burned down their last boyfriend's house. Chicks who used to be strippers but want to settle down...."

"Okay, okay," said Martin. He gripped his tea mug. His knee bounced under the table.

"Think of it another way," said Rob, leaning forward again. "What if you're the perfect man for her? She's got the Powell's bag. She likes books. And look at them chattering away. She's smart. She's an intellectual. She needs a guy like you, a guy who can talk about that shit. You might be doing her a huge favor."

Martin hadn't thought of it like that. This was possibly true. "But what if she's married?" Martin asked. "What if she's seeing someone?"

Rob moved closer still. "Here's the thing," he said. "She probably *is* married. She might have a boyfriend. She could be *gay*. Your odds here, I'd guess, are ten to one. So that means, it's a ninety percent chance she's gonna shut you down. But you know what? You still have to do it. Because what are your options? It's a ten percent chance if you approach. And a zero percent chance if you don't. That's your situation. Do the math."

"Jesus," murmured Martin.

"It's better odds than the lottery," added Rob. "And people play the lottery."

Rob was right. Rob had been right about a lot of things about women and dating. Martin made the conscious decision to let Rob's words affect him. Maybe he *could* walk over there. He tried to internalize Rob's enthusiasm, his confidence.

"Look at her," whispered Rob. "She's cute...nice face...a certain maturity...probably knows what she's doing in the sack. A woman like that is a valuable commodity...."

Martin nodded that this was probably true.

"Or, if you want, I can do it," offered Rob, lightening his tone. "I'll go over there. I'll tell her you're shy, but you want to ask her out. I'll get the number."

"No, no, no," said Martin. He was almost ready to do this. He really was. He sipped from his lukewarm tea. He tried to think it through, what he would say, how he would say it. But he found his brain was not functioning clearly. He was too scared to think.

"You just gotta do it," said Rob. "Walk over there. Say hi. Ask for her number. And then it's over. Your job is done."

Martin swallowed. Why was he even doing this? Why was he hanging out with Rob, his pickup-driving brother-in-law, getting advice about girls, like he was fourteen years old?

"Here's the thing," breathed Rob. "No matter what happens, if you talk to her, you walk out with your head high. Right? You followed through. You took your shot. It's like jumping off the high dive. You gonna crawl back down the ladder after you stood up there and looked down? Why would you do that to yourself?"

"Because it's a fucking suicide mission?" snapped Martin.

"But it's *not* a fucking suicide mission. That's exactly your problem. You're thinking of it all wrong. What it is, it's just some fucking chick over there, blabbering about nothing to her friend. Probably neither of them gives a shit. Probably they aren't even listening to each other. And they're only here because they want some guy to notice them, and think about them, and be attracted to them. Which you are. And even if she doesn't want that, you know she'll be flattered. And impressed. Because how many people, how many *men*, would even have the balls to go over there and say hi?"

Martin was, to some degree, persuaded by Rob's logic.

"Otherwise it's back to OkCupid," said Rob. "Or some chick from your office, which is also a terrible idea. Meanwhile, the one you like, the one who caught your eye, the one who stopped you in your tracks is *that one*. That chick, who is sitting *right there*."

"Stop calling her a 'chick,'" said Martin.

Rob shrugged. He sat back in his chair. Martin, who had been holding his glass tea mug tightly in his fist, slowly placed it on the table. He waited one beat, then another, then rose to his feet.

Rob watched him.

Martin straightened himself, tugged once on the bottom of his coat, and slowly slalomed his way through the tables and chairs. As he approached the two women he saw that Rob was wrong about them not listening to each other. They were fully engaged in their conversation. To interrupt them would be outrageous and rude.

But he'd do it anyway. Rob had shamed him into it. This was on Rob now. This was his idea.

The women ignored Martin as he approached. They were still talking when he stopped beside their table and stood over them. At that moment, the "friend" was speaking while the "target"—Rob's words—was listening. That was unfortunate timing. But there was nothing to be done.

"Hi," blurted Martin. The word fell tumbling out of his mouth like something thrown out of an airplane.

The friend continued to speak as though Martin wasn't there.

"*Hi*," said Martin again, louder this time.

Without stopping her flow of words, the friend turned her face up toward Martin. The target also turned her attention toward him.

"Excuse me?" said the friend. "Can I help you?"

Martin felt his face flush. But he forced himself forward: "Uh...*hi*," he said for a third time. "My name is Martin...." He was speaking to the table, unable to make eye contact with either of the women.

"I...uh..." he stammered.

"Excuse me?" said the friend. "But we're having a conversation? In case you didn't notice? A *private* conversation?"

This was exactly the response Martin had expected. In a way, it helped him relax. He turned to address his target. He lifted his eyes to her and saw that she was visibly alarmed. She was frightened.

"I wanted to say..." said Martin, trying to keep calm. "I'm with my friend." He turned and pointed at Rob sitting at the table behind him. Rob was leaning back in his chair and casually scrolling on his phone. He didn't look up.

"And I happened to say to him, that *you*...." He focused again on his target, and despite being unable to hold eye contact, forced out the words, "that you were...the kind of woman...I would want to go on a date with."

The two friends looked at each other. Martin managed to raise his eyes and glance at the target's face. She didn't look the same up close as she did from across the room. She wasn't quite as pretty. And now she was blushing. He still liked her though.

"That's very nice," said the friend, forcefully, "but like I said, we're in the middle of something—"

"—I'm married," blurted the target.

"*And* she's married," said the friend.

"Oh," said Martin.

"You know, there's a thing called *online dating*," said the friend. "If you're that desperate."

"I'm not desperate," mumbled Martin. "It's just that... um...."

"Okay, that's enough," insisted the friend. "Thank you. But we're not interested." She waved him away with the back of her hand.

Martin wanted to obey the gesture. He wanted desperately to retreat. But his feet remained where they were. There was one more thing he was supposed to say, and he wanted to say it. He refocused on the target. "Can I have your phone number?"

"No!" said the friend. "Are you crazy? Are you deaf? She just told you she's married! Could you please leave us alone? Or do I have to call the manager!?"

The target had not spoken. Martin, with great effort, raised his gaze to her face. When his eyes met hers she shook her head no. But her face had softened somewhat. Her expression was more pity than fear. And a tiny bit of curiosity.

But it didn't matter, she was definitely shaking her head no.

"Okay, thanks," said Martin, turning quickly away.

"That's right! Gu'bye! Thank you very much!" said the friend to his back. To the target she said in her still raised voice, "Can you believe that? What is wrong with men these days? They're *pathetic!*"

Martin lurched back to the café table. He dropped himself into his chair, facing Rob, his back to the women.

the red pill

Rob continued to stare at his phone. "Well?" he said.

Martin shook his head. He put both his hands over his face for a moment. He let out a long sigh.

"She's looking at you," said Rob.

"Who is?"

"The one you like."

Martin started to turn, then stopped himself.

"That other one though..." said Rob. "She's kinda horrible."

"Yeah. I know."

"But you did it."

"I did it."

"And how do you feel?"

"I feel like I wanna get the fuck outta here."

2

Rob was right about internet dating. It was a ghetto. Martin had never met anyone online who wasn't seriously flawed in some obvious way, a judgment he also applied to himself.

Nevertheless, Martin had a date scheduled for that Thursday and dutifully showed up at the Starbucks downtown, near his office. It was a far less dramatic setting than posh, pretentious Café Avignon. That was another one of Rob's rules: never meet a woman in a Starbucks. Ever. Martin had insisted it didn't make a difference, but as he entered, he realized that it probably did.

Shelby, 36, who had stated in her profile that "life was short, so break the rules," sat at a table, her coffee in front of her, thumb scrolling on her phone. Many of his recent dates did this, Martin had noticed. He would arrive exactly on time and the woman would be waiting, beverage already purchased. Maybe they didn't want to appear flaky. Maybe they were worried about making the man pay.

Martin was happy to pay. This was one of the positives of internet dating, the ease and predictability of the routine. You show up. You introduce yourself. You pay for the coffee drinks, splurging sometimes on a cookie or a croissant to share. Then you sat and made polite conversation for forty-five minutes.

the red pill

Martin actually enjoyed the dull talk, the perfunctory life histories, the bland opinions cautiously presented. Naturally, Rob disapproved of Martin's dating style. Rob referred to it as "gallant man syndrome." Playing the polite, respectful guy. Presenting a fact sheet of your life, as if you were applying for a job. Martin didn't understand what the alternative was. Not talking about your life? What else were you supposed to talk about?

Martin bought a coffee and joined Shelby at her table. They began to talk. It definitely lacked the suspense and adrenaline rush of his "cold approach" at Café Avignon. Martin was still thinking about the woman with the Powell's book bag. He'd decided if he ever saw her again, he would walk right up to her, explain about his pushy brother-in-law, and apologize. It was that sympathetic look she'd given him at the end that made him think she would be receptive to this. Women were generous in that way, Martin knew, despite Rob's misogynist arguments to the contrary. Women had that natural ability to empathize, even with a guy they had no interest in. Even with a guy who had fallen flat on his face right in front of them.

"So, you've always lived in Portland then?" said Shelby.

"Yes," said Martin. "I mean, no. I mean, I grew up here. Then I went back east for college and after that I worked for an advertising agency in New York for ten years. Then I left there and came back home and ended up working with another ad guy I knew, and we eventually started our own agency...."

"You have your own business?" said Shelby, her eyes widening.

"Yeah. I mean, my partner already worked with Pacifica. So we mostly work with them. But yeah...."

Shelby took a sip of her coffee. They both watched a mother maneuver a stroller into place at the table beside them. The mother's hair was badly dyed and frizzed out. Even in this relatively nice part of town, the Starbucks had become a sketchy, borderline homeless hangout.

"I used to work with special-needs kids," said Shelby. "It was such a drain on my energy. And my roommate at the time, she was studying acupuncture and massage therapy. And she really liked it. So then I started doing that, but the school was so expensive, and I started to develop these problems with my wrists, you know, from the massage...."

"Was it carpal tunnel?"

"No, it was something else."

"When I was working in New York, I got that," said Martin. "Carpal tunnel."

"No, it wasn't that."

"I'd literally be on my computer for, like, ten hours a day," Martin said. "I had to get those braces for your wrists. To keep them flat."

"My thing is more my immune system," said Shelby. "And my diet. I did herbal remedies."

Martin nodded. He thought back to his twenties, to his office in New York. One of his coworkers was a Rob type. Always hitting on the girls, making an ass of himself mostly but also sleeping with quite a few of them. The frequent sex was probably nice, but Martin couldn't live like that. It was too much work. Not to mention the drama. And nowadays, you could get fired for just about anything. Still, if you were willing to take the risk, then you got the reward. Girls liked guys like that. That was another one of Rob's rules: women want men who have been with a lot of women.

When they ran out of other topics, Martin and Shelby resorted to the old standby: recapping their various experiences on OkCupid.

"Guys are so funny sometimes," Shelby confided. "They put on this big front, but then you meet them and they're nothing like that."

"Yeah?" said Martin.

"This one guy, he was telling me about his big important job, but when he came to pick me up, his car was like from a junkyard. I had to get in on the driver's side and crawl over, because the door was broken. And the window wouldn't close so you had to wear your coat."

"That doesn't sound good," said Martin.

"And this other guy. He only wanted to go to the café at the Whole Foods. And it turned out, his ex-wife worked there and he was stalking her."

"How did you figure that out?"

"He told me. He said he didn't want to have sex with me, but would I mind coming with him to the Whole Foods?"

"That's weird."

"I didn't want to have sex with him either, but I kinda felt sorry for him. And then I wanted to see who this ex-wife was. That guy had one of those things on his leg. An ankle bracelet. He could only go to certain places that were close to his house because he was on probation."

"Probation for what?"

"I don't know. He wouldn't tell me."

"Wow," said Martin. "That's crazy."

"I know it is. I attract them. That's for sure."

When it was time to go, he walked Shelby out of the Starbucks and then waited until she indicated which way her car was. When she did, he said his car was the other direction. He gave her his usual perfunctory hug and walked away.

Martin always did the perfunctory hug. He wasn't sure where he'd picked that up. People in Portland hugged a lot, in general. To Martin a quick hug gave the interaction a sense of closure. And anyway, it felt good, that little bit of human contact. In a way, he needed it. It kept him going.

3

IT WAS SADIE, Martin's sister, who originally suggested he talk to her husband, Rob. This was about three weeks ago. She and Martin had been sitting in her kitchen.

"So how did things work out with the pet shop woman?" Sadie had asked Martin.

"The pet shop woman?"

"Yeah, you liked her. She had the autistic son?"

"Oh, that. Yeah. Nothing happened."

"That's too bad," said Sadie. She was puttering around the kitchen. Martin sat on a stool, at the kitchen island, drinking a beer.

"It seems odd that you can't find anyone," said Sadie.

"I think it's my attitude," said Martin.

"What's wrong with your attitude?"

"I don't know. If I knew, I'd fix it."

"Are you bitter?" asked Sadie, seriously.

"About what?"

"Your divorce. Or women in general?"

"No," said Martin. "I don't think I am. But then a lot of people probably say that."

Sadie ran a sponge around her sink. "Maybe you should go back to therapy."

Martin drank from his beer. "I'm going on the dates," he said. "I'm putting in the time and effort. I'm not sure what else I can do."

Sadie turned on the faucet and washed her hands.

"You know, Rob had this friend," she said, over the water. "This guy from work. He was divorced. He was having a hard time. Rob kinda helped him out...."

"Helped him out how?"

"When Rob was in his twenties he got into that pickup artist stuff. He and his buddies."

"Oh, right," said Martin. He remembered the pickup artist movement. The leader of it was a tall lanky guy in a fur hat. He taught young men strategies for getting women into bed. It was classic '90s-style hokum. But the guy had got a TV show out of it and built up a substantial brand. Martin couldn't remember his name. It was one word. He'd made a lot of money, whoever he was.

"Anyway, Rob always laughed about it," said Sadie. "But he said it worked, especially for the totally clueless guys. It's mostly common sense stuff: Act confident. Dress better."

"Are you saying I'm totally clueless?"

"*No.*"

Martin sipped his beer. "Like, what would he tell me to do?"

"I don't know. Act confident? Dress better?"

"To act confident, you have to be confident," said Martin, staring at his beer bottle.

"Exactly. That's what I mean. Maybe there's stuff you can do. Maybe Rob would have some ideas."

"I'm too old for that stuff. My bar scene days are over."

"I'm just saying. Why not talk to him? It helped that other guy. I think he eventually got married."

"Really?" said Martin, looking up. "Who'd he marry?"

"I don't know, some woman he met. All I'm saying is, it might be worth a try."

And so Martin had agreed to a meeting with Rob. They went to the Arena Sports Bar in a strip mall near Rob and Sadie's house.

Martin had never discussed anything personal with his brother-in-law. Rob and he had significantly different backgrounds. Rob was a talented carpenter and shrewd operator, in his way. He'd risen quickly from a roofer to his current position as a head foreman at a construction company that built suburban subdivisions around Portland. He'd done well for himself and at thirty-eight drove a gigantic $50,000 luxury pickup. Despite Rob's success, Martin maintained an air of superiority over him, based on being better educated, having lived in bigger cities, having a more interesting job, and not driving a $50,000 luxury pickup.

On the other hand, Rob did have a natural competence and leadership quality that people responded to. Martin could see that he was a person other people would turn to for help.

"So Sadie tells me the dating isn't going so well," began Rob.

Martin nodded. "That's right."

"What seems to be the problem?"

Martin smiled. He couldn't believe he was doing this. But he sucked it up and started talking: "I go on a lot of dates. The women aren't very interesting. They don't seem very interested in me. Nothing happens. Repeat."

"I see," said Rob.

Martin looked around the sports bar. It was medium full. There were several basketball games on the different TV screens. The bar patrons were about eighty percent men.

"So what do you think the problem is?" asked Rob.

"I don't know. I was hoping you could tell me."

"Are these women from dating sites?"

"Mostly. Yeah."

"Like, are *all of them* from dating sites?"

Martin shrugged. "Lately?" he said. "Probably. I guess so. Is that bad?"

"No. Not always. I have a guy who works for me, he's about to marry a gal he met online."

"Yeah?" said Martin, sipping his beer.

"The thing about dating on the internet," said Rob, "it's what they call a *buffer*."

"A buffer," repeated Martin.

"It's a thing that allows you to do something, without actually doing it."

"Okay."

"You know, it's easy to write up a profile. You're sitting there in your basement and you write some crap about yourself. Then some girl, sitting around in her sweatpants, she writes something about herself: 'I live life to the fullest, blah blah.'

the red pill

That night, he sat down at his computer and dug up an email Rob had sent, linking to several pickup artist blogs from the "manosphere." Rob had urged him to read from them, especially posts that discussed how to approach. Martin had dismissed Rob's homework assignment, as he had dismissed everything Rob told him at first. But maybe these blogs were worth a look. He made himself a cup of tea, sat down with his laptop, and began reading.

The material was incomprehensible at first. The specialized lingo and endless acronyms forced Martin to constantly stop and look things up on Urban Dictionary or one of the manosphere glossary sites. But he stuck with it. The basic strategies were fairly obvious. You found a "hot babe" (hotness was rated one to ten), started "running game" (teasing, flirting), and then went for "the number close" (asking for her phone number). You could do this at a bar, a party, or the supermarket, as needed.

The overall key to success with women in general was understanding what they wanted. What they *said* they wanted was a nice guy, who treated them with respect, paid for dinner, was reciprocal in the bedroom. But what they *actually* wanted, according to these bloggers, was an obnoxious asshole who was insanely confident and very good-looking. Very good-looking was the most important. Insanely confident was a close second. Not caring about what women thought about you or anything else (Zero Fucks Given or "ZFG") was also crucially important. Women wanted to be shocked by your arrogance, dazzled by your looks, and intrigued by your indifference. Then they wanted to be banged into next week.

Martin chuckled as he read the different variations on this basic idea. It was a pretty archaic view of women, and of human nature in general. It was basically the cave man theory of dating, which every guy had heard, usually during their sophomore year in high school, and most likely in the parking lot.

The act of "waking up" and accepting these "hard truths" about female sexuality was called "taking the red pill." The red pill concept came from the movie *The Matrix*. Of course, it did. Where else could you expect to find such adolescent wisdom than in a Keanu Reeves movie?

Act like a dick. That was the central idea these guys were selling. Martin smiled to himself. He drank his tea.

Still, Martin was entertained enough to continue his study. He went from blog to blog. One of them, P-Crusher, was quite funny. It chronicled the travels and travails of its rude and crude British author, as he circled the globe hitting on unsuspecting local females. He had helpfully posted audio recordings of some of these encounters, which Martin listened to. The lesson here was that P-Crusher, apparently a renowned figure within the pickup community, was as nervous and awkward as Martin had been with the woman at Café Avignon. Approaching different females in a public square in Melbourne, Australia, P-Crusher stammered, stuttered, repeated himself, said stupid things, and was rejected every single time, just like Martin had been.

the red pill

Martin looked through P-Crusher's archives. He found a short post on "Conquering Approach Anxiety" and another more in-depth essay called "The Zone: The Ultimate Approach Mind-set." Both were interesting and instructive, or would be if Martin ever attempted to pick someone up again, which he probably would not.

On another website, he read a post stressing the idea that women *want* you to approach them. The idea that women were offended by male sexual interest, or that such attention was inappropriate or problematic, was simply a construct of our overly feminized society. Was the girl at the coffee shop too busy curing cancer to talk to a cute guy? No. The truth was that attention from guys was the thing girls wanted most. It just had to be *the right guy*.

Martin went to bed that night with a lot to think about. Women *did* want you to hit on them! This explained that last sympathetic look he'd got from the woman at Café Avignon.

The next morning, at EKO, Martin shut the door to his office and returned immediately to the internet. He spent his whole morning poring over P-Crusher's archives. He also spent time in the comments sections. Particularly helpful were the FRs (field reports) where men would describe different situations, different women, how they approached them, and what results they'd had.

Martin was deep in the comment section of one post when he came upon an unexpected diatribe against "niglets" and American "mudsharks." Martin had seen the term "mudshark" on one of the other blogs and now realized what it meant: a white woman who has sex with a black man.

Martin physically recoiled from his computer. Where had this come from? He scrolled upward and read the comments preceding it. There was nothing there about "mudsharks." The original post hadn't mentioned anything about race. An anonymous commentator had just thrown it out there, apropos of nothing. Martin then remembered seeing something about Jews in one of the other comment threads. He'd skipped over it but went back up to P-Crusher's search slot and typed "Jew." Out it came: anti-Semitic GIFS, rants, cartoon caricatures. Martin was horrified. The cartoon images were especially hard to get his head around. They were so crude, so childish, they belonged in a history book from another time. And yet here they were, *right now*. It was like he'd stumbled on an underground vein of some rudimentary human ugliness. Something he'd never seen, and never wanted to see, and yet it had existed all along, just outside his view, just below his consciousness.

Martin did a search for "nigger." That was worse. There were photos. Mangled bodies, lynching memes. A short video of two black girls beating the crap out of each other in a slum in Chicago. And not all of this was in the comments section. Some of it was in the actual blog. P-Crusher himself had some choice words for the "Kebobs" who were invading his beloved England. In some cases, he appeared to be *inciting* his readers. Martin checked some of the other sites; it was mostly the same.

the red pill

Martin got up from his desk and nervously stood behind his chair. So this was the dirty secret of Rob's manosphere: besides being unscrupulous pursuers of sex, they were also racist, right-wing lunatics. He shut off his computer, but then remembered he was in his office. He quickly turned it back on and frantically cleared the browser history. Only when he was sure all traces of the offensive material were gone could he safely leave the room. He went to the bathroom and washed his hands and face.

Rob called on Saturday afternoon. Martin hesitated at the sight of his brother-in-law's name on his caller ID. But he took the call.

"Hey, buddy, what's up?" said Rob.

"Hey, Rob," Martin answered. He was in his two-bedroom apartment, in the southeast district of downtown Portland. He opened the window shades to reveal the usual gray Portland overcast outside.

"How you doing?" Rob asked. "How did that date go last week?"

"It went okay."

"I got Wednesday night free," said Rob, "if you want to hit that wine bar we were talking about."

For the first time Martin questioned Rob's motivation. What was Rob getting out of this relationship? Was he recruiting Martin into some right-wing cult? "You know,

Rob, I wanted to talk to you about that. I was reading some of those websites you sent me. The P-Crusher website."

"Oh, yeah, P-Crusher. He's great."

"Yeah, well, I was reading along, and I got into the comments. And there was all this racist stuff."

"Oh, yeah," said Rob. "That happens. Just ignore it. You know. It's trolls mostly. There's a lot of trolls."

"Whatever it was, it was kinda scary."

"Just ignore that stuff. That's all you can do."

Martin paused for affect. "I don't know if I can do that, to be honest."

"It's just talk. You can't take it seriously. I mean, it's the internet. The minute people think they can say whatever they want, they come up with the worst shit possible. People are fucked up, what can I say? It doesn't take away from the main message."

"Yeah, but the main message is creepy too," said Martin. He'd been thinking about this all day, the "notch count" stuff, the endless pursuit of "pussy" or "tail" or "snatch." "It's sleazy," he told Rob. "And I don't like it."

"Hey, I see what you're saying," said Rob. "But that's kind of the point. It's reality. I mean, do you want to meet someone or not?"

"But like P-Crusher," said Martin, "he goes to these foreign countries and he spends all day hitting on strange girls. *All day*. Does the guy even have a job?"

"That is his job. He sells books. He does workshops."

"Workshops for who?"

"For guys who want to meet girls."

"You mean for guys who want to *fuck* girls."

"Well, yeah."

"And then dump them and go *fuck* some other girls."

"Sometimes."

"And then P-Crusher goes home and writes about how horrible society is because it's full of sluts and whores and Muslims."

"Hey, I totally understand what you're saying. There's a lot of contradictions in this stuff. Those guys are the first to admit it."

"I can't do it. I'm sorry. I searched the word 'Jew.' You should have seen what came up."

"Oh, yeah. You don't want to do that."

"Well, I did it, and Jesus, I mean, I can't do this. And the stuff against African Americans. I'm sorry. I can't get involved with this kinda thing. And I don't care how many girls these guys sleep with. It's evil."

"It's not *evil*," said Rob. "It's the internet. Hey, you date on it."

Martin didn't speak for a moment. Then in a calm, clear voice he said: "Listen, Rob, I appreciate that you were trying to help me. But I can't have anything to do with this. At all. In any way."

"Hey, if you're not comfortable, I understand."

"And I don't think I can do any more of these *excursions*, or whatever. I'm done. Seriously. I'm gonna have to take a pass on all of this."

"Okay. Yeah. If that's how you feel. I get it, I really do."

After this difficult conversation, Martin collapsed onto his sofa, sat for a minute, and then stood again. He felt anxious and out of sorts. He needed to get out of his apartment. He put on his Pacifica Trail Rider rain parka and walked down the street to the New Seasons supermarket.

Martin immediately felt better to be safely within the store's bright lights and high ceilings. There was no racism at New Seasons. Most of the people who worked there were lesbian, gay, and/or people of color. The food was mostly free trade, organic, and otherwise politically correct in whatever ways food could be. Martin found himself wandering aimlessly for a few minutes before he could actually focus his thoughts. Did he actually need anything here? Yes, some half-and-half for coffee, an onion...salad dressing? Maybe some pugliese bread if they had it. He cruised the aisles, mingling with the citizens of his neighborhood, women with their crafted reusable bags, sparrow tattoos, ethnic jewelry. Men in fleece vests, hair buns, Birkenstocks....

In the refrigerated section, Martin grabbed a pint of half-and-half. On his way back to the front, he picked up an onion, a bag of raw carrots, and some ranch dressing.

Standing in the checkout line, the woman behind him began to unload her basket onto the conveyor belt. Martin watched her. She was attractive, his age approximately, a little more conservatively dressed than the other customers. He wondered if he should try a "cold approach," like he'd been reading about. When she looked up, he smiled at her, but she frowned and looked away.

Martin immediately turned and faced forward. He could feel his face turning red. He dug out his debit card and refocused on the young cashier, a heavyset woman, with giant glasses and a ring through her septum. When it was Martin's turn, she asked him how he was.

"Good, good, now that I've got my dinner," said Martin, indicating the onion, the carrots, and the half-and-half.

The cashier didn't get the joke, which embarrassed Martin even more. Maybe he was getting too old to chat people up at New Seasons. On the other hand, compared to Rob and the P-Crushers of the world, these were his people, his tribe. He needed to like them. He needed them to like him. When the cashier rang up his total, Martin smiled kindly at her, slid his debit card into the slot, and punched in his PIN.

5

A WEEK LATER, Sadie invited Martin over for dinner. She didn't say anything in her email, except that their mother was back from her women's painting retreat at the beach. There was no mention of Rob and Martin's falling out.

Martin arrived at the Carr's right on time, with a six-pack of Bud Light, which was Rob's favorite. His mother, Eileen Harris, was already there. She appeared upbeat, still in artist mode with her unkempt white hair and denim overalls. She was now seventy something...seventy-two? Martin greeted his mother and hugged her.

Soon after, six-year-old Jack appeared from the basement and attacked him. He was the oldest of Rob and Sadie's three kids. Martin was careful not to let the ever-aggressive boy actually hurt him. The last time he visited, the boy had wacked him on the shin with a plastic baseball bat. Martin had limped around for days.

Another child appeared from the basement. "Uncle Martin!" called out Ashley, his four-year-old niece. The girl skipped over to him and pressed her stick-like body against him with surprising strength and sincerity. The youngest, Jed, was somewhere else, in his room possibly. Last to emerge from the basement was Rob, tall and rangy, his meaty hand closing the door behind him. The two men made awkward eye contact for a moment, before quickly looking away.

Martin indulged Jack as best he could, narrowly avoiding being hit in the crotch when Jack started play-punching him in the stomach. Jack always attacked him like this, which worried Martin. Had he somehow signaled to the boy that he was available for abuse? "We teach people how to treat us," Oprah had famously said. Probably Martin needed to show the boy who was boss. "Hey...hey!" he told his nephew, deepening his voice. "If you keep hitting me, I'm going to hit you back."

"You can't hit me back!" cried Jack, hitting him harder.

Martin grabbed the kid by the shoulders, roughly spun him around, and then pinned his arms to his sides in a firm grip. He lifted Little Jack off the ground a few times, but this only made Jack scream and kick and struggle more. Now Martin was really in danger of getting injured. Rob, seeing Martin's predicament, took the boy away.

"Stop bothering people, Jack," he said, firmly removing him from Martin's presence.

"Dad-dy!!!" shrieked Jack.

"Go! Get out of here!" commanded Rob. "Down to the basement! Put away your Legos!"

Martin looked to Rob, to thank him, but Rob continued to avoid eye contact.

Dinner was grilled chicken, spinach salad, and small red potatoes that mushed easily, and were creamy and delicious.

Eileen told everyone about her painting retreat at the coast. There were apparently some issues among the elderly artists of who got which cabins. People had tried to claim seniority, having been to the retreat before. Other people simply took the best bunks without asking. Eileen had got stuck in the worst cabin, where there had been snoring and some flatulence.

"We saw one of your commercials, Uncle Martin," declared four-year-old Ashley.

"Which one was that?" Martin asked.

"Captain Obvious!" she said.

"Unfortunately, that isn't one of ours," said Martin.

"I like Captain Obvious," said Ashley.

"Captain Obvious is a dork!" said Jack loudly.

"He's funny," said Ashley, holding her fork against her cheek.

"What product does Captain Obvious endorse?" asked their mother.

"I don't know," said Ashley, losing interest in the subject.

Jed was at the table too. He was approaching two years old and tended not to speak. He had done something with one of his red potatoes, causing it to roll across the table and onto the floor where the dog, Pete, was waiting. Pete swallowed it in one bite.

"Mommy!" said Jed.

"You gotta keep it on your plate there, buddy," said Rob.

Everyone ate. Despite the awkwardness between himself and Rob, Martin always enjoyed being with the Carrs, especially eating dinner in their bright, well-appointed dining room. The sights, sounds, and smells of a genuine family gathering, Martin not only enjoyed the activity personally, but kept an eye out for the small details of family life that could be useful to him in future advertising campaigns.

Rob was the most efficient eater of the group, Martin noted. He halved his grilled chicken strips with the edge of his fork and dispatched them quickly into his mouth. Martin, who'd always been finicky with food, took his time. The children were having trouble getting anything at all into their mouths. Jack especially was mostly stabbing at and moving his food around the plate.

"Captain Obvious is what they call a *spokesman*," said Martin, in the silence.

The kids weren't listening, but Martin continued. "A spokesman is an interesting person, or a character, like on a TV show. And once you have a good character, you can create different stories around them."

"Why do they call him Captain Obvious?" said Ashley.

"Because everything he does is *obvious*," said Jack, with a sneer.

"That's right, Jack. Good call, buddy," said Rob.

"He's also kind of stupid, which makes him funny," added Martin.

"Jed is kind of *stoopid*," said Jack.

Jed did not defend himself. He was busy trying to spear one of his round potatoes onto his fork by bracing the fork against the table and pushing the potato down onto its prongs.

"Do you guys know who Flo is?" Martin asked the kids.

They didn't.

"She's the woman dressed in white, from Progressive Insurance?"

The kids had lost interest.

"Anyway, if you're making a commercial," said Martin, "you always want to have a central character who people will remember. And who is funny or interesting in some way."

"Funny *looking*," said Jack to himself.

"I like Captain Obvious," said Ashley. "I wish we had a cat. Then we could call him that."

"We have a cat, honey," said her mother.

"I mean another cat, that we could name!" said Ashley.

Martin addressed Jack directly. "Do you have any people in your class who are always making jokes? Like the class clown?"

Jack didn't answer.

"Because those kind of people," said Martin, "even if they don't get good grades, when they grow up, they can go into advertising. Because they're funny."

"Can we get another cat?" Ashley asked her mother.

"Jed!" said Rob. But it was too late. Jed had stabbed himself in the hand with his fork and begun to cry. And, of course, another potato had rolled off the table and into the mouth of Pete.

Later, while the kids scattered elsewhere, the adults remained at the dinner table. Sadie, Martin, and their mother were on one side looking at photos of Eileen's painting retreat on her iPhone. Martin followed along on this photo tour for as long as he could. He finally retreated to the kitchen, got himself a Bud Light, and took a seat on the other end of the table where Rob was.

So there they were.

Martin took a long drag off his beer. Rob did the same. They had not spoken since they had talked on the phone. Martin had said nothing to anyone about the offensive content on the websites Rob had recommended. Martin would keep that to himself.

"Did you catch the Blazer game last night?" Martin asked Rob.

"Yeah, a bit of it."

They both sipped their beers.

"Mother, you painted that?" said Sadie, at the other end of the table. "That's beautiful!"

The men remained where they were. "Yeah, I thought the Blazers had that," said Martin. "But their defense. They can't stop anyone."

"Yeah," said Rob. "They've been doing that all year."

Rob was leaning back in his chair, like he had the night they were at Café Avignon.

Martin tried to think of something else to talk to Rob about. What else was there?

"Been fishing lately?"

"Nah," said Rob. "Been too cold."

"Yeah, weirdly cold for April."

"Neighbor said his pipes nearly froze," said Rob.

"Yeah," said Martin. "It's gotta be pretty cold to freeze your pipes. That's the good thing about renting."

"Better to own," said Rob, a sentiment he often expressed. "Renting, you're paying someone else's mortgage."

Martin said nothing. He was glad to rent. No worries. No problems. And when you figured in the countless hassles and expenses of owning a place....

"Listen," said Rob, quietly clearing his throat and setting the front legs of his chair down on the floor. "I'm sorry for sending you to those sites on the internet."

"Nah. Don't worry about it," said Martin, also lowering his voice. "It's no big deal. Weird shit on the internet."

"I don't want you to think I'm into that stuff."

"Nah, of course not."

They both sipped their beers. Martin watched his mother, scrolling through her pictures.

Rob leaned back in his chair again. "Yeah, so Little Jack's got tryouts for tee ball this year."

"Yeah? What position will he play?"

"I don't know if they have positions at that stage. Probably they just rotate everyone around."

"Sure," said Martin. "Give everyone a chance."

"I saw they got rid of Pee Wee football though. Banned by the state. Too dangerous, I guess."

"Yeah," said Martin. "Concussions. That's a big thing now."

"Too bad. I mean, whatever. All the kids around here play soccer anyway."

"Yeah, soccer's big now," said Martin.

the red pill

"It's a physical game too, in its way."

"You gotta be in great shape," said Martin. "Those guys run for hours."

When it was time to go, Martin felt like it had been a productive evening. His mother was in good spirits. Things had been somewhat normalized with Rob. Everyone said good-bye at the door. The children were called and things got complicated with a lot of hugs and some punching to avoid. Martin made sure to look Rob square in the face at one point, but Rob pretended not to see. Whatever. Martin had done his best. He walked down the driveway, got in his Audi A4, and drove away.

Heading back into town, Martin wasn't quite ready to go home and headed instead to Powell's Books. He parked and went inside. The studious quiet of the place at the late hour was comforting and calming as usual. He wandered among the tall rows of literary fiction, letting his eyes bounce along the titles and names and book covers. When he came around a corner, a familiar face appeared.

It was her. The woman from Café Avignon. The married woman.

Martin balked and averted his eyes. He turned quickly toward the bookshelf beside him. His instinct was to walk away, but he found he couldn't. Though they barely knew each other, one thing had been established between himself and this woman: Martin didn't flee.

And so he didn't.

"It's you…" she said. "From the café."

"Yeah," said Martin, daring to turn toward her and finding that it wasn't so difficult. He had rehearsed what he might say if he saw her again but now he said nothing. Instead, he watched her face, enjoying the bemusement, the embarrassment, the mutual surprise and pleasant excitement that vibrated between them.

"I have to tell you something," she said quickly.

"What's that?"

"I'm not married."

"You're not?"

"I know. It's weird. I'm not sure why I said that. It just popped out. You caught us by surprise."

Martin watched her.

"It was because of Gina, my friend," said the woman. "She was being so…. She gets like that sometimes. I guess I was trying to defuse the situation. And give you an easy out."

"Oh," said Martin. "Thank you."

"I felt bad for you. The way you came up to us like that. Do you always do that to strange women?"

"No," said Martin. "I never do that."

"Because I just…well…the both of us, we were caught off guard."

"Sorry about that."

"No. It's okay. It was funny…. I'm Rebecca, by the way."

"I'm Martin."

They smiled at each other, then awkwardly shook hands.

"What have you got there?" said Martin, pointing at the books in her arms.

"Oh, nothing much..." said Rebecca. "Some stuff for a class."

"You're a teacher?"

"I'm an adjunct, up at PSU. We're doing *Middlemarch* this term."

Martin nodded his approval. "I remember *Middlemarch*. That's a classic."

"Yeah. Hopefully the students will actually read it...."

"Would you like to get a drink sometime?" asked Martin. It was like a different person speaking when he said this. The clarity, the calm, the smoothness.

"Oh. Um. Like...when?"

"How about Wednesday?"

"I mean...I don't know.... I guess I could. I'd have to check my schedule."

"Why don't you give me your number and I'll text you," said Martin. It was like he was a robot. Or someone in a film. Someone who knew exactly what to do and did it.

6

THE AFTERNOON BEFORE his date with Rebecca, Martin sat in his office at EKO, flipping a pen around on his desk and staring out his window. He felt an uncomfortable compulsion to call Rob. For what, though? Last-minute tips? A pep talk? He didn't need those. He knew how to go on a date. He especially knew how to go on a date with an adjunct professor of English lit. Martin had been an English major himself. This wouldn't just be easy; it would be fun.

The other fun thing: Rebecca was hot. She knew how to dress. She had beautiful eyes. Rob had definitely been right about that, the casual indifference of a Tinder date versus someone you actually *wanted* to go out with, someone you had picked out of a crowd. He had forgotten how exciting and nerve racking that feeling could be.

Dylan, one of the agency's younger guys, happened to walk by his office at that moment. "Hey! Dylan!" called Martin when he saw him pass by.

"Wudup?" said Dylan, sticking his head in the door.

"Dude, I got a date tonight," said Martin.

"No shit," the younger man said. He came into the office and closed the door. He took a seat on the small couch across from Martin's desk. "Anyone I know?"

"Nah," said Martin, grinning. "Some woman I met in a coffee shop."

"Oh yeah? She hot?"

"Yeah. She kinda is. I first saw her at this coffee shop.... Anyway, it's a long story. But I saw her again and I got her number."

"No shit? Way to go...."

"I know. I'm not usually so bold," said Martin.

"That's what you gotta do," said Dylan. "Go after what you want."

Martin smiled to himself. "She's an English professor at PSU. An adjunct."

"That's awesome. She'll be smart. How old is she?"

"Thirties, late thirties?"

"Okay," Dylan said and nodded. "Perfect."

"Yeah, I'm psyched. The thing is: I'm fucking nervous!"

"That's okay. It'll be fun. Have a couple drinks. Don't sweat it."

Martin thought about this. "Yeah, that's good advice. Have a couple drinks."

"The thing I always tell myself?" said Dylan. "They're nervous too! So, whatever."

"Yeah," said Martin.

"If they like you, you can't really fuck it up, right? I mean, it's a matter of getting through it, moving past the awkwardness."

"Right, right," said Martin.

"So what's the date?"

"Drinks," said Martin.

"Perfect. That's the exact right thing to do."

"I don't want to get too drunk. I might drink too much if I'm nervous."

"Nah, go ahead. Get a little drunk. Just don't make an ass of yourself. Get her drunk."

"Really?"

"Why not?" said Dylan. "I mean, if she wants. Whatever. Roll with it. See how it feels."

"Yeah."

Dylan checked his watch. "Hey, I gotta drive out to Beaverton. But, dude, sounds like you scored on this one. Good luck, man. You're gonna kill it. *Slay-ah!*"

With that Dylan bounced out of the chair and out the door.

⊙

For lunch Martin left the building and walked downhill to a sushi place he liked. Generally, Martin preferred to eat lunch alone, and today especially, he needed time to think about his date. What would he tell Rebecca about himself? At the restaurant, a strange sadness came over him. He spent an awful lot of time alone, was the truth about his life. How was he going to explain that exactly?

Not that he was so unusual. A lot of people were like that now. He'd just read an article about it in *Advertising Inc.* "Atomization and the Consumer" was the title. It was the usual stuff: how Americans were becoming increasingly separate and solitary, with their phones and their single apartments and their isolated pod cars. This was good for the economy, it turned out. Two people who were single consumed more than two people who lived together and pooled their resources. Paying rent by yourself, eating alone in restaurants, buying frying pans or laundry detergent or vacation packages by yourself: this was the costliest way to exist in the world. Plus, you were more vulnerable to advertising when you were alone. Who else was talking to you except your TV? And since most people still wanted a partner, or thought they did, it also kept the pressure on to constantly pay to improve yourself, to buy products that made you more desirable. It was a depressing scenario, overall, but good for business, if you were in advertising.

When he was done with his sushi, he took the long way back to his office, enjoying the mild Oregon weather. It was May now, and there was a warm wetness in the air. He thought about Rebecca, the panicked look on her face at Café Avignon, and how different she appeared at Powell's. She seemed *impressed* by Martin then. Rob had been right about that: women understood how hard it was for a man to approach them. They respected that courage. No matter what else happened, if you dared to speak to a woman in a confident and forward way, they were going to remember you. They might not *like* you, but that didn't matter. You gained their respect by risking their rejection.

Standing at a corner, waiting for the WALK signal, a young woman appeared beside Martin. He glanced at her once. She looked college aged. She wore an interesting vintage toggle coat. She was too young for Martin, but there she was, a single female, beautiful in her youth, walking down the street. As a young man, how many times had he seen such a woman and thought, *too bad I can't talk to her*, when, in fact, he could have talked to her. He could have said hi, and just started talking, P-Crusher style. Think of what Martin had missed out on, not understanding the possibilities of the "cold approach." Knowing about such a thing would have been useful information twenty years ago.

Back in his office, Martin spent a few minutes going over a production budget. But with his date with Rebecca looming ever closer, he found it impossible to concentrate. He imagined the initial meeting, what he might talk to her about. Obviously, the English lit stuff would be a good start. Since her class was reading *Middlemarch*, he googled the novel and read some of the plot summary. *This will be fun*, he assured himself. Talking about books with an attractive woman, what's not to like? She was very good-looking. He had seen that at Powell's. And she had a nice body, from what he had seen. Jesus, what if this lead to something? A real girlfriend? A wife even? Martin swooned slightly in his seat, at the thought of it.

He refocused on the project budget for a few more minutes and then stared out his window. Then he reached for his cell phone and called Rob.

The phone answered after two rings. "Hello," said Rob in his deep, professional voice.

"Rob, hey, it's Martin."

the red pill

"Hey, buddy," said Rob.

"Hey. You gotta second?"

"Yeah, sure, what's up?"

"Well, um, you'll never believe what happened. I ran into that woman again. The woman from Café Avignon. The one I talked to."

"No kidding."

"She was at Powell's of all places."

"Right. She had the Powell's bag."

"Yeah, exactly. So I saw her there. And I kinda asked her out for a drink."

"Wow. That's great."

"So yeah, so I asked her out, and she said yes, and now I'm like…I'm meeting her tonight. And I'm a little nervous."

"Yeah, sure you are."

"The thing is…I sorta…I feel like I'm in foreign territory here. And I was wondering if you had any words of wisdom."

"Huh. Okay. Well, I'm not sure what to tell you."

"Because like the way I met her. It was so unusual. I don't know how to follow up on it. If that makes sense."

"No. Sure. Of course, it does. As for what to do, I guess the main thing is, try to be cool. Not like *sunglasses* cool. But just, you know, let her do the talking. And don't be too into it. Even if you are. It's always good to hold back a little."

"Okay. Hold back."

"So when you saw her, what'd she say?"

"The first thing she said was she wasn't married."

"No shit. That's funny."

"Yeah, it was."

"The gods are looking out for you, my man. Fortune favors the bold."

"I guess so. If I don't blow it tonight."

"Hey, don't think like that. Even if it doesn't work out, it's all good. This is practice. You're learning how to do this."

"I'm a little late to be practicing, at *forty-one*."

"Hey, no disgrace in that. And be positive. Don't put yourself down."

"Okay."

"No, seriously, when you're around her, no self-deprecating humor. Like what you just said. About being forty-one."

"Okay," said Martin, a little surprised that Rob even knew the word "self-deprecating."

"Do women not like that?" asked Martin.

"No, they don't. And it's a bad habit. Don't do it."

"But women like it when you're funny...."

"Not in that way they don't."

"Okay. Okay," said Martin. This was like the anti-Star-bucks stuff. Rob and his rules. As if women were farm animals and could be led around by simple manipulations of language.

"And *outcome independence*," said Rob. "You don't care what happens. That's key. This is practice. You're just starting."

"It's not like I've never been on a date before."

"Trust me. You're just starting."

"Okay. Okay."

There was some sort of loud machine noise on Rob's end. "Listen, they need me here. But that's it. Don't talk too much. Listen to her. Keep your cool. And don't pay for her drink. All right. Gotta go. Good luck!"

the red pill

"Okay, thanks Rob," said Martin, as the connection ended.

Martin placed his phone on his desk and stared out the window. He mulled over his brother-in-law's advice. It all sounded good, except for the part at the end, about not paying for her drink. Had Rob been serious? What kind of person wouldn't pay for her drink? That didn't even make sense.

7

MARTIN ARRIVED DOWNTOWN at 8:15. He had agonized for days over where to meet Rebecca and had eventually picked the Sevens Hotel bar after reading an online article entitled "Portland's Top Romantic Spots for People over Forty." The Sevens Hotel bar was their number two choice. They called it a "splurge." An accompanying picture showed two attractive well-dressed Portlanders, with champagne flutes, snuggled against an outdoor railing on a summer evening.

Unfortunately, it was raining when Martin parked several blocks from the Sevens Hotel. As he walked through the wet streets, he reassured himself that this was a good idea. Hotel bars were classy; they were adult. And the Sevens was the hot new hotel that everybody talked about.

He entered through the main door. The insides were predictably pretentious: minimal industrial-style lobby, glowing plastic white walls, the chilly reception desk with the two well-groomed young men behind it. Somewhere a low electro-beat throbbed. Obvious as it was, the interior design made Martin feel shabby and middle-aged in his wet shoes and rain parka. Martin politely asked where the hotel bar was. He was directed to the elevator. Inside, and faced with a row of buttons, he was reminded that the bar was on the roof.

the red pill

That was the moment Martin felt his first flush of cold, hard fear. He'd maybe not done this right. This was going to be too fancy. *Don't be too into it*, Rob had advised.

The elevator doors opened and Martin stepped into an empty nightclub-style bar, which would have been fine except that there was not a single human being in sight. Martin walked stiffly forward to the stainless-steel bar. He glanced around the empty room and spotted the bartender, another meticulously dressed young man, who was drying glasses. Martin continued forward and reluctantly took a seat at the bar. A reggae beat played quietly on the stereo. It wasn't too loud at least. Martin removed his Pacifica rain parka and slung it over the back of his chair. His feet were wet from the walk. He had insisted on wearing his new Adidas, instead of the L.L. Bean "duck shoes" he usually wore on rainy nights. Once Rebecca got here, he wouldn't be thinking about that. But for the moment, he felt damp, cold, uncool, and unprepared for what was coming.

"What can I get you?" asked the expressionless bartender. He placed a single square napkin in front of Martin on the cold, stainless-steel bar.

"I'll have..." began Martin, feeling that nagging fear in his chest again.

The bartender, who looked like a male model of the "rugged" type, stood over him, an impatience showing in his face.

"You know what?" said Martin. "I'm waiting for someone. Maybe I'll hold off and wait for her."

The bartender's expression did not change.

"Maybe a glass of water?" Martin croaked. "Until she gets here?"

A glass of water appeared. Martin got out his phone. It was 8:27. The date was for 8:30. There were no messages from Rebecca, except for her confirmation of when and where to meet from two days ago.

Martin put his phone away. He sipped the glass of water. He looked around the room. Behind him were large glass windows, or maybe they were sliding doors, that led to the roof of the Sevens Hotel. This was the spot the online article had featured, where you could see the stars and all of downtown Portland spread out before you, while sipping champagne.

Deciding that the bartender wouldn't mind, Martin slid off his stool and walked over to the sliding glass doors. It would probably be nice here on a warm summer evening, with all these doors open. Martin walked around to the other side of the bar where, from inside, you could see down onto Pioneer Square, Portland's central public space. It was a nice view despite the rain-blurred glass. Maybe this wasn't such a bad choice. Maybe Rebecca would think it was okay. Whatever. He was practicing, according to Rob. He needed to remember that tonight.

the red pill

Because the bar was so empty and quiet, Martin heard the quiet ding of the elevator when it opened at 8:41. There she was, Rebecca, looking a little lost, a little confused. Martin hurried over to her from the other side of the bar.

"Hi!" he gushed.

"Hi," she said smiling. She looked great. A cute dress, an elegant overcoat. She had makeup on. Lipstick. Her hair was silky clean and hung loosely around her shoulders.

"You look great," said Martin, not quite in control of himself as he beheld the most attractive woman he'd been on a date with since college.

"Oh," she said back, batting her eyelashes for a moment. "I was kind of lost. I didn't know there was a bar here."

"Yeah, it's kinda dead," Martin said. "Someone said it was good though. So I thought it might be worth a try."

"No one's here," she said.

"Well, yeah, we can still get a drink though. Unless you want to go somewhere else."

Rebecca looked around at the empty room. "No, this is okay. It's a little cold."

"It is a little cold. It's actually the roof. See those windows? I think it's probably more for summer."

"Yeah," said Rebecca, looking around. "I guess this is okay."

"We might as well," said Martin, leading her to where his coat hung over the back of the chair. She took her time removing her coat, putting her bag on the bar, and arranging herself. The handsome bartender appeared, which cheered her somewhat. Martin climbed up onto his stool.

Rebecca had to check something on her phone and so for a second both Martin and the bartender found themselves waiting for her. When she realized this, she told Martin to go ahead and order. Martin was given a list of Hotel Sevens' special cocktail menu. Martin perused the cutesy names of the drinks, also noticing how wildly expensive they were. It didn't matter. He had plenty of money.

The bartender went away. Rebecca studied the drinks. Martin did too, saying to her, "These sound kind of lame."

"I just want a sidecar," said Rebecca. "They must have that."

"I'm sure they do," said Martin. "I'll get a vodka tonic." Martin had learned this in New York. The always-safe drink order was a vodka tonic. It sounded cool, they couldn't fuck it up, and if you were nervous or afraid, it gave you a chance to sound decisive.

Rebecca continued to study the drink menu. "But some of these do sound interesting...."

"The bartender is good-looking anyway," said Martin, trying to make a joke.

"Is he?"

Martin changed the subject. "It's weird how empty it is. The hotel, I mean. I wonder if the Sevens is making any money. Maybe it's too sophisticated for its own good."

"I don't know," said Rebecca looking around. "I sort of like it. I mean, it's kinda dead tonight though...."

"Yeah, no..." said Martin. "I think Portland needs more places like this." He didn't actually believe that and wasn't sure why he said it.

The bartender returned. He did not speak but stood over them.

"Can you make a sidecar?" asked Rebecca.

"Of course," he said.

"And I'll have a vodka tonic," said Martin.

The two of them continued to settle themselves as the bartender made the drinks. They made small talk. Martin found himself talking about a recent news item involving Pacifica, the giant sportswear company his small agency did most of their business with. Their workers in Vietnam were protesting. It wasn't terribly interesting.

When the drinks came, the bartender stared at Martin, who obediently dug his wallet out of his back pocket. He found his credit card and handed it over.

"Do you want to start a tab, sir?" asked the man.

"Uh...yeah, sure," said Martin.

The bartender took the card and walked to the other end of the bar.

"Thanks for the drink," said Rebecca, smiling.

"My pleasure," said Martin, stuffing his wallet a little too forcefully back into his pocket. "That's funny," he said. "A guy at work was saying he didn't pay for his date's drinks when he went out. And we were like, what? Like who doesn't pay for their date's drink?"

"Some people don't," said Rebecca. "But it's a nice thing to do, I think."

"I mean, if you ask someone out for a drink..." reasoned Martin. He was speaking too quickly but he couldn't seem to stop. "And, like, if you're the man. I mean, not that the man always has to pay…."

"It's just nice," said Rebecca. It was clear she didn't need to hear all of Martin's thoughts on this subject.

And yet Martin couldn't resist saying one more thing: "It seems like an asshole move. That's all. Like, if you're the person who asked, and you picked the place, you don't leave the other person in the lurch like that. I mean, I guess that's kind of sexist in some ways. But it's not like you gave the person a choice."

Rebecca didn't respond. She sipped her sidecar through her straw. Martin forced himself to shut up, and did the same. The vodka and tonic tasted sweet and soothing, especially after he'd drank half of it. Dylan had been right about that. Alcohol was the key to a high-pressure first date.

Ninety minutes later, after what Martin considered a decent conversation—though it included no English literature—Martin and Rebecca climbed off their chairs and walked into the elevator together.

By that time the bar had a half-dozen customers and downstairs a small crowd was milling around in the lobby. Martin, after two vodka tonics, let Rebecca lead the way out of the elevator. Pleasantly buzzed, he glanced around at the Sevens staff and their guests.

Outside, it was raining and he and Rebecca huddled for a moment under the awning. It wasn't as much of a huddle as

Martin would have preferred; he had not physically touched Rebecca yet. It wasn't that he expected a good-night kiss, but to not have touched her at all would not be good.

"I'm parked up the street at the Smart Park," said Rebecca.

"Okay," Martin said, nodding. For the first time that night, he began to find himself, to feel comfortable. Maybe it was the cold, or the wetness in the air, or maybe the alcohol. He felt something come into his posture and his tone of voice, a confidence, a feeling of control.

Still, he had no idea if Rebecca wanted to kiss him. How had she done that? Left him so up in the air like this? She seemed to like him. She seemed to enjoy talking to him. But here at the critical moment, he had no idea what she was thinking.

Fortunately, he was drunk. So he went for it. He touched her shoulder, stepped in front of her, and went for the kiss.

It didn't work. His mouth ended up on her cheek. He was going for a hug too and messed that up as well. It was pretty much a fail all around. In any event, a few seconds later, she was gone and he was walking through the rain, along the wet street, to where his car was parked.

8

HE HAD HER…. He fucking had her…!

Martin sat in the passenger seat of his sister Sadie's minivan. It was Saturday and they were running errands. Sadie was inside the Country Village Bakery getting a birthday cake for Jack. *Rebecca liked him. She gave him her number. She wanted to go out with him. How had he blown it so badly?*

One particular moment stuck in his head. About thirty minutes after Rebecca had arrived, the bartender had wandered away, and then suddenly the music got louder. The bar had still been empty, but suddenly the music was blaring from speakers right over their heads. Rebecca had looked around. Martin did too, thinking it would be his responsibility to locate the bartender and ask him to turn it down.

But the bartender had disappeared, leaving the two of them alone in the cold, empty room, at the cold, metallic bar. Martin and Rebecca had had no choice but to continue their conversation with raised voices. Eventually, when some other customers showed up, the bartender reappeared, but by then it seemed too late to say anything and Martin had let it go. Still though. The loud music. The negligent bartender. The ridiculous Sevens Hotel. Jesus. Why didn't he take her to a normal bar? Or some cozy neighborhood wine place?

She had looked so good. She had dressed up for him. She had worn *lipstick*. And by the end she wouldn't even kiss him! That's how badly he had fucked up.

He had disappointed her. That was the truth of it. It was terrible to contemplate. Well, Jesus, what did women want? What was he supposed to do? Okay, so obviously the hotel bar was a mistake; it had set the wrong tone. But was it a total date killer? Couldn't she forgive him for that one mistake?

Apparently not. That was the lesson in Martin's mind: *Don't try to be something you aren't*. Go somewhere you would normally go. *The Sevens*. Jesus. What was he thinking? And what was he doing reading articles about "hot dating spots for people over forty"? He was forty-*one*, not sixty! It was like a switch had gone off in his head. The stupid switch. He literally could not have picked a worse place.

Sadie came out of the Village Bakery with a large pink box. Jack was turning seven the next day; this was his birthday cake. Martin distractedly watched his sister approach the van and then struggle for a moment to open the sliding side door. Belatedly, he realized she needed help. He hopped up from his seat and opened the door for her.

Their next stop was picking up an extra coffee maker and some other party supplies from Sadie's friend Libby, who lived with her husband and infant daughter nearby. Sadie pulled into Libby's driveway. The house was not big enough to be considered a McMansion, but it was the same idea: new, clean, exactly like the houses lined up beside it.

Libby let them in. Her young child was asleep somewhere, so the initial conversation was conducted in whisper voices. Sadie and Libby embraced and made quiet female sounds. Martin, who had met Libby before, smiled and offered his hand. She rejected it and gave him an enthusiastic hug as well. The three of them went into the kitchen, petite, excitable Libby patting around in her bare feet.

"Do you guys want coffee?" she said.

"No, no," said Sadie. "We don't want to take up your whole afternoon."

"Oh, my God, you're not. Please stay. I'm so glad to have Delilah asleep. Please, do a girl a favor and keep me company."

Sadie looked at Martin. Martin was not against hanging out. Libby, thrilled, hurriedly loaded up the coffee maker and then busied herself finding coffee cups, soy milk, various forms of sweeteners.

They settled on stools around Libby's kitchen island.

"So how's Kevin doing?" asked Sadie.

"He's in Tacoma this weekend, at a conference," she said. "So I'm here with Del." She turned to Martin: "That's my daughter, Delilah, who is mercifully asleep at the moment."

"How is Del?" said Sadie. "Can we see her?"

"Good God, no, she's finally asleep. When you leave maybe. How are you guys? Martin, I haven't seen you in ages."

"I'm good," said Martin.

"Yeah, so I'm here all alone for the weekend," said Libby. "But I'm definitely coming to Jack's party tomorrow. My mom said she could babysit, so I'll get a break for that."

"I think we invited too many people," said Sadie. "I'm a little concerned."

"Did you get your cake from Country Village?"

"Of course," said Sadie. "Marianne said she baked it herself."

"Oh, my God, I love Marianne. She's *amazing*."

"Isn't she, though?" said Sadie. "And so helpful."

Libby poured everyone coffee. She sat across from them at the island and drank from hers. She was clearly relieved to have people over. Martin felt bad for her. This was the part of marriage he never got to. The babies and the infant children, how cute they were, but how exhausted and desperately tired and bored everyone got. And the women, they definitely got the worst of it. No doubt Kevin, Libby's husband, was happy to be away. The one time they'd met, Kevin had seemed a little short-fused for the fathering business. That was Martin's impression. Kevin was one of those rage-y guys you gave a little extra space to.

Libby turned to Martin: "And how's the advertising business going, Mr. Boss Man!"

Martin smiled. "Good. Really good. There's talk we might sell EKO to Pacifica. That's what my partner wants to do."

"You're going to sell your business? Is that a good thing?"

"I think so," said Martin.

"It is," Sadie interjected. "It's a very good thing."

"What does it mean?"

"What do you think it means?" Sadie laughed. "When Pacifica wants to buy you out, they don't mess around!"

Libby did a funny bit for Martin, suddenly acting flirty and starstruck. "So you're gonna be *rich*?"

"Well, I wouldn't say *rich*," said Martin

Sadie shook her head. "Don't listen to him. They'll do very well if Pacifica buys them out."

"Will you still work there?" said Libby, with genuine interest.

"That's the plan. It's not so much a buyout as a 'folding in.'"

"That must be *so* interesting," mused Libby. "To deal with a company like Pacifica in that way. You don't work for Pacifica. You work *with* Pacifica."

"It's very exciting," said Sadie, looking proudly at her brother. "Even if they don't do it, that Pacifica would consider it."

"I wish Kevin would do something like that," said Libby, still looking at Martin. "Break out and do something on his own. Working for someone, making a salary, that same boring number every two weeks. You're so at the mercy of everyone else. And the way the world works these days, you never get ahead."

"Well, at least you have health insurance," said Sadie.

Libby gasped. "Do you and Rob not have health insurance?"

"No! Of course, we do," said Sadie. "We have great health insurance. But in general."

"You know, Jen and Wyatt lost theirs," whispered Libby.

"Oh, my God," said Sadie. "And with three kids!"

"I know," said Libby. "And now Jen's totally freaking out."

"The premiums," said Martin. "They went through the roof this year."

"That's terrible," Sadie to Libby.

"Like, what if you had a little business," said Martin. "That kinda increase would kill you." He looked at Libby for affirmation. She gave it, totally, smiling at him in complete agreement. She then continued to gaze into his face. Martin had to look away.

The two women moved onto other subjects: mutual friends, their children. Martin sipped his coffee. He glanced surreptitiously at Libby. She was "the nutty friend," among Sadie and Rob's circle: long, mussed black hair, wild eyes, cute mouth. Cute in general. But feral, a little.

When they left, Libby gave Sadie a big hug at the front door, and then did the same with Martin. "So nice to see you Martin!" she said. "I never hang out with single people anymore. It's like they all moved away to another planet!"

"I'm pretty sure I'm still on the same planet," said Martin.

"Ha-ha!" laughed Libby. "Well, you look great! Are you dating? Are you doing Tinder?"

Martin smiled. "Unfortunately, yes."

"And you still haven't met anyone?"

"Oh, sure," said Martin. "I meet people."

"I don't know why he doesn't have women all over him," said Sadie. "He's a total catch."

"Well, maybe I can think of someone," said Libby.

"I wish you would," said Sadie.

"I'll put my thinking cap on. And I'll get back to you."

Martin smiled.

"Would that be okay?" Libby said to Martin, touching his upper arm. "I'll really do it, if you want."

"Sure, do it," said Sadie.

"Yeah," said Martin. "Do it."

Back in the car, Martin and Sadie fell silent as they continued to the next errand. Martin's thoughts returned to the pressing issue of his day: what had gone wrong with Rebecca?

"So when you and Rob were first dating..." he said to his sister, "did he pay for stuff?"

"Rob? Yeah, I guess so. What do you mean?"

"Like, if you went out. Like, on your first dates. Did he buy the beer?"

"Sure. Yeah. Why wouldn't he?"

"I dunno."

"I mean, we were younger. He wasn't making so much money. If that's what you mean."

"No, but, like, between you. Did he pay or did you pay?"

"Um, he paid. And I probably paid too. I don't remember. Why? What difference does it make?"

"I don't know. I'm reviewing my dating practices."

"Your problem is who you're dating. You need to find better people. I still think you should take that dance class. A lot of people our age do that. It's the normal thing for singles. And it's not online. It's real. The person is actually there."

"Yeah, maybe," said Martin, looking out the window.

the red pill

Back home that night, Rebecca was still on Martin's mind. He opened a beer and sat on his couch in his silent apartment. He wondered if he was perceiving this situation correctly. One of Rob's pickup blogs, not P-Crusher, had mentioned that. Guys who lacked confidence tended to misread situations. They'd assume they fucked up, when they actually hadn't. Was it possible that the Sevens date wasn't as bad as Martin thought?

He tried to do the math on it. He'd assumed it was a total fail: 100 percent. But what if there was still a chance, a ten or twenty percent possibility that if he called her up and acted like nothing bad had happened, she might go out with him again?

He picked up his phone and scrolled back through their text messages. Rebecca had sounded so cheerful, so up for it. God, women were so inscrutable. If she liked him so much, how could she not forgive him for one bad date location?

He stared at her number for a minute. She had responded positively to his boldness in the café. Maybe that's what he needed now. He hit dial.

"Hello?" said Rebecca.

"Hi, Rebecca. It's me, Martin."

"Oh," she said. "Hi, Martin."

Martin adopted a jaunty tone. "I wanted to thank you again for coming out the other night."

"Sure. No problem."

"I kinda felt like...in retrospect, I didn't like that place. I'm sorry I picked it. I was thinking maybe we should try again.

Go somewhere more normal, more neighborhoody." When she didn't respond immediately, he added, "If you want."

She sighed on her end. "The thing is, Martin, I've kind of been seeing someone recently. And it feels like it might go somewhere. So I want to give that a chance."

"Oh," said Martin. "Like a boyfriend?"

"I wouldn't call him a boyfriend. He's someone I've been seeing."

"Oh. You didn't mention that."

"No. Generally, you don't mention other people on a first date."

"Right, of course," said Martin. "Sorry." He tried to laugh lightly at himself.

Rebecca, on her end, remained silent.

"So you don't want to give it another chance? Not even on a friends level?"

"It's not that; it's this other situation. Like I said. But it was nice to meet you."

"Okay, all right..." he said. "Well, good luck, with every-thing. And with your class, and with *Middlemarch*. We didn't even get to talk about that."

"No, we didn't. I should go. Good-bye, Martin."

"Good-bye," he said back.

Martin turned off his phone and threw it on the coffee table.

9

Martin avoided Rob at Jack's birthday party. Not physically, that was impossible, but in a psychic way. Through gestures and body language, Martin made it clear that he didn't want to discuss anything of importance with Rob today. He didn't need any advice, or any pep talks; he wasn't going to discuss his date with Rebecca. This was Jack's day, after all.

This was bullshit, of course. Martin was a mess. The Rebecca phone call had been the clearest indication yet that he had no clue how to conduct his own romantic life. Why wasn't he getting smarter about such things as he aged? He had done fine with girls in his twenties. He'd had flings, girlfriends, long-term relationships. He'd been *married* for chrissakes. What had happened? He was decent looking, he was smart, he co-owned a successful business! How could he not find someone to go out with? It was the great mystery of his life.

He poured himself a cup of coffee and sat at the Carr's kitchen table surrounded by a swirl of parents, young children, his sister, Rob, and then Libby who appeared—without Delilah—in a cute summer romper and sneakers. At different times Ashley, God bless her, came over to say hi and explain something to Martin in her adorably skewed four-year-old-girl logic. Sadie moved around quickly, putting out fires, keeping things moving. Libby was her abrupt, funny self. The twenty or so grownups were all having a great time, in their harried parental way. Rob remained tall, composed, fatherly. He really did have the dad-thing down. It was a little annoying.

After the chaotic serving and consuming of cake and ice cream by the kids, everyone moved into the living room for presents. Martin found himself on the couch with a young father he didn't know, but who appeared so bland and inconsequential, Martin didn't bother to introduce himself. Libby at one point sat on the couch too, and as people bounced up and down, she ended up beside Martin, giving him a gushy smile and picking something off his shoulder.

When it was time, Jack tore through the presents with breakneck speed. Ashley tried to help and was pushed away by selfish Jack, who was admonished by the crowd. He was indifferent to this criticism and continued in his own brutish style. Among his presents were toys, games, and educational items that had to be explained to him and that would supposedly challenge his young intellect. Pictures were taken and videos. Baby Jed left the room in tears at one point.

After the presents, the party wound down. The more heavily scheduled parents left first. A core group hung around and settled in the living room. Libby rejoined Martin on the couch and the two of them made small talk. Wasn't the party fun? Wasn't Sadie great with the kids? Had Martin planned on having children when he was married?

"Yes, but we never made it that far," Martin told her.

"Oh?" said Libby. "What happened?"

Martin shrugged. "I'm not sure. I think everything took too long. We dated too long. Then we were married too long. We should have just done it, and not thought about it so much."

"How long were you married?"

"Five years."

"Kevin and I did the opposite. We just dove in. Before we thought about anything."

"Of course, if I'd done that," said Martin, "I'd probably still be married to my ex, who I didn't like very much. And who didn't like me."

"That doesn't matter though," said Libby. "I mean, you're gonna like them as much as you like them."

"That's true."

"You never know," said Libby. "That's what I think. And how much does it even matter anyway? It's just this other person, living in your house, who you have to deal with."

Martin nodded along with this. That was one of his favorite things about marriage, kids, family: it humbled people. Anything could happen. Even the most powerful person on Earth had no defense against the cosmic vagaries of family.

"Oh, my God, look at Ashley!" said Libby.

Martin found her in the crowd. She was trying to help one of her departing friends get her toddler jacket zipped up. The two of them, with their tiny fingers, could not get the zipper sides to align. Ashley did the smart thing and found her father among the many towering adults. Rob bent down, studied the problem, and solved it effortlessly.

Which, of course, made him the hero to all involved. Which he was anyway.

Rob, thought Martin, with irritation. *What the fuck?*

Eventually, Libby had to go too. She ran around, saying good-bye to everyone, and then focused in on Martin.

"We should hang out more," said Libby, when she'd cornered him near the door.

"Yeah, sure," said Martin.

"I mean it. Maybe I can help you with your love life. But also, you seem like...."

Martin didn't know what she was going to say.

"You seem like you need a friend."

"Yeah," he said. "Maybe I do."

"Well, you know where I live. The coffee is always on. Text first, of course. Do you have my number?"

Martin shook his head no. Expectantly, she waited for him to dig out his phone, and so he did. She took it from him and entered her number, quickly, smoothly, and did so with her back turned slightly, away from the rest of the room.

"Done!" she said quietly, slipping the phone back into his coat pocket.

After she was gone, Martin made himself useful, gathering up the scattered wrapping paper and then cleaning up in the dining room. He found himself interacting with Rob. At one point, the two of them had to lift the extra table, one on either end, and walk it back to the den, which was a tricky maneuver and required them to work together.

When they were done with that, Martin returned to the living room, where Ashley and Jack were having a conversation.

"If you're not careful, people aren't going to like you, Jack," Ashley was telling her older brother.

"I don't care," said Jack.

"You should care. Because who are you going to be friends with?"

"Anyone I feel like."

"Yeah, but people don't like it."

"You should mind your own business."

Jack was trying to open a bag of gumballs someone had given him. After tearing at it from several different directions, the bag burst apart, sending gumballs across the room.

The two children watched in surprise as the gumballs bounced and rolled across the carpet in all directions.

"I told you," said Ashley.

But Jack was not listening. He dove onto the floor and made a game of collecting the gumballs, gently herding them with his hand, guiding them, talking to them, moving them into one central community of gumballs in the middle of the room.

Finally, with the guests all gone and the Carr household back in order, Martin got his coat.

Only then did Rob approach him. "Thanks for coming by," he said to Martin.

"No problem. That was fun."

"It was," said Rob, smiling and looking around the room. "Who knew the rug rats could be so entertaining?"

"You've got some serious entertainment value going on," said Martin.

"How are you doing?" Rob asked, watching Martin's face.

"I'm doing great," said Martin.

"Did you end up going on that date? With the woman from the café?"

Martin put on his coat. "Yeah, I did."

"How'd it go?"

"It was okay," said Martin, straightening his coat, adjusting his arms inside the sleeves. "I might have screwed up when I picked the place."

"How so?"

"We went to a hotel bar. Which I thought might be interesting." He adjusted his collar. "But it wasn't so great."

"You gonna see her again?"

"I doubt it."

"You didn't like her?"

"No," said Martin, with some formality. "She didn't like me."

"Oh."

"I paid for her drinks," said Martin, with a sudden hostility in his voice. "Maybe that was the problem."

"Well, if the chemistry's wrong, something like that isn't going to make any difference."

"No, I guess not," said Martin. He headed toward the door. Rob accompanied him.

Martin opened the door, and then turned to Rob. "What was that supposed to do to her anyway?" Martin asked, quietly. "Not buying her a drink? Make her feel like shit or something?"

Rob shrugged. "Sometimes if you start right off buying them stuff, it sends the wrong message."

"And what message would that be?"

"That you're too into it. That you're too invested. You're trying too hard."

Martin didn't respond.

"And..." continued Rob, "to be honest, that seemed like your mind-set going in."

"So not buying them a drink? How would that have helped?"

"I don't know if it would have. I'm just saying, women lose interest in a guy who lays down at their feet. They like to chase too. They like a challenge."

"So I gotta be more of a dick."

"You gotta not be so obvious."

"Buying someone a drink is not being obvious," said Martin. "It's following the basic protocol so you can move forward. So you can talk and hang out and figure out if you actually like the other person."

"Sure. You're right. There's a million different ways to do this stuff."

Martin was ready to leave but he lingered. He wanted to hear what else Rob had to say.

"And anyway," said Martin, "how do you even get to that place where you don't give a shit, when you obviously *do* give a shit?"

Rob didn't answer.

"And who has the energy to put on all these acts, or personas, or whatever this stuff is supposed to be. I'm a grown man. I'm about to sell my business. I don't have time to create some *character*. I'm too old for that. I am what I am."

"Hey, I understand," said Rob. "Like you say, you're doing great. But you're not *acting* like you're doing great. Some guy, who started his own company, and built it up, and now is going to sell it to Pacifica? I mean, Jesus. That guy must be a serious dude."

Martin said nothing.

"And this idea that you can't change, that's bullshit," said Rob. "People change all the time. You get a new job? You get a new girlfriend? What's the first thing that happens? You change. You adjust yourself. You can't help it."

Martin looked at him. He detached and reattached the bottom button on his coat.

Then Sadie called for Rob from the kitchen. Rob looked at Martin one last time. "Hey, I don't mean that as a criticism. Just something to think about. Thanks for coming over. Always nice to have you around. The kids love to see their uncle."

"Yeah," said Martin, pushing out through the door. "Likewise."

10

"...So THEN I had this friend in New York who worked for an advertising agency. He got me a job there and I did that for a while...and met my ex-wife...so then that became the plan, to stay there, maybe start a family...but then things didn't work out with her, so I came back to Portland, to regroup...."

Cynthia, 38, whose interests included family, friends, and the environment, sipped her latte. They were at Martin's same Starbucks, the one near his office. The sun was still up at 9 p.m., in early June, but that only exposed the grim atmosphere around them. There were two homeless guys camped out in the back, an obese woman in a T-shirt complaining to someone on her phone, two sad-looking emo kids looking out the window. There wasn't even any music on to mute the depressing sounds.

To make matters worse, Cynthia was very strange. She looked strange; she acted strange. Martin was afraid to let her talk. She appeared woozy; she was probably on drugs. Dylan and Martin had compared notes recently on the preponderance of heavily medicated women on dating apps. It made sense in a way. As a woman, what could possibly be more nerve racking than a Tinder date? A strange man, in a strange place, with no backup, no friends in the vicinity. Dylan had recited the oft-repeated factoid: men fear their internet dates will be fat. Women fear their internet dates will kill them.

Dylan had a girlfriend at the moment but he'd done his share of online dating. He liked it for the easy sex. "But they're all on drugs," he'd added. "That was the feeling I got. Prescribed stuff, nonprescribed stuff. Or their therapist is making them 'get back out there.' So, of course, they're gonna need some meds for that."

Cynthia did look significantly altered. She had dyed black hair, weird bangs. The blankness in her eyes was unnerving. And so Martin kept going with his story: "…so then I ran into this old friend from high school. He'd worked at an agency in LA. He wanted to start his own shop. So the two of us pooled our resources and the next thing I knew, I was a business owner."

This was the point where Martin most often got some kind of response. Usually the woman's ears perked up at least. Cynthia was not interested, however. She carefully placed her cup on the table and in a weird, slow-motion movement, lifted her phone out of her coat pocket to check the time.

They said good-bye outside the Starbucks fifteen minutes later. "Sorry if I was boring you," Martin said.

"It's okay," said Cynthia. She was wearing a long black coat, in the middle of summer. There *was* something sexy about her vacant face. But she was so checked out it was embarrassing. Further interaction was pointless.

the red pill

It was all so tragic in a way. These lost women, their damaged souls. Walking back to his car, Martin felt nauseous and awful and like his heart was being ripped from his chest. He feared he had reached the final burnout threshold. He would never go on another Tinder date again.

But that had happened before. Terrible, soul-sucking encounters would make him swear off the dating apps, but then, a couple weeks would go by and there he'd be: swiping back and forth again.

On the way home Martin stopped at New Seasons. He wandered the aisles in his usual daze. He came here a lot lately. If he bought things one or two items at a time, he always had something to do at night.

He did a slow cruise through the store. There was an attractive fortyish woman near the frozen pizzas. Martin slowed to glance at her once. She was slender and wearing gray-colored yoga pants, which rendered her basically naked from the waist down. Since he'd just finished a date, he considered himself "off the clock" and felt no obligation to talk to her. Besides, her hair was dirty, and sloppily pulled back. She was wearing a man's sweatshirt.

Nevertheless, something came over him and he stepped recklessly forward, opened the glass door beside her, and pulled out one of the frozen pizzas, a brand called California Kitchen.

Keeping his eyes on the pizza box, he said to her, "Are these good?"

The woman was startled by his comment but answered the question. "I don't know. I haven't had that one."

"I usually get the DiGiorno's," said Martin.

"Yeah, those are good."

"These look kind of tasty though," said Martin, turning the box over. "I like the packaging." He looked up and found that she was studying him. They smiled at each other. She was obviously nervous, but seemed willing to chat more, if he wanted to.

"The best *un*-frozen pizza, I've found, is that new place down the street," said Martin. "The by-the-slice place? I used to live in New York and there hasn't been a good place for a slice until that place."

"Oh, yeah," she said. "I've heard it's good. I haven't been there."

"Yeah, it closes early though. Otherwise I'd be there now."

"Yeah," said the woman. "The pizza in Portland isn't the best."

"Where are you from?" Martin asked.

"Minnesota, originally. My husband and I. We've been here three years."

Martin glanced into her face again. She remained nervous, but also curious, and possibly interested. But she had a husband. Martin wasn't sure what to do next. "Yeah," he said, placing the pizza-for-one in his carry basket. "It seems like everyone's moving to Portland nowadays."

the red pill

Back in his apartment he preheated the oven and slid the pizza into it. He thought about the married woman. Should he have pushed that more? Was there an opportunity there? Despite the husband?

But then he remembered a blog poster who had blown it with one particular woman and was beating himself up over it. A commentator had immediately jumped in: *C'mon! It's not like there's no other women around. There's a million of them. Look around you. They're all over the place!*

This had seemed so true at the moment Martin had read it. There really were women "all over the place." And they weren't all married, or crazy, or on drugs. The trick was to keep moving, keep your eyes open, stay positive.

At work the next day, with his afternoon to kill, Martin decided to check back in with P-Crusher. *What's ol' racist P-Crusher up to these days?* he snarked to himself, as he typed the blog's name into Google. One of the more interesting aspects of the manosphere was that it was so freely found on the internet, even with its racist rants and multiple use of the N-word, the C-word, and pretty much every other word a normal person was forbidden to use.

He found P-Crusher and opened the site. It had been awhile. The big news in P-Crusher's world was that he and another pickup artist, Natty D., had met up in Prague and had interviewed each other. This meeting was presented as a momentous event in human history, as if two great heads of states, or two legendary artists, had come together for the first time. Martin chuckled to himself and clicked on the link. With ironic excitement, he braced himself for the great knowledge about to spill forth.

Unfortunately, this epic summit, this convergence of the pickup titans, had been audio recorded in a pub that was so noisy and echoey it hurt your ears to listen to it. Also, P-Crusher was British and his accent was not exactly elegant or concise. The other guy, Natty D., was American, but his high-pitched screech of a voice was equally abrasive. No wonder Natty D. had dedicated himself to fooling females with psychological manipulation. He sounded like an over-excited six-year-old when he spoke. After a few minutes of the tinny noise, Martin gave up and clicked back to the original site.

He went from there to some of the other sites he could still remember. They were pushing the same stuff: (1) act like a jackass and you'll get women, and (2) the world is going to hell, thanks to the _____ (insert: blacks, gays, immigrants, feminists, SJWs, and so on). It was like a hidden army of twentysomething Archie Bunkers. The weird thing was, these bloggers weren't stupid. They were often talented writers. And, as before, they were very funny.

There was also a lot of stuff about Donald Trump, who had recently secured the Republican nomination to run for president. To most normal people, this was a mixed blessing. The bad news was that Trump had made it so far, which demonstrated just how insane the world had become. The good news was it practically guaranteed that Hillary Clinton would win the presidency.

The manosphere, however, did not share this view. Trump was their man and Trump was going to win. Period. Out of morbid curiosity, Martin paused to read a few pro-Trump posts. It was disorienting, their contrarian love for "The Orange One." It was as if these people inhabited a completely separate reality. Did they not see what everyone else saw every day on the news? That the man was a pathological liar, a con man, and probably a clinical narcissist?

As the evening wore on, and the EKO staff went home, Martin remained in his office, glued to his computer. He was back to the subject that most concerned him: the art of chatting up females. For instance, the pizza woman at New Seasons: he had "opened her," meaning he had successfully begun a conversation. But what then? According to the bloggers, once you'd managed the "cold approach," you wanted to keep them talking for a few minutes, "building familiarity" and "establishing shared values." Then you went for the "numbers close," saying something like "I gotta go, but we should talk more. Can I get your number?" Martin couldn't quite picture himself saying that but he grasped the effectiveness of the message: I'm busy. I'm important. But I am definitely interested in you in a romantic/sexual way. Which, according to these blogs, was precisely what a woman wanted to hear.

It was 10:30 at night when he finally shut off his work computer. His eyes hurt from reading so obsessively. The office was empty and silent when he shut off the lights, as was the parking garage as he unlocked his Audi A4. Pulling onto the deserted city streets, Martin felt like a secret operative, his head full of the manosphere's forbidden language and radical ideas. No wonder it was all young guys who were into this stuff. It made the world feel like a spy novel. It made you feel like Jason Bourne.

11

It was late July and Martin had been swimming laps at the YMCA. Standing at his locker with a towel around his waist, he found a text from Libby on his phone:

Unusual request. Got new bookshelves. Can't figure them out. Kevin's on the road again. If convenient swing by?

Martin had no plans for the night. He felt awake and invigorated after his swim. It was only 9:30. Libby was fun, easy to talk to, and it was a lovely summer night.

Thirty minutes later, Libby answered her door. She was holding a glass of wine. "Shhh," she said, as she beckoned him in. "The baby is sick. She's sleeping but she keeps waking up."

Martin nodded his understanding. He stepped quietly into the house and followed Libby, who led him into the kitchen. She excused herself to do a quick check on Delilah, leaving Martin to stand alone for a moment and silently take in the surrounding household. This was the home of a young married couple, both about thirty, one child, middle-to-upper-middle class. This was Martin's advertising self, doing the demographics.

Despite his scrutiny, he got no particular vibe off Libby's kitchen. It was strangely neutral. On the counters there was nothing distinctive: a cheap toaster, some other Target-bought appliances.

"Oh, my God," said Libby returning from the hallway. She was wearing sweatpants, slippers, a light bathrobe cinched tight around her waist. "I'm sorry we have to be so quiet. It was so hard to get her to bed. I refuse to drug her or whatever."

Martin nodded. Did people drug their babies? Probably.

"Aaaanyways…" said Libby, sighing. "Let me get you some wine or something. Or do you want a beer?"

Martin was dehydrated from his lap swimming and took the beer.

"Oh, crap, we only have Coors. Or wait. No. Here's a pale ale. Do you like pale ale?"

"That's fine," said Martin.

"I don't know what kind it is. Something weird that Kevin likes." She opened the bottle and set it in front of him. "Sit. Have a seat. Here." She patted one of the island stools.

Martin sat. She sat next to him. Martin could see the curve of her butt as it flattened against the round wooden seat. He drank his beer. It was rich and thick and delicious. "Very cold," he said, lowering his bottle.

"Yes. Kevin likes it that way. He makes me put them in the back, on the top shelf, where it's extra cold."

"Coldness matters," said Martin. "According to the surveys, coldness is the most important quality a beer can have."

"You're a beer expert?"

"I'm in advertising," said Martin. "The greatest minds of my industry have dedicated themselves to the sale of American beer. Especially light beer. Because how else do you sell piss water to middle-class Americans except through advertising?"

"Ha-ha!" laughed Libby.

"American beer and American advertising. It's a love story."

"But it's a *cold* love story," said Libby.

Martin laughed. "Exactly. Americans want their love *cold*. Like their revenge. Ha-ha."

"I like my revenge cold and hard!" said Libby.

"Who have you ever had to take revenge on?" asked Martin, grinning at her.

"Oh, a few people," said Libby, with a flirty face.

"I bet you have," said Martin.

"Ha! Wouldn't you like to know!" said Libby.

Martin took a deep draw from his pale ale and then placed it back on the kitchen island surface. The beer had an antique motorcycle on the label. In a 1930s art deco style, the motorcycle's front tire was positioned to make it look enormous and about to run you over. A lot of the advertising from that era had that same gigantism. Or was there another word for it? Monumentalism? Making things look big and overpowering was the point. Nowadays they called certain architecture "brutalist." He and his partner, Simon, used to joke around like that. They'd make up their own words for styles and fonts from the different periods of American design. They didn't care what the correct word was; they'd make up their own. This was back during that first year or two, when EKO Agency became very hot, very fast. Everything they did had a sharpness to it, a crispness. At the height of their sudden fame, they'd been profiled in *Influence Magazine*, Martin and Simon's faces pictured like they were a musical duo. Now, as their work had streamlined into a more consistent and less edgy mode, they would quietly sell the company to Pacifica, make a killing, and keep their illustrious creative reputation intact.

Martin asked about the bookshelves.

"Oh, it's nothing," said Libby. "Don't worry about it. Kevin can figure it out."

"No, but I'm curious."

"Seriously?"

"Just let me look."

"Okay. But I'm telling you."

Libby stood up and re-cinched her bathrobe. She led him down the carpeted hallway to the farthest back room in the house. Martin followed behind. In the McMansion tradition, everything in the house felt new and cheap and insubstantial.

The room they entered was in the early stages of becoming an office. There was an IKEA desk, a high-backed office chair with rollers, which didn't make sense since the room was carpeted. A newly assembled standing bookshelf stood against one wall. On the other wall, slotted metal strips had been screwed vertically into the wall. A stack of metal supports, which would eventually hold up the wooden shelves, lay on the floor. A couple of these supports were hanging crooked out of the slots, upside down.

"I think I see the problem," said Martin.

"What is the problem that you see?" said Libby. She was staring at him, an amused look on her face. She sipped her wine.

"These things are upside down."

"What things?" said Libby, but she didn't bother to look. She was staring at Martin.

"These support things," said Martin. He reached out and pulled one free of the metal strip, turned it right side up, and easily slipped the tabs into the slots so that it was sticking out from the wall like it was supposed to.

"Oh," said Libby.

"See how that works?" said Martin. He did it again, showing her how you tilted the support piece upward slightly, before slipping the tab in the slot and then letting it come down so that it locked into place.

"I knew it was going to be something obvious," said Libby. "Now you think I'm an idiot."

"No, I don't think you're an idiot."

Libby sipped her wine, her eyes still on Martin.

"Here, we can put them all in," he said. He picked up three of the supports and began putting them in.

Libby didn't help. She watched, her slender forearm crossed over her stomach, exposing her thin, feminine wrist. "Don't tell Kevin," she said.

"Don't tell him what?"

"Any of this," said Libby. "How stupid I am."

"You're not stupid," said Martin, picking up more of the supports.

"Yes, I am. When it comes to stuff like this. I can't figure out which way is up."

Meanwhile, the baby had begun to make noises in the next room. Then it began to cry. "Oh, Jesus," said Libby. She left the office, taking her wine with her. She began to coo and make baby noises in the hallway. Once inside the baby's room, she shut the door and the house became quiet again.

Martin continued fitting the supports into the metal strips. He didn't know how far down Libby or Kevin would want the shelves to go. Since they had an infant daughter, they would probably want them higher up, so Martin kept the bottom row a good eighteen inches above the carpet.

When that was done, he found the wooden shelves, stacked beneath the window, and began putting them into place. After he'd done a couple, he realized they were upside down and had to start over. When it was finally done, Martin stepped back and surveyed his handiwork. He looked around at the office. It occurred to him that he was in another man's home, drinking with another man's wife. She was wearing a bathrobe and it was—he checked his watch—11:15 at night.

Martin rapped one knuckle lightly on Delilah's bedroom door. "Hey, Libby?" he said.

"Yes?"

the red pill

"I got the shelves sorted out. I should probably go. I didn't realize it was so late."

"Oh, yeah," she said through the door. "It is late. Can you wait a minute? Until I finish up in here?"

"Sure."

"Wait in the kitchen."

"Okay."

Martin returned to his stool in the quiet kitchen and drank the last sips of his pale ale. The refrigerator made a noise. He sat and waited. An ugly cat appeared. Trying to stay hidden from Martin, it silently moved under the dining room table to a silver cat food dish that was unfortunately empty.

Martin watched the cat, then did a slow scan of the dining room area and the half of the living room that he could see from his stool. There was something not right about this house. It was too new, he decided, too empty. It was not yet a home.

Martin heard Delilah's bedroom door quietly open and shut, and then Libby reappeared. She seemed different. She hadn't closed her robe, for one thing, so that for a moment, he saw a tract of pale skin, from her neck to her bellybutton, and a bit of one breast. She went to the sink and washed her hands, and only then pulled her bathrobe closed and cinched it. She seemed flushed and dopey. "Breast feeding," she said. "It kinda gets you high sometimes. They don't tell you that, of course. They don't tell you a lot of things."

Martin, embarrassed, couldn't quite look at her. "I think I got the shelving situation squared away."

"Oh, great, thank you. And would you mind, really, not telling Kevin about this?"

"Of course. Not a word. My lips are sealed."

"Good, good," murmured Libby to herself.

Libby let him out. She touched his arm in the doorway. "Thank you so much for coming over," she said. "And helping me out."

"It was nothing," said Martin. "It was fun."

"So you live alone?" asked Libby.

"That's right."

"All alone? In an apartment?"

"Yup."

"Well, I'm glad you could come over." She still had her hand on his arm. "Will you come over again sometime? We can...I don't know, *get drunk*. Ha-ha."

"Getting drunk and hanging out is always an option," said Martin, smiling.

Libby smiled back. They both drank in the other, in a momentary pheromonal exchange.

It was Libby who went for the kiss. She leaned forward, stretched onto her tiptoes, and slowly kissed him on the cheek. Martin did not respond, even as he found the sensation of her wet lips on his face tantalizing.

But it was time to go, and Martin left, moving through the doorway and into the fragrant summer night. "Bye," he said.

"Bye," said Libby.

12

MEANWHILE, LITTLE JACK'S summer soccer league season was in full swing. Sadie kept bugging Martin to come to a game. "It's the funniest thing you've ever seen in your life," she claimed.

So here he was, in a crowded parking lot on a Saturday morning at the Westview Parks and Recreation Center. It took a while to find a space. One poor family was packing up to leave. The father, in cargo shorts and sunglasses, was trying to get a miniature netted soccer goal into the back of his SUV while his blonde wife tried to read her phone, control a tote bag, and simultaneously maintain contact with two toddlers in baby soccer outfits. The soccer goal was not going to fit. The poor father was going to have to take it apart. *Oh, the trials of the young parent,* thought Martin. It was reassuring to see such scenes. Martin had successfully avoided ruining his youth with parenthood. Or perhaps he had squandered his youth by avoiding it. It was hard to tell.

Once parked, Martin walked down the hill toward the soccer field. The sidelines were crowded with parents, children, folding chairs, coolers, soccer equipment. Inside the white lines, an assortment of seven- and eight-year-old soccer players were in the middle of their game. Martin stopped at the edge of the playing field. Sadie was right.

The game was total chaos. It was pretty amusing. The ball would roll around. A gaggle of kids would swarm around it, kicking lamely at it, missing, kicking each other, falling, knocking each other down.

Martin noticed they were well outfitted: Pacifica cleats, Pacifica socks, Pacifica shin guards. Their team shirts—one team in green, the other in yellow—also displayed the Pacifica logo. The players seemed to have only a vague concept of what they were doing. Or maybe it was a problem of attention span. That was something you sometimes forgot about kids: they didn't care very much. Watching for a full minute from the sideline, Martin could see there were a few potential athletes in the group. Of course, they were totally smothered and thwarted by the incompetence of the others. Such was life.

The parents, to their credit, seemed pretty calm. But you could feel the self-control being exercised. Even the most indifferent, hipster mother couldn't resist lowering her locally roasted coffee for a moment and shrieking, "Kick it, Aiden!" before laughing at herself and returning to whatever low-grade gossip she was engaged in with her fellow moms.

Martin began to move a little, working his way down the sideline, taking it all in. Soccer moms, soccer parents, they were still a thing. The parent-child dynamic was one of the most crucial relationships in Martin's line of work. Advertisers thought about it constantly. His impression was that the days of the hover parent were waning and there had been a return to something like normalcy in this area of the culture. Of course, kids were now addicted to their phones, which was also not healthy, but at least the parents weren't following their eleven-year-olds around, asking if they wanted Thai or Ethiopian for dinner.

Sadie and Rob, for instance, seemed to have struck the right balance in their parenting style. Rob especially seemed to understand that it was more about presence, less about activities and interaction. To be a good father, what did you really have to do? Be solid. Be a rock. What else did a kid need? Martin's father had been like that: more a presence than a playmate. An influential attorney, Martin's father had been too busy to hang out with his children. But so what? He'd been a competent human male. If the car broke down. If the power went out. If someone was hurt or got in trouble, Dad appeared. Dad would handle it. If Dad was there, you were safe.

You'd think, though, that with such a solid role model, Martin would have been more productive as a heterosexual male. One short marriage. Zero kids. Living alone in a rented apartment at forty-one. Martin had calculated that he'd been with someone for only forty percent of his adult life, and that was counting his marriage. The rest of the time he'd been single. Was that on him? Was it possibly generational? His parents were boomers. He was Generation X. And weren't the Gen-Xers the ones who got screwed the worst? Of course, the millennials were having their own problems. People teased them for being spoiled. But Martin, who had studied the data, knew the truth: the millennials were walking into a shit-storm.

"C'mon, Shane!" yelled someone's mother, a little too close to Martin's ear. He continued along the sideline until he reached a small section of aluminum bleachers, where he spotted Sadie and Rob and climbed up to join them.

"So where's Jack?" he asked his sister.

"Number thirteen."

Martin searched the field for his nephew.

"He's over there," said Rob, and Martin spotted him standing on the sideline across the field.

"He's not in right now," said Sadie.

"He'll go back in," said Rob.

Meanwhile, the raucous scrum was moving to their side of the field. The three adults watched the tiny children chase the relatively large soccer ball as it bounced and rolled randomly among them.

"That Edelman kid, he can actually kick the ball," observed Rob to Sadie.

She nodded.

"The cream is already rising," said Rob to no one. Martin didn't respond. He watched. The amusement he'd felt initially was fading. He wondered how much longer the game would last.

Later, they went for smoothies with another couple, Courtney and Wayne, and their soccer-playing son, Guthrie. Since there were only two children present and they were occupied with their oversized straws and thick smoothies, the five adults had no choice but to talk among themselves.

the red pill

Courtney, who was plump, clean, and cheerful, spoke first. "Did you hear what Trump said about Mexicans?"

Everyone nodded that they had, though it was unclear what everyone thought about it. Wayne, who was thin and had a beard, grimaced slightly but reserved comment. Rob sipped his own smoothie. Martin said nothing. He knew how conservative suburban Portlanders could be. But then sometimes they were the exact opposite.

"I mean, he's running for *president*," said Courtney.

"He got the nomination," said Wayne.

"Not that I want a million Mexicans running around," said Courtney. "But you can't insult a whole group of people like that."

"He can't win," said Sadie. "That's all I care about. He'll never beat Hillary."

"Unless Bernie goes Independent and splits the vote," said Wayne. Wayne's beard was not as trim up close as it looked from farther away, Martin noticed, sitting close beside him. But that was always the case with beards. The closer you got, the worse they looked. The poor women who had to put up with them. Maybe you could do an ad like that: something funny about women and beards. *She wants to kiss him but where's his mouth?*

"The guys who mow our lawn are Mexican," said Courtney. "And they're very nice."

"They're a family-oriented people," said Wayne.

Rob avoided the issue by helping Jack get his giant straw back inside the hole on the top of his smoothie's plastic lid.

"I can't stand Trump," said Sadie. "I mean, Rob is more.... What do you think, Rob? Rob thinks he has some good ideas."

Rob straightened up. "He probably shouldn't be insulting Mexicans," he said.

"It just sounds weird," said Courtney. "Like if you're running for president...there's things you don't say...."

"Maybe he doesn't want to win," said Wayne. "Maybe it's a publicity stunt."

"Martin used to live in New York," said Sadie. "What do people in New York think of Trump, Martin?"

Martin shrugged. "I think he's considered a joke. In New York City, anyway."

"He won't be a joke if he wins," said Rob.

"Rob likes him," Sadie said to the group, looking at her husband.

"I'm just saying," said Rob. "He's not that different from other Republicans. Other people have said the exact same things."

"See what I got here?" Sadie said to Courtney. "I married a Republican."

"Wayne is like that sometimes," Courtney confided to Sadie. "I think we agree and then I realize he's off in his own little world."

"I think you have to give it time," said Rob. "See how it plays out. The real campaign hasn't even started yet."

"Did anyone watch his TV show?" Courtney asked.

No one had.

"I did," she said. "It wasn't great. But it wasn't terrible."

the red pill

"Nobody's into Trump at my work," said Wayne, who did something tech related. "At least not out loud. Management's totally anti-Trump."

"Well, he won't win, so we don't have to worry about it," said Sadie.

The group fell silent for a few moments.

"So you and Rob...?" Courtney asked Sadie. "Do you guys disagree often about politics?"

Sadie looked at Rob. "Sometimes," she said.

"Not always," said Rob.

"I would say we do, especially lately," said Sadie. She turned to Courtney. "Do you guys?"

"No," said Courtney, looking at Wayne. "I don't think so. Do you think we do?"

"No," said Wayne. "Not about anything important."

"Not that there's anything wrong with it," said Sadie.

"It's good for everyone to have their say," said Wayne.

"Keeps things interesting," said Sadie, looking back at Rob, who was talking to Jack, who had slid off his chair and was under the table for some reason.

Courtney looked across the table at Martin. "What did you do in New York?"

"I worked in advertising."

"Oh," she said, smiling at him. "Are you married?"

"No," said Martin.

"But he's looking," said Sadie. "If you know of anyone."

"Have you tried online?" asked Wayne.

"Yes, he's done everything," Sadie answered for Martin. "He's really made an effort. It's just very difficult right now."

"It is!" said Courtney. "My sister-in-law, Wayne's sister? She can't meet anyone. She's tried everything."

"How old is she?" asked Sadie.

"Oh, Martin wouldn't like her. She's very active in her church."

Martin didn't know what that meant. But everyone dropped the subject.

"Well," said Courtney, finally, "we probably need to get these little athletes home and into some clean clothes!"

13

It was a week later, while Martin was visiting the Carr household, that Sadie kicked her brother and husband out for the night, so she could host a baby shower for a friend. Rob and Martin drove to the Arena Sports Bar. Though Martin and Rob's issues over the racist manosphere blogs had long been put aside, it was still an odd moment when they found themselves walking into the bar together.

Inside, Rob spotted some coworkers by the pool tables and went to talk to them. Martin stayed at the bar and watched the baseball game over the bartender's head. The Arena on that night had its usual high ratio of men. Occasionally bits of political conversation would drift to Martin's ears. People were pretty worked up about the election and there were still three months to go. Martin was not worked up. Hillary was boring and Trump was evil. What sort of choice was that? The interesting thing to him was how evenly balanced the general public always turned out to be. Always, it was half conservatives, half liberals. How did it work out like that? Perhaps it was a biological imperative; the society splits itself evenly in half, like cells do during reproduction. In politics, though, it wasn't always perfectly symmetrical. Sometimes there were factions or a third-wheel threat, Bernie Sanders, in this case. Fortunately, in America, it never got too complicated, not like in Europe, where they had multiple parties morphing, shifting, converging with each other. No, a steady back and forth between two clearly defined poles, that was the American way. Reagan for a while, then Clinton for a while. Then Bush, then Obama. Who was president didn't affect things very much and probably the slow gentle swinging of the pendulum was the best-case scenario. Any one party would grow toxic if left in power too long. Politics in America was more of a sporting event, with the added touch that if your team won a couple times in a row, it was almost guaranteed that the other side would get their chance.

    "So, like, all your construction buddies, they're all full-on Trump guys?" Martin asked Rob, when he returned.

    "Pretty much," said Rob.

    "Don't they worry that he has no experience?"

    "That's why they like him."

    Martin drank his beer. "But he lies about stuff. He lies about everything."

    "He has his own style."

    "Well, it's an interesting turn of events anyway," conceded Martin. "Doesn't seem like he has a chance though."

    "Maybe not," said Rob.

    A new female bartender had come on shift and Rob ordered another beer.

    Martin felt like talking. "So I've been reading those pickup blogs again," he told Rob.

"Yeah?"

"They're helpful," said Martin. "I gotta admit. Just in terms of making you more aware of what you're doing."

"Sure, sure."

"The political stuff…" Martin shook his head. "Some of it's so over the top. I honestly don't know how they can post it on the internet."

"It was a lot different when I was into it."

"How did you first get interested in this?" asked Martin. "Were you bad at meeting women?"

"It wasn't that I was *bad*. I just needed to be reminded of certain things. The true nature of women."

"And what would you say that is?"

"They're designed a certain way."

"Like…what way?"

"They're emotional. They're nurturing. They're the ones who have the kids. We don't have the kids. We're built to defend the kids, and defend the cave or the village or whatever. We're built to fight."

"Yeah?"

"All animals are like that. The male and the female are different. They have different roles. It's not some evil plot. It's not the oppres-sive patriarchy."

Martin drank his beer.

"And that's why we like what we like," said Rob. "Men want women who are young and healthy and can have lots of babies. And the women want men who are dominant and aggressive and can protect them."

"To breed with…."

"Even if they're not breeding. That stuff is hardwired into us. That's what we're attracted to."

"I don't know," said Martin. "Most women I know would not say they want an aggressive, dominant man."

"Of course, they wouldn't. Because they don't know it themselves...."

Martin had read this argument on the blogs. It sounded suspicious to him, that women didn't know their own minds.

The female bartender appeared and placed Rob's Bud Light in front of him.

"Hey," Rob said to her. "Can I ask you something?"

The bartender was tall, with a pretty face, probably in her mid-thirties. "Sure."

"What do you like best in a guy?"

"Like physically?"

"Yeah."

"Well," she said. "I sort of like tall guys." She smiled at Rob, as she thought about it. "But I'm sort of tall myself...."

"What else?"

She shrugged. "I dunno. Nice abs, I guess."

"Nice abs? That's pretty specific."

"Well, everyone has their things they like. I sorta like that whole region."

"Oh really?" said Rob, suggestively. "The 'whole region.'"

"Not like that!" the bartender laughed. "I just don't like beer guts. I see enough of them!"

"How about finances?"

"Finances? Yes. That's definitely important."

"So you like rich guys?"

"They don't have to be rich. But it's nice when they have their shit together."

"But, like, if a guy pulls up in a brand-new Mercedes...."

"No, I don't care about that."

"What about personality?" asked Rob.

"Hmmm," she said. "Personality...."

"Or five general things," said Rob. "What are the top five qualities you want in a guy?"

"They need to be nice," said the bartender, pouring a beer for one of her waitresses.

"Okay, nice," repeated Rob.

"And funny. I definitely like funny guys."

"Funny," said Rob. "Everyone likes that."

"And just...I don't know. Kind. And sweet. And smart is good. But not like nerd smart. More like a person you don't mind talking to, who has interesting things to say."

"So you don't just want nice abs," said Rob. "You want the whole package."

"Yeah. I'd say so," she answered. "What's wrong with that?"

"Nothing, nothing at all," said Rob. "What about bad boys?"

"Bad boys?" she said, blushing slightly. "I mean, that's kind of its own category."

"In what way?"

"Bad boys are...well, they're different."

"How are they different? Like in a good way?"

"Yeah. Sometimes," she said. "They're fun. There's definitely a time and a place for that."

"Like what?"

"Like when you're younger. And when you're into that. When you crave that *excitement.*"

"You don't crave it anymore?" asked Rob.

"No. Of course, I do. I just know better."

"So bad boys are more fling material."

"I mean, bad boys grow up too," she said. Then she leaned closer to the two of them: "*Fuck boys,* that's what the girls call them around here."

"Yeah?" asked Rob.

"I mean, I don't go in for that sort of thing myself. But some of the girls...."

"Like if they want to have a good time," said Rob.

"I guess so," said the bartender, filling a beer pitcher. "I mean, girls like to have fun too. Nothing wrong with that. Or do you not approve?"

"I approve," said Rob. Martin was not part of the conversation at this point. But he nodded his head in approval as well.

"What about you? What do you like?" asked the bartender, eyeing Rob.

"Me?" said Rob, smiling. "I'm married, unfortunately. So it's not something I think about much. Martin here though... this is Martin...what's your name?"

"Danielle."

"Hi, Danielle. This is Martin."

The female bartender was not interested in Martin. She and Martin nodded to each other and then Danielle returned her full attention to Rob.

the red pill

"What brought this up?" she asked him.

"Oh, nothing," said Rob, "We were discussing the nature of women. And men. And sex."

"I could talk about *that* all night," said Danielle.

But just then a large group appeared on the other end of the bar. "Excuse me," she said.

When she was gone, neither man spoke. They both sipped their beers and stared at the big TV screen above the bar.

Heading home, Martin and Rob climbed inside Rob's F-250 LX pickup. It sat higher up than a normal truck. After a couple beers, it took some effort for Martin to get into it. He buckled his seat belt.

"Jeez, Danielle really liked you," said Martin, as they pulled onto the main road.

"Yeah," said Rob. "When you're married it's easy to flirt. No consequences."

"Yeah, but you're good at it."

"I'm not that good at it."

Martin stared out the window as they drove. What would he have said to the bartender if he had been in the bar alone? He would have said nothing. He wouldn't have dared.

"So how would you rate Danielle on the number scale?" Martin asked. He kept seeing women rated like this on the blogs, but he'd never used the system in real life.

"I'd say a seven. Six or seven. And she was a little older, so a definite seven if accounting for age."

"I was thinking an eight."

"Naaah," said Rob. "She was cute. But she wasn't an eight."

"She liked you though. Whatever she was."

"She liked the idea of having a fun conversation," said Rob. "Girls always want that."

Martin stared out the window.

"Seriously," said Rob. "Think about it. They can't play football. They can't get in fights. They can't get drunk and pass out on the lawn, like you or I could. They can't go camping by themselves. They can't walk around at night by themselves. If they get a flat tire, they gotta call some dude to come out and fix it for them. Everything they do has to include other people. It's always gotta be a group. And then they got men, who are their only real source of entertainment, and most of them are morons. So there you are, you spend your whole life depending on these clueless dudes, who harass you all the time. Think of how old that would get."

Martin nodded at all this.

"Women want to do stuff," continued Rob. "They wanna have adventures. Even just a fun conversation. So that's what you give them. A fun night. A fun chat. Do them a favor. Don't be another idiot."

"Yeah," said Martin.

"And don't fucking believe any of this bullshit that you're to blame for their situation. You're not to blame. Nature did this. Nature made us like this. Our job is not to lie down and spend our life apologizing for whatever the fuck we supposedly did to them. Our job is to go have an interesting life, and do interesting shit, and bring them along. Share it with them. Include them. That's what they *want*."

"I dunno," said Martin. "That's not what they say they want."

"Okay then, do the eye test. Look around you. Who's happy? Which kind of women that you see walking around are actually happy?"

Martin didn't know.

"The ones who are married, that's who. The ones who have three kids. Your sister, for one. They're occupied, they're busy, they're doing what they were intended to do. And I'm not saying I did that. I'm saying she knew what she wanted and so did I and we lucked out, finding each other. It ain't that hard. I do the dude shit. She does the chick shit. And it works out pretty good. I wouldn't trade places with anyone. Not one fucking person. And neither would she."

Martin found this last bit a little embarrassing, and so didn't respond immediately. Libby came to mind. And a half-dozen other married women he knew. They didn't seem so happy.

But there was probably some truth in what Rob was saying. Rob did seem to understand certain things, to an alarming degree. Even riding in his ridiculous pickup truck was shockingly comfortable, and what a pleasing sensation to be up above the other cars, riding smooth and steady through the world.

"And so you're gonna vote for Trump," said Martin, quietly in the dark.

"Fuck yeah, I am."

14

WALKING BY THE screening room one afternoon, at the EKO offices, Martin saw people had gathered to watch a Trump rally in the Midwest. It was August now and Trump was wearing his usual business suit, standing on a stage, in the middle of a sweltering cornfield.

Martin stepped inside to watch. It was almost funny how Trump said whatever random thought came into his head. He didn't go "off script"; he appeared to have no script to start with. Instead, he bragged, boasted, bullshitted. The latest trend in the media was to fact-check his nonsense. Which was hilarious.

"There he is," Martin said to Dylan, who was sprawled on the couch, sneering at the screen. Melissa, the office manager, was there too.

"Look at these people," said Dylan, to no one in particular. "Eating out of his hand. The guy lies about everything. Literally, every word that comes out of his mouth is a lie and these fucking hillbillies lap it right up!"

"My brother-in-law's voting for him," said Martin.

"I've got some cousins in San Diego," said Melissa. "They love him."

"What if he wins?" said Martin.

"How is he gonna win?" said Dylan.

"I don't know," said Martin. "How did he win the primary?"

"Dude is not going to win," said Dylan. "I can promise you that."

"He better not..." said Melissa.

"It's like, what could you possibly like about this guy?" said Dylan. "You want to look at that smug face for four years?"

"Or his hair," said Melissa.

"I'm a face guy too," said Martin. "I liked Obama's face."

"Obama was the bomb!" said Dylan. "And now we go to this? I mean, Hillary...whatever. But at this point? You better fucking vote for her. Or we're in serious trouble."

"I thought you said he couldn't win," said Martin.

"He can't," said Dylan. "I mean, who knows what could happen. Have you seen those dudes who do security for him? They're a bunch of ex-convicts. He's, like, walking around with a bunch of neo-Nazis for backup. It's like Mussolini."

"Yeah, I noticed the Mussolini thing," said Martin. There'd been a rash of recent Facebook videos comparing the two. The likeness was uncanny.

"And these fucking women who like him," continued Dylan. "Look at them! They're right there in the crowd. Fucking Christians! Hey, ladies, he's not a fucking Christian! He's fucking *lying* to you!"

At that moment Simon Howard, Martin's partner, walked into the conference room. He had a bunch of papers. "What is this?" he said, looking at the screen.

"Trump."

"Oh, Jesus," said Simon. "Gimme a fucking break."

"What's it mean, though?" asked Martin. "That he's gotten so far?"

"It means we're all going to die," said Simon, getting out his phone and checking something.

"I'm serious," said Martin. "It makes you feel like you don't know your own country. And that's our job."

"It's not my job to know that shit," said Dylan.

"The thing is," said Simon, looking up at the screen, "you knew there'd be a push from the conservatives. Which is normal. Black president or whatever. Not to be racist. But the Midwestern white people, they're gonna want one of their guys again, right? So you think maybe Romney, or someone like that. Something that wouldn't be the end of the world. Not this guy."

Simon handed Martin a multipage contract of some kind.

"What's this?" asked Martin.

"Sign on the checkmarks," he said.

Martin pulled a pen from his shirt pocket, moved to the table, and began flipping through the document, signing on the checkmarks. "What do the Pacifica people think of Trump?" Martin asked.

"Nothing," said Simon. "They don't care. I mean, they hate him. Of course, they do. They think Hillary will win. I'm sure they're giving her boatloads of cash."

"Obama couldn't do anything," said Martin. "Even if Trump got elected, he'd be in the same boat. No experience. Everybody hates you. How much damage could he do?"

the red pill

"He won't get elected," said Simon. "We shouldn't waste one second of our time thinking about it. He's a dick. I mean, all politicians are dicks. But that's his primary essence. That's *all* he is. Pure, unadulterated *dick.*"

Simon took back the contract Martin had signed. "And with that, gentlemen and ladies, I will take my leave."

Martin went back to his own office, where, on that particular day, he didn't have much to do. With his door closed, he went online and checked some of the manosphere blogs. What did they think of Trump's growing popularity?

As before, the young men of the manosphere were 100 percent the opposite of Martin and his peers. They loved Trump. They worshipped him. There were already memes from that day's rally, showing Trump's eyes turning into laser beams and vaporizing all the "libtards" and the "soyboy weaklings of the Left." There was a short video of Trump's head on top of the Hulk, throwing Hillary around like a rag doll.

"Hey, Martin," said Regan the new intern, opening his door without knocking. Martin instantly closed the window.

Regan came in. She was famous around the office for her bizarre, high-fashion outfits. She seemed to be channeling Bjork, though at twenty-one, it was possible she didn't know who Bjork was.

"Hey, Regan," he said, not looking up.

"Can you sign this card for Raj Taheed?" she said.

He took the large card, opened it, studied the many signatures that were already present. "Who is Raj Taheed?"

"He's Pacifica. In the San Francisco office. He must be important. They said we should all sign the card."

It was an elaborate card. It played classical music when you opened it. Martin wrote *Happy Birthday, Bro* and handed it back to Regan, who was standing beside him at his desk. She was wearing another startling outfit: an unusually patterned yellow blouse, which was so sheer you could see every detail of the white bra beneath it. For pants she wore very tight, high-waisted pink pastel jeans.

"Where do you shop for clothes?" he asked her, returning her pen.

"Oh, everywhere."

"You're always wearing something interesting."

"I know."

"I would think it's hard to find stuff in Portland."

"I go online. And I go home to LA sometimes. That's where I'm from."

"Yeah? You grew up there?"

"Yes."

"That makes sense," said Martin, sitting back. "I feel bad sometimes. I dress so boring. But I love it when other people wear cool stuff to work. The agency I worked at in New York, GGI, you kinda had to. Like if you showed up at a job interview there, and you didn't have something going on style-wise, you wouldn't get hired."

"What was your style?" she asked him. "Back in New York?"

"Me? Same as now. Nothing spectacular. Preppy hipster. High waters. Weird shoes. I went through this moccasin phase at one point. I guess to show off my Oregon roots."

"I like your style."

Martin laughed. He rolled his chair back from his desk and looked down at himself. He was wearing Levi's skinny jeans, a dark blue J. Crew shirt, old white Tretorn sneakers.

"It's a nice mix," commented Regan. "Youthful but not too much. It's low-key. It's perfect for someone your age."

Martin smiled at that. It occurred to him that he and Regan were having a conversation. Like Rob had with Danielle at the sports bar. They were pretty deep into it too, talking about their clothes, teasing each other, looking each other up and down. Too bad she was so young...and worked at his company.

But he could still practice. That was fairly standard advice on the pickup sites. *Be the fun guy. Flirt with everyone. Be the guy who lights up the room.*

Martin glanced up into Regan's face. She was grinning at him. She was enjoying this. At least she was enjoying it more than walking around with a birthday card.

"Yeah these Tretorns," said Martin pulling his feet out further, to show off his sneakers. "They're pretty comfortable."

"I like them."

"The thing about Tretorns is," said Martin, "I remember them from when I was a kid. They were tennis shoes. Like for actually playing tennis. Like in the nineties. They're like Volvos or something."

"Volvos?" said Regan, skeptically. "Like the car? Are they Swedish?"

"No, no, they're just...*nostalgic* in a way," said Martin. "Maybe Volvos aren't the best analogy...." Martin looked down at his shoes. He was momentarily stuck for something else to say. "How long have you been in Portland?" he asked her.

"Not long."

"Like one year, two years, three years?"

"Four months."

"Four months. Oh. So you're brand new," said Martin.

She nodded. Martin again struggled for something to say. "How do you like it so far?" he asked.

"It's okay."

"Just okay?"

"I like LA better."

"Yeah, LA's probably more fun than Portland." He swung his chair from side to side.

Regan watched him.

"So who are your fashion icons?" said Martin, smirking slightly.

"My 'fashion icons'?" said Regan, laughing. "Are you serious?"

"What's wrong with that?"

"It's a weird question."

"Why? I'm curious. Who do you like?"

"I don't know. Different people," she said. "You probably wouldn't know them."

"Try me."

"You wouldn't," she said. "And anyway, I have my own style."

"No, you obviously do," said Martin. "That's not what I meant...."

"I don't *copy* people."

"No," said Martin. "I didn't say you did. I just thought there might be some kind of influence."

He'd screwed this up. How to recover?

"I better finish getting this card signed," she said.

"Do you like Bjork?" he tried.

"Bjork?" she said. "The musician?"

"You know, we did a shoot with her once, back in New York," said Martin, realizing a half-second too late that this was a mistake. Bringing up a celebrity you've worked with, to make yourself seem interesting, was always a mistake. And that wasn't from the manosphere; he knew that from his own life.

"Really?" said Regan, without enthusiasm.

"Yeah, she was...well, you can imagine."

Regan pursed her lips. "Hmmm," she said. "I better keep moving. They want everyone to sign the card."

"Okay," said Martin.

When she was gone, Martin rolled himself back into place at his desk. He paused for a moment, to reflect on the conversation. He tried not to be too hard on himself. So he got self-conscious; that happened. And the Bjork thing was a mistake. But he still gave himself a B, or maybe even a B+, overall. The trick was not to think too much, just roll with it. And don't apologize if you fuck up. And don't ask boring questions. *So how long have you lived in Portland?* Yeah, that was bad. That was probably where he lost her.

At New Seasons after work, he felt good though. Waiting in a long checkout line, he noticed the woman behind him had a big plastic tub of animal crackers.

"Oh my God, are those animal crackers?" he said to her. She was about his age, with an intelligent face and nice eyes.

"Yes, they are."

"Where were they?"

"Over with the cookies. On the end."

"I should get some of those."

"I could hold your place," she offered.

"Yeah?" Martin said, thinking about it. "Nah. I can come back. I just live up the street."

"They might be gluten free." She looked at the tub. "That's probably why they're here."

Martin smiled at her. "I love those. I used to bite off the little feet. The little arms."

"My kids love them," she said.

"How old are your kids?"

"Four and six."

"I got some nieces and nephews that age. Prime animal cracker years."

"Yeah, the kids will be excited."

Martin paid for his small allotment of groceries and then stopped by the exit to check a message that had dinged on his phone.

The animal cracker woman came out behind him, with her shopping cart. They smiled at each other as she moved past him into the parking lot. Martin's message was from Dylan, something work related. He typed a quick answer, sent it, and started through the parking lot himself. The animal cracker woman, meanwhile, had opened her trunk and was loading her groceries into it. As Martin walked by, her cart began to roll away from her. Martin was right there, so he grabbed it.

"Your shopping cart's trying to escape!" he said to the woman.

"Oh!" said the woman. "Thank you!"

"Yeah, they should level out this parking lot," said Martin. He held the cart while she put the last bag into her trunk. He watched her. He tried to think of something else to say but couldn't think of anything.

"Thanks…thank you…" said the woman.

"I got the cart," said Martin, pushing it into the cart corral a few feet away.

The woman, who'd been flustered for a moment, regained her composure. "So, you live around here?" she asked, pushing her hair behind one ear.

"Yeah, just up the street," said Martin.

"I live in Sellwood," said the woman. "But my kid's dad lives here. A couple blocks that way. Sometimes when I drop them off I come here and buy stuff I know they'll like."

"That's nice," said Martin. Was she hitting on him?

"Yeah," she said. "So I come to this store a lot. Since I'm in the neighborhood."

"Yeah," said Martin. "New Seasons is the best. I'm lucky to be so close."

"Yeah," said the woman. She was watching him, holding eye contact.

"I heard they're building another one in Northeast," said Martin.

"Oh, right, I heard that too."

"They must be doing pretty well," said Martin. He studied the woman's face. Outside, in the natural light, despite her pretty eyes, she wasn't very attractive. Also, her clothes weren't great. And yet she looked at him hopefully, waiting for him to speak.

He understood this was the moment to ask for her number, or make a date, or invite her to coffee right then. He recognized the moment as it came. And watched it as it passed.

She wasn't the one. But he'd done everything right this time. It was there, if he wanted it.

15

"WAIT, BUT YOU do consider yourself a feminist though, right?" said Petra, 31, bisexual, whose interests included valerian tea, Beach House, and "NOTRUMP." She was sitting across from Martin in the Powell's Books coffee shop.

"Of course," said Martin.

"But you think that women might be happier if they didn't have a job."

"*Might* be happier. In some situations. It's just something to think about. It was my brother-in-law—"

"—Women *have* to work," interrupted Petra. "You know that, right? It's not, like, a choice. We can't depend on men anymore. Men don't help us. Men are basically our worst enemy."

"Hey, I'm with you. I'm just saying that a classic family structure, in some cases, can be...like my brother-in-law—"

"And you do understand that women still get paid less than men. *Way* less than men. Even now they do."

"Right, but that's not—"

"If I get a job, they will literally pay me *less* money than they pay some dude for the exact same thing."

"Not always."

"Yes. *Always.*"

"What kind of job is it?"

"What difference does that make?" said Petra.

"Listen, all I was trying to say is," argued Martin, "if you would let me finish—"

"I don't want to hear about your *brother-in-law*."

"I'm not defending that, I'm just saying—"

"Are you a Trump supporter?" said Petra.

"Me? No. Of course not."

"But you're a white male," she said.

"So what? You're a white female."

"Next thing, you're going to deny your privilege!" she spat, sitting back and staring at him hard across the table.

Martin took a breath. He continued: "All I'm saying is…I have, *myself*, in my own life, known many women, who, when they get into their thirties, they really want to have a kid. It's biology. It's the biological clock, which everyone makes fun of—"

"It amazes me the kind of sexist bullshit men still cling to. *Still*. Do you honestly believe that? The best thing for a woman is to get *pregnant*? Do you have any idea how stupid you sound?"

"It's not me who's stupid."

"Are you sure about that?"

"Yeah, I am sure about that. You're the one who sounds stupid. You can't let one new idea into your head. You sound like you're brainwashed."

Petra fumed. She wore a vintage summer dress that revealed elaborate tattoos on both her pudgy shoulders. She had short hair, dyed rust orange. Her face was quite pretty: blue eyes, full youthful lips, which was why Martin had swiped right on her. When he'd suggested getting coffee, he suspected it would turn into something like this. He just thought...well, he hadn't really thought. He was bored. And his office was nearby. So he'd made the date.

"How old are you?" asked Petra.

"I'm forty-one," said Martin.

"Oh, so you go for the *young* girls."

"You're not that young."

"Ohhhhhh," said Petra. "Look at you! With the *stinging comeback!*"

"Is this what you always do on dates?" asked Martin. "Piss off the guy as much as you can?"

"Yes," said Petra quickly. She stared down into her tea.

Martin believed her. He sipped his latte. He looked around the Powell's coffee shop. The other customers were not on dates. They were involved in more constructive activities: nerding out to *Star Wars* trailers, studying numerology, converting to Wicca.

Martin wanted a family. He did. He didn't want to be sitting in these coffee shops, surrounded by dorks, talking to the Petras of the world.

Jesus. He was turning into Rob....

But no, he wasn't. He was still himself. He glanced back at Petra again. Why was he still sitting here?

"Do you want to get a slice of pizza?" asked Petra.

"What?"

"You heard me. I'm hungry. I want a slice of pizza."

✺

They walked down the street to the nearby pizza place. Martin bought them both a slice of pizza. There was some daddy issue at work here, he decided. He'd heard about women like Petra. Rage-disordered women who wanted to argue or wrestle or punch you during sex. Martin had never been with such a person himself. He tended to bail when things strayed too far out of the ordinary.

It was nice out at least, a breezy end-of-summer day. Martin and Petra sat at a metal table outside, on the dirty sidewalk. A large umbrella shaded them as they bit into their pizza slices. A gang of grime-covered street kids had gathered two tables down from them. A dog lay at their feet, tied to the table by a rope leash.

"So what kind of name is Petra?" asked Martin.

She chewed her pizza for a moment. "Are you seriously asking me that?"

"Why wouldn't I?"

"It's boring, for one thing."

"But isn't that how these things go?" reasoned Martin. "You taunt me into a fight at the coffee shop, then we cool down with some bland chill-out conversation? Then we rile each other into a frenzy again?"

Petra didn't answer.

"What's your sign?" asked Martin.

"Scorpio."

"Yeah, that makes sense."

"What are you?"

the red pill

"Virgo," said Martin.

"Figures."

The two sat there in the cool breeze of the afternoon. Petra was wearing oversized sunglasses. She had nice skin. And the curve of her neck looked sexy in the shade. It was too bad about the bad tattoos. And the chubbiness. And the terrible personality.

"Are we going to have sex when this is over?" asked Martin.

"No."

"Okay. Just checking."

But they did have sex. It took another two hours of driving around and insulting each other. They ended up at her group house, across the river. It was no doubt home to several other sullen, sketchy young people, though the house was thankfully empty when they entered. They went upstairs to her room, which was dominated by a huge bed and tangles of unwashed bedding. The rest of her personal space was a trash heap of spiritual/feminist/gothic knickknacks. Books on her floor: Rebecca Solnit, *Lesbian Magick*, Phoebe Gloeckner's *Diary of a Teenaged Girl*.

They got right to it. Petra was so mannered in her make-out style, Martin imagined a different guy went through this process every weekend. Most of them probably younger and more "alternative" than him. But maybe not. Maybe variety was the name of the game here.

In any event, Martin did his best to give Petra her money's worth. Casual sex was not something he'd experienced often, and he assumed a solid effort was expected of him. But again, Petra was so self-focused, this was not a problem. She knew what she wanted and that's what they did. It was a strange, soulless, mechanical act.

Afterward, there was nothing to say, though Martin tried hard to think of something. He was greatly relieved to let himself out the front door, passing by the old couch and the bicycles on the porch outside. He dropped down the wooden steps in front and strode across the street. It wasn't until he was inside his car, with the doors safely locked, that he let himself relax.

Later though, he felt differently. He had, in this awkward encounter with Petra, ended the single worst sexual drought of his adult life. It had been almost eleven months since he'd last had sex.

His mood the next morning reflected this accomplishment. At EKO, he bounded out of the elevator and settled into his office with great satisfaction. As he worked his way through the items of the day, he took frequent breaks, sitting back in his chair, braiding his fingers behind his head, and doing nothing but smile to himself and enjoy the view out his window.

Later, when the office cleared out, he went online to check in with P-Crusher. He felt like a peer now, as he read through several of the P-man's recent field reports. Martin himself had managed an F-close, as well as the even rarer SDL (Same Day Lay). It was like being in high school again, the giddy irrepressible joy of knowing that he, Martin Harris, had met some chick, maneuvered through her bullshit, took her home, and banged her. And all in one day! Of course, he also acknowledged to himself that finding Petra had been dumb luck. He happened to try the door that was unlocked. Well, whatever. Sometimes it was better to be lucky than good. And he was in the game, at least. He had to give himself credit for that. If you slog through enough dates, sooner or later.... And Jesus, had it really been almost a year since he was last with a woman? It had. That was not good. It wasn't healthy. This point was often stressed in the blogs: Sex is good for you. Sex is natural. And most important of all: *Women want sex as much as you do, so don't be fooled if they pretend otherwise.*

Martin, with his renewed confidence, wanted to read more about that. He surfed around the internet, searching different things: "How often do women need sex?" "Is abstinence bad for women?" "What do women consider a dry spell?"

This last search led to a Reddit post by a young medical student. In it, the young man shared a conversation he'd overheard with three female employees at his hospital. To them a dry spell was *three weeks!* One of them claimed she couldn't even go *one week!* Martin was stunned by this information. Was that possible? Who did this woman have sex with if she was between boyfriends? Or maybe she was never between boyfriends. Or maybe she had a phone full of standbys.

She probably did. A lot of women probably did. Martin felt the harsh truth of this thought move through his body. He'd been trying to get a girlfriend *for years*. The least sexually active of the hospital workers claimed she had once gone two months without sex. The other women were horrified. Two months? Why would she deny herself like that? When she claimed she needed the right man or she didn't feel comfortable, her friends laughed at her. "After two months, you don't worry about the man," they told her. "You do what's good for you."

This particular blog post, which was no worse than many others he had read, festered in Martin's brain the rest of the day. That and Petra, and her me-first sexual style. *Women consider sex an entitlement. While men have to struggle and fight for every scrap they can get.*

Before he left his office he called Sadie and asked if he could come over. Rob was helping a friend build a garage that night, so when he arrived it was Martin, Sadie, and the kids. This was fine. Martin didn't feel like talking anyway. He wanted his sister nearby. And the kids. And some semblance of routine and familiarity.

He helped himself to a Bud Light and settled on the couch to watch *Frozen*, which the kids were only allowed to watch on special occasions. Martin sprawled on the couch, a child on either side of him, and watched the Disney animated fairy tale.

the red pill

In this way he distracted himself while his brain processed the day's revelations. *Women didn't give a shit about guys.* How had he gotten so old and yet still understood so little about the world? Or maybe he *had* learned this lesson and forgotten. Life was funny that way; it never changed, but you did. And every time you changed, you had to go back and learn the same things all over again.

16

"IT's A VERY small window we're dealing with," Simon Howard told Martin over drinks at Kelly's Bar and Grill. They were discussing Simon's most recent talks with Pacifica, and the acquisition of EKO.

"How so?" said Martin.

"Their last quarter profits were down and they're restructuring," said Simon, contemplating his drink for a moment. "And now there's some new people involved. That's the hard part. The people we're dealing with keep changing."

Martin, as usual, accepted Simon's assessment of the situation unconditionally. Simon was the business guy. The two had known each other since they were teenagers. They'd lived in different areas of the city but had run in the same circles of Portland's elite high school kids. As he had in their company, Simon tended toward "leadership" roles as a teenager. He knew everyone. He knew where the parties were. He was generous with his friends, almost like a politician at times, but then occasionally became cruel and selfish, in the proportion necessary to maintain his high social standing. He was very popular and he slept with many, many girls.

"We just gotta be patient," continued Simon. "And trust the process. It does make me nervous though. All the delays. And these new people. Now there's this guy in San Francisco—"

the red pill

"Raj Taheed?"

"Yeah. How did you know? What do you know about him?"

"Nothing. I just signed his birthday card."

"Fuck. He's a weird dude. Can't read him at all. He's somehow got himself involved in this." Simon shook his head. "A guy like that, he comes out of nowhere, and suddenly, you can't get your deal done. And you look at him like, what does he want? A payoff? A cut? How do you get rid of this guy?"

"Does that happen? That someone wants money?"

Simon snorted and downed the rest of his drink. "Fuck yes, it happens. When there's millions of dollars involved all sorts of fucked-up shit happens."

Martin nodded along with this. "And would we do that? Pay him off? How do you even do that?"

"I don't know. But I'm gonna find out. I'm meeting with this new lawyer in LA next week."

Their office mates Regan and Melissa walked in a few minutes later. Regan, who was barely old enough to be in a bar, was wearing another one of her avant-garde outfits.

"Look who's here!" called Simon from their place at the bar.

Martin was not thrilled to see Regan, not after blowing it with her the other day with the "fashion icon" comment. But whatever. He picked up his beer and the four of them got a table.

Then as soon as they sat down, Dylan and Nick Chen appeared. "We have the whole company here!" said Simon, making room at the table.

Nick and Dylan pulled up extra chairs. The waitress came and took drink orders. They all made small talk for a while and then Trump came up.

"Dude, he's gonna win!" exclaimed Nick, who was twenty-four and their newest hire. "I'm serious. I don't bet, but if I did, I would bet on him. I would! I would bet one thousand dollars!"

"He can't win. How's he gonna win?" said Dylan.

"People hate Hillary," said Nick. "They do."

"Do you hate Hillary?" asked Dylan.

"Yes," said Nick. "I mean, no. I don't care myself. But yes. People hate her. So many people hate her."

Melissa didn't agree and made a look of disgust with her face.

"People are *racist*. That's what it is," said Dylan. "If Trump wins it's only because people are way more racist than they admit."

"Yes! Yes, they are!" said Nick. "They're totally racist. That's what I'm saying."

"Trump is like if David Duke ran for president," said Dylan.

"Who is David Duke?" asked Nick.

"A famous racist guy," said Martin.

Nick was getting excited like he did. So much so, it was making his colleagues uncomfortable. "People are sick of diversity!" he said. "And on Facebook, everyone attacking each other."

"People aren't sick of diversity," said Dylan.

"Yes, they are!" insisted Nick. "People are so racist. And then they accuse other people of being racist. And you can lose your job. Even if you notice the smallest thing. Racist! Racist! You're a racist! I'm Chinese. I know."

Several people chuckled.

"Maybe in China," scoffed Dylan.

"No! No!" sputtered Nick. He was talking very fast. "I swear to you, I swear to God, you guys. You watch. He's going to win!"

Martin shifted his attention away from this conversation and began to watch Regan. In the office she often appeared bored and indifferent, but here at Kelly's, seated next to her rock-star boss, she was more fully her young, beautiful self. She seemed to glow in the dark congeniality of the bar, as she sipped demurely at a rum and Coke through a straw.

Simon began to argue with Nick. Regan ignored the conversation. There was something odd about how she sat there, so at ease, so self-contained....

"Trump is a horrible person," Melissa was saying. "If he gets elected, I swear, I don't know what I'll do. I think my head will explode."

"It's hard to imagine," said Dylan.

"No, but you guys! You guys!" Nick interjected. "Think about it...."

Martin went back to watching Regan. They had not spoken since their conversation. Had she thought he was hitting on her? Probably. She probably thought everyone was hitting on her. He regretted the conversation now. She was a serious nine, or possibly even a ten by Portland standards, plus she was twenty-one years old, the absolute prime of her beauty and sexual power. Well, whatever. It was practice. No harm, no foul. He looked around at the rest of the bar. More people had come in. The after work crowd. People in suits. There were no single women that he could see.

When he'd finished his scan of the place, he glanced back at Regan again and noticed a smirk on her face. She was indulging in a smug, secret delight in something. What was going on with her?

And then he knew: *she was fucking Simon.* Of course, she was! Jesus. Where had Martin been? He almost laughed out loud but restrained himself. He sunk back into his chair. Simon was fucking the intern! How predictable. How fucking cliché. And as usual, Martin was the last person to figure it out.

When the party broke up, Martin slipped away and went for a walk along the river by himself. Other people were out, enjoying the September night: young couples, gangs of kids, bike people with their helmets and Lycra outfits. One thing about Portland, it wasn't as white as it once was. And yet for some reason, it didn't feel particularly diverse either. Probably because of the proximity to East Asia and Mexico. People of mixed Asian/Hispanic/Caucasian ethnicity became hard to identify. They weren't black; they were just sort of...tan.

None of this was anything you could say out loud, of course. Martin had always been interested in such things but was used to pained looks whenever he talked cultural or "population" anthropology with friends. And that was before everyone had become so touchy. His favorite theory was that Asians had originally settled North America, crossing the Bering Sea on foot or on boats, during the last Ice Age. You could look at Native Americans or indigenous Central Americans and see the resemblance. Some of the languages spoken in isolated parts of South America shared common roots with Chinese. Or so he had read. But of course, even speculating about such things was now considered racist and unacceptable.

Martin found a bench and took a seat. He checked his phone as he sat and found a new text there. It was from Petra of all people.

Hey. Do you want to come over?

Martin studied the text for a moment and wrote back:

Is this a booty call?

Petra answered:

Call it whatever you want.

Martin felt a zing of excitement. She was serious. She wanted him to come over and have sex, like right now!

He jumped up, jamming his phone in his pocket, but then stopped himself. Maybe that wasn't the best move. He steadied himself, then sat back down on the bench. He remembered what a pain in the ass Petra was. How joyless the sex had been. What her bathroom looked like.

He went back to his phone and read through their correspondence again. She'd been snippy, annoying, demanding throughout.

On the other hand, *sex.*

You always have options, he reminded himself. The manosphere constantly advised him to think that way. Even if it wasn't true. In this case Martin *didn't* have any options. But what would happen if he acted like he did?

He decided to find out. He went back to Petra's message and read it again. Then he typed:

I'm busy

It felt good to push send. Really good. But then it didn't seem like enough. So he went back to her number and blocked it. This also felt good. And then a moment later, in a fit of exhilaration, he deleted Petra from his phone completely. That felt the best of all.

17

THERE WAS ANOTHER guy Martin had grown up with who he'd been thinking about lately. William Belknap, whose father had also been a lawyer and whose grandfather had been a senator from Oregon. In grade school, William had been one of the popular kids. He was roughly equivalent to Martin in the male social hierarchy, a decent athlete, dressed cool, was a little on the shy side, but was considered one of the "cute boys" by the girls of their class. But somewhere around seventh or eighth grade, just when things were getting interesting, he'd withdrawn from his natural peer group. Martin remembered this about William because Martin had been slow to pick up on this social change and had insisted on including William, and inviting him to things, long after the other kids had figured out to exclude him.

Martin was sitting at his sister's dinner table while he pondered this. His mother was across from him, with the Carr family around them both. They were eating pasta and apple sausage, with a delicious salad containing halved cherry tomatoes. The conversation was the usual: the kids' day at school, Rob's new subdivision, a new stoplight in the neighborhood that needed to be explained to Jack for when he got old enough to walk to school.

Martin slipped back into his memory. What had happened to William Belknap? In high school, he lost more ground. He had acne, Martin remembered, but lots of kids had that; it wouldn't necessarily hurt you socially. Whatever it was, William lost most of his guy friends and never got near the girls. Martin had been surprised by this. There weren't that many cool boys, and William should have been one of them. Why didn't some girl coax poor William out of his shell? Wouldn't it have been worth it? But the girls had steadfastly avoided William. They didn't care about potential; they wanted the boys who were popular now.

Among the guys, it was wondered if William might be gay. But there was no indication of that. It was more that he was unable to socially integrate; he couldn't relax and just *be*. Or maybe he didn't want to compete for status. Or perhaps the world in general was too much for him; he was overly sensitive.

William became even more remote and bookish as an upperclassman, Martin recalled. He won several scholarly honors at graduation. But that wouldn't have been hard, if you were reasonably smart, which he was.

William disappeared after that. He either didn't go to college or didn't tell anyone if he did. During Martin's college years, while home for holidays, Martin would often ask Portland friends about him, and occasionally someone knew something. At one time he was in India, doing nonprofit, or possibly church-related volunteer work. To Martin, this confirmed his own private suspicion: William was some kind of modern monk type. An ascetic. There were people like that, even in contemporary America. It was weird, but totally possible. Another time he heard William was in San Diego, possibly doing something secretive with the military. That didn't really make sense, or maybe it did; maybe his senator grandfather had got him a job.

But then, a few years ago, the weirdest news of all had filtered back to Portland: William had supposedly married a Vietnamese woman, through a foreign-bride marriage service. The people he heard this from seemed not particularly surprised. How else would a person like William find someone? Especially as he got older and didn't have a career or any obvious accomplishments to speak of?

When dinner was over, Martin organized the cleaning up. Ashley and Jack were supposed to help but only Ashley showed up in the kitchen. Ashley handed him the dishes, which he rinsed and put in the dishwasher.

Later, sitting with his mother and sister over coffee, Martin asked Sadie about William Belknap.

"I don't remember him," she said. "He was in your class?"

"Yeah, he was this odd guy, popular in middle school, but in high school, he kind of faded off the scene."

"And his grandfather was a senator?" said Sadie.

"I remember him," said their mother. "The Belknap boy."

"The last I heard he got a mail-order bride," said Martin. Sadie scoffed. "I don't think people still do that."

"I think they do," said Martin. "Or something equivalent." Rob was in the front room doing something. "Rob!" called out Martin. "Do people still get mail-order brides?"

"Why are you asking me?" said Rob from the other room.

"Maybe *you* should try that," Eileen said to her son. She was serious.

"Mom, I'm doing a lot better with women nowadays."

"You don't even have a girlfriend."

"He is doing a lot better, Mom," said Sadie. "Rob is helping him."

"How is Rob helping him?"

"He's fed me the red pill," said Martin.

"What's that?"

"Rob is teaching Martin how to meet women in real life," said Sadie. "So he doesn't have to go on dating sites."

"How do you do that?"

"You 'cold approach' them," said Martin.

"'Cold approach'?" said his mother. "That doesn't sound good."

"It's a technique, Mom," said Sadie. "They practice it. They learn things to say."

"Like what?"

"Like you insult the girl, to lower her self-esteem," said Sadie. "And that makes her like you."

"*What!?*" said her mother.

"That's not what it is," said Martin.

"Isn't that what *negging* is?" said Sadie.

"You learn to tease women," Martin told his mother. "And have fun with them. And not take it too seriously."

"You shouldn't need someone to teach you that," said his mother. "Not if you're a man."

"I know, Mom," said Martin. "But I'm an idiot. So that's what I'm doing. I'm improving myself."

"Did Rob do that to you?" Eileen asked Sadie, seriously.

"A little bit."

"What did he say to you?"

"Oh, God, I don't remember."

"And did it work?"

"Sure. I mean, I already liked him. So I let him say his stupid lines. And pretended I was falling for it."

"We didn't play all these games when I was growing up," said Eileen.

"You didn't have to," said Martin. "Women liked men in your day."

"Why don't they like them now?"

"We still like them," Sadie assured her mother. "It's just that a lot has changed."

"There's sexual harassment," said Martin.

"The world is more political," said Sadie. "There's more at stake."

"More at stake?" scoffed their mother. "Then in my day? When you married one man, and were stuck with him for the rest of your life? No, there's *less* at stake now. A lot less. That's your problem."

Later, driving home, Martin tried to picture William Belknap standing with flowers in an airport, awaiting his foreign bride. She'd get off the plane and there she'd be, in America. What would that be like? Walking her out to your car. Introducing her to the American freeway, the American strip mall, the American suburb. Driving home, you'd talk a bit. Hopefully she knows a little English. If not, you begin the long difficult game of teaching it to her.

And then a few months of getting her up to speed: how to drive, how to pay for stuff, how to work the remote. You'd help her find things to do: night classes, crafting, activities where she could make friends. You might take her to the mall. Teach her the rules of American fashion. What not to wear as well as what to wear, depending on what sort of village she came from. (Martin saw such a woman as a country rube, though that might not be the case.)

There'd be some rough spots, no doubt. She'd be lonely. She'd get frustrated. She might not like America. She might not like *you*. And God only knows what weird habits and hygienic practices a rural Vietnamese female might have. There'd be some adjustments, some teary nights, some moments of total incomprehension. But maybe not that much worse than you'd experience with an American wife.

And then sex. That would be strange. But maybe good; maybe at first sex would be the glue that held you together. And then pregnancy and childbirth, which would give everyone something to focus on. Once born, the kids would grow up relatively normal, Americanized, with the slight variance of the unusual mother. Since she'd be married to William Belknap, who still had family money Martin assumed, the house would be nice, the local schools good, when it got time for that.

And the day-to-day life, what would that be? That was the interesting part. Would there be some noticeable difference in how she treated her husband than how an American woman would? Was the foreign bride actually going to be nicer to you? More helpful? More traditional?

Probably it would all even out. Humans were humans after all. And then someday her kids would have kids and she would become the beloved grandmother, still with the accent and the funny customs that everyone teased her about. And eventually she'd die and William too and no one would even remember the odd random way they had found each other.

It didn't sound that bad, Martin decided, as he parallel parked his car in the street below his apartment. Still, Martin wouldn't do it. He'd never be that desperate. If his normal way of life could not produce a workable marriage, then he would accept his fate. He just wasn't suited to it. Or he'd been born at the wrong time.

18

THE FIRST PRESIDENTIAL debate, on September 29, 2016, had everyone buzzing in Portland. Martin hadn't planned on watching it but got dragged to a bar by Dylan and Nick Chen to view the proceedings. Martin hadn't seen Trump debate during the primaries, except for the short clips that circulated nightly on the internet and the late-night talk shows. In the bar, he got his first prolonged look of Trump's debating style. There he was, with his bizarre hair and hard, remorseless face. He really did look like the classic school-yard bully. Dylan and Nick Chen were teasing each other. Nick Chen kept insisting he wasn't *voting* for Trump but still believed he would win. Dylan was there "for the lulz," waiting for Trump to do something "heinous." Martin watched for a while, then got bored, then ordered a beer and scanned the crowded bar for women.

One possibility was only a few feet away. An office worker of some sort; she had a fit every time Trump spoke. "Oh my God! What the *fuck?* I can't even...." She was attractive, pretty face, business attire, probably early thirties. Her two friends were less vocal but they looked the same: serious, intelligent, sixes or sevens on the beauty scale. They'd obviously just got off work at the courthouse or one of the downtown office buildings. While Nick and Dylan argued, Martin studied this threesome. Any one of them would probably be good girl-friend material. This was exactly what Rob kept telling him. Approaching women in real life was the only way to access competent, sane females.

Martin casually wandered over and stood by them. The first woman was too incensed by the debate to talk to, but after laughing with her at some Trump gaffe, Martin made a sly pivot move, circling behind her and ending up beside her red-haired friend.

When the TV cut to a Toyota commercial, he casually turned to the redhead. "Can you believe Trump?" he asked.

"I know," she replied.

"Hillary seems to be handling it okay," said Martin, holding his pint glass against his chest.

"Yeah."

"You *are* rooting for Hillary?" joked Martin.

"I hate Trump," said the woman without smiling.

She didn't seem interested in discussing it further and Martin considered his situation. The general advice on the manosphere was: never force it. If you get a lackluster response, keep moving. Try someone else.

"Who's your friend?" said Martin, indicating the third woman. But that was too forward. She wasn't going to introduce her friend. And anyway, they'd come back from the commercial, and all the women had refocused on the TV. The crowd booed loudly when they showed Trump at his podium. They cheered when they showed Hillary.

Martin made his way back to Nick and Dylan. Trump was speaking and Martin actually watched him for a few seconds.

He didn't seem as ridiculous as he did on the clips he saw online, but he did keep repeating the same basic phrases over and over. Hillary wasn't much better. She had that difficult monotone voice. He looked over at the three women, who'd been scowling at Trump. They were still scowling.

The next weekend, Martin joined Dylan and Nick on another excursion, this time to a high school football game. Dylan had been urging them to come, claiming it was a great demographic study. You could see actual American teenagers, up close, what they wore, what they did; you could hear their slang and speech patterns. Also, it was fun to watch a real football game.

And so Martin went along. It was a beautiful Friday night: early October, a smoky chill in the air. Two of the better teams in the city were playing. Martin, Dylan, and Nick took their place in the bleachers, in the parents' section of the home team.

When they were halfway through the first quarter, Nick began to complain.

"We're in the old-people section," he said to Dylan.

"Yes, we are."

"I thought we were going to be where the teenagers are," said Nick.

"Don't worry, there's plenty around."

It was true. There were teenagers everywhere. Occasionally a thirteen- or fourteen-year-old would come over to the parent section to check in with Mom or Dad. But the older teens were somewhere else, in their own area.

"I thought we were going to sit with the high school students." said Nick.

"We can do that," said Dylan. "I thought we could start here. You can walk around if you want."

But Nick didn't want to walk around by himself. And he didn't like being surrounded by middle-aged parents. Nick himself could have easily passed for being in high school.

They sat through the rest of the first quarter and part of the second. "Let's go sit over there," said Nick, pointing to the student section. "That's where things are happening."

"Okay, okay," said Dylan. "At halftime."

"Why don't you go check it out, Nick," offered Martin. He also preferred sitting with the adults. The teenagers looked scary to him. They were bigger than he remembered. Also, they moved so fast. They bounded up and down the bleachers like giant beasts. They were physically dangerous.

Nick became annoying. "I thought. You said. The purpose of coming here..." he began. He was going to pester them until he got his way.

So they got up. They walked through the packed stadium until they found a place between the student section and the marching band, who were at that moment down in the end zone, getting ready to perform at halftime.

Martin, Dylan, and Nick seated themselves. It turned out Nick was right. It was more fun to be closer to the young people. They were bouncy and excited and full of mischief. The girls especially; they flirted, schemed, whispered to each other.

So that was fun. It was also fun to watch the game. Watching live, Martin saw things you didn't see on TV. The wide receivers blocking on a run play, the referees slipping in the muddy grass. Since the players were high school students, they were not always the proper sizes for their respective positions. Some of the guys were too big, some too small, some so skinny you wondered if they could survive a collision. Also, you were close enough to see the disparities of age. Some of the players had the faces of children, others the grim determination of grown men.

Unfortunately, after halftime, the marching band returned to the bleachers. The three advertising men had to make room for the forty pimply musicians. And then they began to play. It became so loud Martin put his hands over his ears. They endured this for a few minutes and then Dylan insisted they return to the adult section. So back they went, cramming themselves in among the parents again.

"I still haven't heard any teen slang," Nick complained.

"We're *absorbing* the *atmosphere*," insisted Dylan.

"I don't like the atmosphere. It's boring."

"Go for a walk then," said Dylan. "And stop whining. I wanna watch the game."

"But you said...."

Martin was getting bored too and as the third quarter dragged on, he decided to walk back to the concession stand and get a coffee.

the red pill

This small errand was quite enjoyable. Walking by himself, Martin did get a feeling for the contemporary high school scene. The frenetic energy of the teenagers. How happy and excited they were, despite their oily skin and awkward bodies. The parents, too, were full of light and sparkle and sexual possibility. There was also the grumbly old grandpa types, lifelong fans of the local school, with their team hats and windbreakers. Most energetic of all: the youngest kids, the little brothers and sisters, nine and ten and eleven years old, racing through the crowd like tiny demons. Someday, far, far in the future, they too would be initiated into the sacred mysteries of *high school*....

Martin found the concession booth and got in line. It was mostly parents inside, volunteers. When it was his turn Martin asked for a coffee, and got one, in a small Styrofoam cup. When he asked if they had creamer, the volunteers weren't sure, and before he could stop them, they began a frantic, all-encompassing search. Finally, an old plastic container of powdered creamer was found, a big chunk of which dropped into Martin's cup, ruining it. He was forced to ask for another coffee. And so the whole process began again.

When he finally had his coffee, he stepped aside and stood against a cinder block wall, watching the stream of kids and parents flow past.

"Well, that was quite an ordeal," a woman said to him. She had been stuck behind him in the line and took the place next to him, against the wall.

"I know," said Martin. "Sorry about that. I should have known not to ask for anything special."

The woman also had a hot drink of some kind and took a tentative sip of it.

"What's that?" Martin asked.

"Cider," said the woman.

"Hot cider. Good call. Good night for it."

No sooner had she lowered her cup then two young girls came running up to her.

"Omigod!" they squealed. "Miss Parker! Miss Parker! Have you seen Bryce? Or Justin? Or those guys?"

"No, I haven't," said Miss Parker.

"Because...omigod, omigod, because Justin said. Well, you know how Justin said that stuff about Carmen? It's like, I need to talk to him, like *right now*, like *right now*...."

"No, Brianna, I haven't seen any of those guys. Have you looked in the student section?"

"No because...because..." said Brianna. She was twirling her hair wildly with her finger and bouncing up and down on her tiptoes. She had large, super-nerd glasses.

"I don't know where they are," said Miss Parker.

"Um...um..." stammered Brianna. "What...what do you think of Justin? Do you think he's a bad person?"

"I don't know Justin and if I did, I wouldn't have an opinion about him. I'm your teacher, Brianna, not your BFF, remember?"

"Omigod, omigod, because...I mean, Justin has said a *lot* of things about Carmen.... You know...he shouldn't talk about people like that...."

Suddenly the friend grabbed Brianna by her arm and pointed. There he was! Justin! Or Bryce! Or whoever.

the red pill

"Good-bye, Miss Parker!" they shrieked as they took off running, on their wobbly, colt legs.

Martin stood with his coffee, smiling at this. He looked into the woman's face. It was a serious adult face, but with humor in it, and a certain wisdom, Martin thought. "So you're Miss Parker," he said.

"Yes, I am."

"And you teach those kids?"

"Yes, I do."

"That's funny. I'm in advertising. I try to sell them stuff."

19

Two weeks later, Angela Parker snored softly beside Martin. They were at her house, in her bedroom, in her bed. This was their second date, not counting the conversation at the football game.

Angela was naked. Martin lay on his side next to her, also naked. He stared at her back in the dim light. Her body was incredible: full, warm, inviting, heavenly. The entire evening had been incredible. Angela had made it clear she was ready to take things to the next level. And so they had moved effortlessly from a restaurant meal, back to her house, into her kitchen, where they made hot cider in honor of the football game that had brought them together. It was Angela who initiated the kiss, which was also incredible, exquisite, and yet relaxed and dreamlike. *How easy things went when it was the right person!* Martin had thought. *How little you had to rely on games or attitude or manipulation!* They'd made out for several minutes, and then done a silent slow dance around the kitchen, his fingertips gradually exploring her neck and face and bare shoulders: everything happening slowly, calmly, as if they had all the time in the world.

In bed, he'd finished a little quick. She was tired, she'd said, so she was probably glad. She was literally asleep sixty seconds after he moved off her. Martin tried to imagine her life as she breathed rhythmically beside him: single, with a thirteen-year-old daughter—*thirteen!*—that alone sounded like an all-consuming life challenge. And her daily work routine: up at 5:30 a.m., coffee, the car, and then walking into that blast of adolescent energy each morning.

He found himself touching her hair as she slept. He stroked the side of her head. Then he scooted closer, sliding his leg over one of her thick thighs. The warmth of her, the welcome softness of her skin. Martin was so happy he could cry.

At work on Monday, Martin ran into Regan, who was handing out some sort of health insurance disclaimer.

"I thought we weren't doing these," Martin said to Regan.

Regan shrugged. "Simon wants everyone to sign it."

"Do we have to read it?"

She shrugged again. "I never sign anything I don't read."

Martin watched her leave the room. She was wearing... what did they call those...a pencil skirt? Narrow and long. Vintage, it looked like. With it she wore a pressed red blouse with frills around the neck.

Martin put the form aside and found the one budget proposal he needed to finalize that day. But he couldn't focus yet. He sat back in his chair, braided his hands behind his head, and stared out the window. Angela Parker. He thought of her house. He thought of her bedroom. He thought of her daughter. What would she be like? Thirteen. That was possibly the worst age a human could be. Fortunately, at least on the dating sites, most women stressed that their children were not part of their romantic life. "You will not be meeting my son/daughter," they often announced in their profile. So probably it wouldn't be an issue.

He thought about the sex. Several vivid images had stayed very clearly in his mind. Angela had left the lights on, obviously aware of how good she looked. *She'll be at school now*, he thought, glancing at his watch. In fact, she had been at school for four hours already.

Regan was still wandering around when he went to lunch. Martin avoided eye contact. He was afraid of Regan now. Not only had he embarrassed himself flirting with her, but he was convinced she was sleeping with Simon. It was a hard situation to untangle. Did she now have a special status within the office because of that? He tried to picture himself, as her boss, telling her to do something. He couldn't really see that happening. He would have to ask. And ask nicely. And he wasn't sure she would do it.

Once he was on the street, he felt better about things. He forgot about Regan and enjoyed the special lightness in his heart caused by Angela Parker. No, it wasn't a perfect situation. People would have issues with it. Rob would disapprove. "Don't get involved with single mothers" was the conventional wisdom in the manosphere. But the manosphere was primarily for twenty-five-year-olds, in which case that was excellent advice. At Martin's age, a prospective girlfriend having a kid was likely a sign of sanity. Probably, it was more of a red flag to *not* have a kid by forty.

the red pill

It didn't matter. He'd gone on two highly enjoyable dates with an attractive, lively, intelligent woman, approximately his age, open to him, interested in him. They'd had amazing sex. They would probably have more amazing sex. He already wanted to call her and tell her about his day. It was truly shocking how a little female affection could turn your life around.

After lunch, Martin checked in with Sadie and asked if he might come over for dinner that week. She told him to come over that night, which he did, arriving early and running into Libby in the kitchen. She was also staying for dinner. Martin didn't want to talk about his new relationship in front of Libby, so he kept quiet, got a Bud Light out of the fridge, and stood at the kitchen island eating pretzels out of a bowl.

"His polls are dropping. He can't win," Sadie was telling Libby.

Libby wasn't much into politics though.

"What are you hearing?" Sadie asked Martin.

Martin shrugged. "We have this Asian guy at work, he's twenty-four. He's guaranteeing that Trump will win."

"Guaranteeing? How?"

"He says he would bet a thousand dollars," said Martin, chewing a pretzel.

"Well, he'll lose," said Sadie.

"I don't know, he's a pretty smart guy. He's got his finger on the pulse."

"What are you, a Trumper now?" asked his sister.

"No. I'm just saying," said Martin. "He's a twenty-four-year-old Asian dude, and he's convinced. He says we're all racists. Meaning Americans." Martin got some Dijon mustard out of the refrigerator and spooned some of it onto a plate. He'd learned this in New York: dipping pretzels into mustard. It was delicious but nobody did it in Oregon.

"I feel weird about it," said Sadie. "I have this bad feeling. Like, nobody that I know wants him. And none of the commentators on TV want him. And every day they show him doing something idiotic and giving very clear and definite reasons why he is not fit to be president. But his supporters, it's like *they don't see it.* These people, whoever they are, it has no effect. And they stay with him. It's like this army of...I don't know what."

"Deplorables," said Martin.

"Or not even that," said Sadie. "People who are immune to common sense. I mean, I understand conservatism. I do. And if he's going to claim to be a Christian, well, OK...but that's not what he is. What he is, is a used car salesman. He *looks* like a used car salesman. How do they not see that? Or am I crazy? Am I missing something?"

"You're right. You're totally right," said Libby, who had seen Martin dipping his pretzels in the mustard and had come over to try it. She bumped up against him as she dipped.

"Yeah, but you have to understand how they feel," said Martin.

"How do they feel?"

the red pill

Martin had read a *New York Times* article about this that afternoon. "They feel like nobody cares about them. The TV mocks them. And lectures them. And tries to force stuff down their throat. And they're sick of it. They're butt-hurt."

"Butt-hurt," said Libby. "That's a good word for it."

"I'm sorry but it scares me," said Sadie. "And what does this mean for the future? So we stop him and then what happens? Someone else will try the same thing, except that person will be smarter, and an actual politician, and he won't make every mistake in the book, like Trump is doing."

Libby and Martin enjoyed their pretzels. Martin was thinking about Angela. It was unclear what Libby was thinking about.

"Where's Delilah?" Martin asked her.

"Home with Kevin."

"How are you guys doing?"

Libby smiled with her usual faux flirtiness. "Okay."

Sadie finished what she was doing and poured herself a glass of white wine. She sat at the kitchen island with them. She tried one of the pretzels dipped in mustard.

"It's so weird to think of people in places like Texas or Idaho...." said Sadie. "Like do they really not believe what they see on TV? Like every day they watch the news and think: *That's not true, that's not true, that's not true?*"

"Fake news," said Libby.

"I know," said Sadie. "It's Trump's way of neutralizing the truth. It's like Fascism 101. It's, like, literally, by the book, *totalitarianism*. And stupid Americans. Do they even know this? Do they know history? Do they know anything?"

◈

Rob arrived late. He was sweaty, dirty, with dried mud on his jeans and plaster dust in his hair. He had to take a quick shower before they could begin.

Finally, they sat down to eat. The meal was good but uneventful. The kids were quiet. Rob said nothing. Libby tried making conversation with Sadie with limited results. Eventually, Martin couldn't contain himself any longer. "So I met someone," he said to the sound of multiple chewing mouths.

Sadie was the first to swallow. "Oh my God, who?"

"A teacher. A high school teacher."

"How'd you meet her?" asked Rob.

"I went to a high school football game with some guys from the office. I was standing by the concession stand and this woman was standing there and we started talking."

"You met a teacher?" said Jack.

Jeb was banging something.

"Jeb! Stop it, buddy!" said Rob.

"And what happened?" asked Sadie.

"We hit it off. She was funny. And the students kept coming up to her. She's pretty popular, I guess."

Libby's face glassed over a bit.

"How old is she?" asked Sadie.

"Forty."

"And she's single?"

"Yeah. But she has a kid," clarified Martin. "A daughter. Thirteen."

"Oh," said Sadie, thinking for a moment. "Well, that's okay. There's nothing wrong with that."

Libby poked at her food with her fork.

"So she's divorced?" said Rob.

"Yeah," said Martin. "The dad lives nearby. They split time fifty-fifty."

"What's divorce?" asked Ashley.

"It's when two people who are married stop being married," said Sadie.

"Why do they do that?" asked the girl.

"Because," said Sadie. To Martin she said: "That's great news."

"Yeah, I'm kind of excited," said Martin.

"I could tell you had a secret," said Libby.

"So what's happened so far?" asked Rob.

Martin thought for a moment before he spoke. Somehow Rob was going to turn this into a bad thing. There would be some rule, some reason not to go forward. But he didn't care. Rob's stuff worked for Rob. Martin was a different kind of person.

"Well," said Martin, "we were standing there and we started talking and it was like...an instant connection."

Everyone at the table was rapt.

"So then, the next week, she invited me to come to a play rehearsal they were doing at her school. Which was totally fun. Her name is Angela, by the way. Angela Parker. And of course, the kids all call her Miss Parker, which is super cute."

"Sounds super cute," said Libby.

"It sounds great," said Sadie.

"And what then?" asked Rob.

"And then last weekend, I took her out to dinner. This nice Moroccan place downtown. We had a great time."

"That's wonderful, Martin," said Sadie. "And you're going to see her again?"

"Yeah. Of course. I assume so."

"What does she look like?" asked Ashley.

Martin smiled. "She's about this tall," he said, holding his hand about even with his own head. "And she has pretty brown eyes. And long brown hair, which she sort of gathers up on the top of her head in a messy kind of way."

"I hate teachers," said Jack.

"No, you don't," said Sadie.

"Yes, I do," said Jack. "They're mean and they put you in time-out."

Everyone chuckled. Martin was glad for the comic relief. Also, he was just so happy. He couldn't stop grinning. He actually tried to stop. But he couldn't.

20

"IT'S NOT RECOMMENDED, what you're getting into, with the single mom thing...." said Rob.

This was a couple days later, at the Arena Sports Bar. Martin had a feeling this was how the conversation would go. "What the fuck, Rob," he replied. "Don't give me a bunch of shit about this. This is serious. This could turn into something."

"What's it going to turn into?"

"I don't know. Maybe nothing. Or maybe I'm gonna get laid a bunch by a smokin' hot high school teacher who I actually like. Someone I can actually talk to for a change."

"Okay. Yeah. Sounds great."

"And I'm definitely going to play it out. I'm not going to stop doing it because there's some rule, on some website."

"I wasn't suggesting that."

"I'm not fucking twenty. I understand that would be good advice for the younger guys but at my age, most women, if they have their shit together at all, they're going to have kids."

"But what if you want to have kids?"

"I could still do that. Why couldn't I do that? For now, I'm enjoying this for what it is."

Martin didn't like this thing of other men telling him what to do. Or male friends saving you from the clutches of some duplicitous female. "Guys hanging out" was a big theme in advertising. According to surveys, every male on earth wished he had more or better guy friends. But, really, male friendship was overrated.

"Have you met the kid yet?"

"Dude, I've gone out with her twice! No, I haven't met the kid. And I'm probably not going to. Women don't want you to meet their kids."

"Where's the dad?"

"He lives nearby. They get along. It's fine. Seriously, Rob, everything's fine."

"Okay. All right," said Rob, lifting his hand in surrender.

"You got lucky with your situation," said Martin. "The rest of us aren't you. Angela's great. She really is. The sex was amazing...." Martin paused for comic effect. "Except that she fell asleep like thirty seconds afterward."

Rob chuckled. "Really?"

"Her schedule's brutal. But she can handle it. And it'll be good anyway. It'll keep things from going too fast."

"I'm sure she's fantastic," said Rob.

"Look," insisted Martin, "it's not like I'm not self-aware. Obviously, I'm falling for her and I'm not supposed to do that. But you know what? It's fun to fall in love. I'm enjoying it. I haven't felt like this in a long time."

"Hey, I'm behind you. I am. But I still feel obligated to warn you."

"Warn me about what?"

"That no matter what you want from it, no matter how casual it is, certain rules still apply. If you gush all over her, if you make her the center of your universe, you're gonna lose your edge. And then you'll lose her. Nobody can respect someone who acts like that. Man or woman."

Martin shook his head in frustration. "Dude, it's so not like that. Listen, no offense, but this is the difference between you and me. She's not some hot babe. She's not twenty-one. She's a nice, solid, middle-aged person, trying to make a difference, doing the teacher thing. And she's smart. She understands things. Even from the couple times we've been together, there's already an understanding between us. There's a calmness. A normalcy. And it's fucking great. It's exactly what I want. Do you understand that? It's not even *about* sex. It's way more basic than that."

Rob nodded. He looked up at the closest TV for a minute. The broadcasters were discussing this weekend's football games.

"I just want things to work out for you, that's all," said Rob.

"Thank you," said Martin. He sipped his beer and looked up at the TV. In his mind, though, he'd already made some decisions. No more meet-ups with Rob. No more discussions about Martin's love life. He was glad to have gotten closer to his brother-in-law. This whole experience had been educational and—Martin was the first to admit—had helped him with his confidence and his overall mind-set with women.

But honestly, he was glad this phase of his life was over. He'd got what he came for: a real girlfriend. Now Rob and his sex theories and P-Crusher and the right-wingers, they could all quietly ride off into the sunset and out of Martin's life. He was not like that. He was a normal guy.

Meanwhile, time seemed to accelerate as the days got shorter, the air got colder, and the presidential election came into view. Suddenly, it was November, and soon after, voting day. Martin woke up early, dressed, and drove to an elementary school near his apartment. He parked in the parking lot, greeted an old woman, stood in line, and then voted for Hillary Clinton, Democrat, and a few other local names he'd heard of. His vote was unnecessary. Hillary would win Oregon easily. But it felt good to be there: the polling place, the random citizens, the bad coffee from the urn on the cafeteria table. This was America. This was what you did.

At the office the TV in the big screening room was on all day, people checking in with the early results. Nothing unusual seemed to be in the works. People assumed the outcome. At five, Martin left and went to the YMCA for his Tuesday night pickup basketball game. Nobody was talking about the election, he noticed. The first game he played in was mostly older guys like himself. The pace was exaggeratedly slow. People kidded each other and made jokes about their aging bones and feeble reaction times. In the second game, though, some newly arrived younger guys joined in. They were more serious, and Martin's older team lost badly. He spent the next game in the bleachers, recovering. He sat with a towel around his shoulder drinking water. Someone on the bench below him had a phone out and was watching the election. Another guy scooted closer to look.

"Trump's gonna win Ohio, it looks like," said the guy with the phone.

"Jesus," said the other guy, running a towel over his sweaty bald head. "What if he pulls the upset?"

"He won't."

"He might."

"He can't. He's been down in the polls all week and fading...."

An hour later, between games, word spread around the fifteen guys standing around with basketballs: Trump had won Ohio. Nobody said much in response, except for a single blond kid, college age, who raised his fists in the air in victory, whooped, and did a monkey strut around the court for a few seconds. He seemed oblivious, or maybe he didn't care about the other men glaring at him.

But after that, there was a new energy on the court. The guys played harder. The whole gym seemed to crackle with electricity. Occasionally, more unexpected election news would circulate among their group. Martin, watching the final game from the bench, felt a twinge of anxiety move through him. The world was getting more dangerous, he sensed. Some new force was being released into the collective consciousness, or maybe the better word was *unleashed*.

After the last game, he went downstairs to the locker room and sat in the steam bath. Then he took a long shower. Back at his locker it was after 10 p.m. The locker room was mostly empty. "What's happening?" Martin asked a guy who was looking at his phone.

"Trump got Florida."

"What does that mean?"

"It means he could win."

"Like he *will* win? Or he *could* win?"

The guy shook his head in disgust and said nothing more.

By the time Martin got home, it was over. Trump had won the presidency of the United States. Martin switched on the TV and took some Advil with a swig of lime Gatorade. The TV experts struggled to make sense of the results. Martin was having trouble identifying his own feelings as well. One image that came to mind was gangs of Nazi brown shirts, driving in vans through the streets of Portland, harassing people, and hauling some of them away. Could something like that happen? And who would they come looking for? Muslims? Mexicans?

But Trump couldn't do that. Presidents could barely do anything. Over the last month, Martin had tried to remind his frightened liberal friends how powerless Obama had been. Obama had been president for eight years and couldn't even shut down Guantanamo Bay. But, of course, nobody believes you in the heat of the moment. And it gets worse when they're pissed.

Angela came over on Friday. Martin made dinner. Angela fixed herself a strong drink. She was not taking the election news well. Martin hadn't realized she was such an adamant Hillary supporter. She was so upset they couldn't even talk about it.

After the meal, Martin led her to the couch, removed her shoes, and gave her a foot massage. She enjoyed this, closing her eyes, and perhaps even dozing off for a second. Then she came back to life, smiling at him and drinking more of her drink. Eventually she sat back up, scooted closer, and they began kissing.

She was different that night sexually. She crawled on top of Martin and rode him forcefully for a long time. Martin loved it: Angela's large breasts and deliciously curvy body. Later, thoroughly spent, the two collapsed in a tangle of arms and legs.

Once Angela was asleep, there was no waking her, and Martin, who often stayed up late, found himself wide awake. He slipped quietly out of bed and in the living room turned on CNN. It had been three days since the election and the commentators were still freaking out. It was funny, everyone had been so worried about what craziness Trump might resort to if he lost. Now that he'd won, it was the on-air commentators who were acting bizarre. Furious and outraged, sputtering their rage and then lapsing into stunned silence. The impossible had happened, the unthinkable. It was very compelling television. It was political disaster porn. You couldn't look away.

Martin, realizing he was not tired in the slightest, put some water on for tea. He returned to the bedroom and checked on Angela. She was dead asleep, parts of her not entirely covered up by the tangle of bedding. Martin carefully tugged and pulled at the blankets so that he could lay them over her the correct way. He kissed the side of her head.

Then he went back to the main room, made himself a cup of Earl Grey tea, cozied up on the couch, and began to surf around on his laptop to see what the manosphere was saying.

The next morning, Martin and Angela walked down the street to one of the foodie breakfast spots in his neighborhood. It was wet outside, gray skies, a typical November day. Checking the faces of the people walking by, Martin noticed no discernable difference. People looked happy, thoughtful, distracted, the usual variety. If the TV news anchors couldn't let the election go, most normal people had, it appeared.

In the restaurant, they grabbed a table right away, as there was a slight time problem with Angela needing to pick up her daughter, Michaela, at noon.

"I couldn't sleep so I watched the news again last night," he told Angela, as they settled in. "People are still freaking out."

Angela studied the menu and said: "The French toast looks good."

"Yeah, it is," agreed Martin.

The waitress came with waters.

"And then I was bored," said Martin. "So I checked out the manosphere. Do you know what that is?"

"No," said Angela.

"It's blogs for men. Guy talk, I guess. It's usually stuff about dating and women, but it's gotten pretty political lately. Anyway, so those guys were going ape shit. They love that Trump won. They'd made these Photoshopped pictures of Trump flying around on his victory horse, through the gates of heaven, with a crown on his head and his golden sword. They call him the God Emperor."

"That sounds awful."

"I know. But that's what it's like. When people say, who voted for Trump, that's who did. These young guys. The 'alt-right,' they call themselves."

"Why were you on these sites?"

"It's a long story. I went through this period where my brother-in-law tried to give me dating advice. He told me to read them. Back then they were mostly pickup blogs. Like how to talk to girls. It made sense. After my divorce."

Angela didn't seem impressed. She sipped her water.

"My sister was worried about me. It was her idea."

The waitress came. Angela ordered the French toast and eggs. Martin did the same.

"Yeah, in a way, it was pretty interesting," Martin said, when the waitress was gone. "Me and my brother-in-law. I mean, he was genuinely trying to help. But these blogs...oh my God...they're like every kooky right-wing conspiracy theory... racist stuff...videos.... Occasionally there's something intelligent. And like this one guy, P-Crusher...he's made himself into this James Bond character, 'banging chicks around the world.' It's pretty funny. And some of these guys, they literally make a living doing this. They have seminars and videos. Buy their book. Private instruction. I can only imagine what that would be like. I did learn a few things, I suppose."

"What did you learn?"

"Oh, obvious things, be more confident. Act like you know what you're doing. And don't worry if you screw up. It's just a game. Have fun."

Angela checked her phone quickly for messages from her daughter.

Martin adjusted his silverware. "It's funny to think about," he continued. He was finding it cathartic to talk about the manosphere out loud. It felt good to get it off his chest. Nobody but Rob knew he'd been reading these blogs. It was his one dirty secret and he wanted to be rid of it. "I kinda got into it, in a way. This underground world of masculinity. Like *Fight Club* or whatever. Sometimes you need that, I think, if you're a guy. You need that encouragement. I mean, it isn't anything I would talk openly about. I was terrified I'd leave something up on my computer at work. But I did read a lot of stuff on there. And politically, I mean, at least I have an understanding of what the other side is thinking. Especially these young guys. They're not even Republicans. They're something new. The alt-right. It's interesting on a cultural level...."

Their breakfasts came and Angela put hot sauce on her eggs. Martin dug into his. After the good sex, and now the unexpected euphoria that came from unburdening himself of his manosphere secrets, he felt very good, and very hungry.

21

Two MONTHS LATER was the presidential inauguration. By that point Martin and Angela were an official couple. At least in Martin's mind they were. Angela made dinner at her house and they watched the coverage of the ceremony on tape delay, all three and a half hours' worth.

Angela was beyond disgusted, of course. She kept going back and forth from the kitchen to the living room. At different times she began chopping carrots or celery on a cutting board. The loud chucking of the knife was audible from the couch.

Martin was less emotionally invested. He was more interested in the spectacle of it and noting the acute and obvious abnormalities of the ceremony. Trump, it seemed, had no friends. Nobody wanted to be there. The emptiness of the streets and the audience area, it was eerie, almost frightening.

And where was Bon Jovi? Weren't they supposed to play? Or was that someone else? They kept mentioning the alternative '90s band Three Doors Down. But they seemed to be missing as well. Maybe their manager talked some sense into them at the last minute.

Despite everything, Martin found that he couldn't genuinely hate Trump. He'd never hated anyone in the political realm. They all seemed like characters to him, in a not terribly important play. In college, he'd taken a course called

Presidential Politics: From the Civil War to World War One.
It was deadly boring. But the one thing he'd learned was
how comical the various "leaders" were. The blunders, the
posturing, the idiocy, it was all good wholesome fun. Maybe
Trump would be different. Maybe he was as evil as the media
claimed and would destroy the world or enslave the Mexican
people, but Martin seriously doubted it. More likely he would
flounder and do nothing. The public would get used to him;
they'd make fun of his hair. He would serve out his term, or
quit, and then some new attractive person or TV celebrity—
Oprah possibly—would beat him in 2020.

When the inauguration coverage was over, Angela told
Martin she would prefer it if he didn't sleep over. This was
unexpected and left Martin disoriented since it was a Friday
night, a night he usually spent with her. But she was apparently upset, so he didn't make a fuss. He left and drove his
Audi A4 to Powell's and drank a latte in the café while looking
at photography books. He wondered if Angela was angry with
him. Had he not hated Trump enough?

Things got back to normal soon enough. Martin and
Angela had a nice stretch after that, a month or so of Martin
sleeping over on a regular basis, eating meals together, establishing a domestic routine. Martin even met the daughter,
Michaela, ahead of schedule when she unexpectedly had to
stay with her mother during what was usually Dad time. This
meeting hadn't amounted to much. The girl had stayed in

her room for most of their one evening together under the same roof.

It was about mid-February when Angela began to act strangely. Martin couldn't identify what was happening. And then one night, while they were eating popcorn in the middle of a Netflix documentary, she turned to him and said that she was thinking about getting back together with her ex-husband.

Martin absorbed this surprising and unexpected information. He did not react or speak and maintained his sitting position on the couch. He did not look away from the TV. Angela then asked him, in a moving and sincere sequence of sentences, if the two of them could take a break for a time, so she could continue her conversations with Jonathan. Martin had no choice but to say yes.

So that happened. Martin left soon after and from that moment onward found himself without a partner. Except for a few terse check-in emails, he didn't speak or see Angela for four weeks. During the same time, Martin avoided hanging out with Rob and Sadie, knowing what Rob would say. His brother-in-law had more or less predicted something bad would happen. No doubt, he would counsel him to bail immediately. But Martin clung to his original strategy: play it out. What did he have to lose? A little time maybe. And he could see other people. Angela had urged him to. But who were they kidding? Martin was a one-woman-at-a-time type of guy. Angela was the person who made him happy.

It was during her spring break that Angela reached out to Martin again. Her daughter and ex-husband had gone camping for the week, and Angela invited Martin over for dinner, which he accepted. They ate and chatted about superficial things. Then, while cleaning up, they found themselves making out in the kitchen. This led to intense sex in her bedroom. Afterward, Martin lay staring at the ceiling, in the dark, his chest filled with dread.

"I'm getting back together with Jonathan," Angela told him from her side of the bed.

"I had a feeling."

"It's been so hard," she said. She was naked, on her stomach, her face partially buried in her pillow. "You don't think things are going to work out like this. The bad husband...versus no husband...versus being single and never quite finding that thing that feels right...no offense."

"None taken," said Martin. He turned onto his side, facing her, one hand propping up his head. With the other hand he began to lightly caress the smooth warm curve of her back.

"And with Michaela in the middle of it," said Angela. "God only knows what damage I've already caused her."

"Yeah," said Martin.

"And Jonathan...I guess there's a certain point where you have to face reality. He's the father of my child. It's a biological fact."

"Yeah," said Martin again. For a long time, neither spoke. Martin continued to glide his hand over Angela's back.

"I hope this hasn't been too hard for you," she said, her words muffled by the pillow.

"No..." he said. He looked at her beautiful hair, her beautiful neck. "No, it makes sense," continued Martin, in a soft, calm voice. "Just the way things are, and with Michaela being a teenager, it's probably better this way...."

"Yeah, I think so," said Angela.

And thus, Martin did the right thing, the honorable thing. He released Angela to return to her ex-husband and keep her family together and do what was best for troubled Michaela, while at the same time leaving himself with nothing.

PART TWO

April 2017

22

THE JACK LONDON Bar and Grill was the hot new singles bar in Portland, according to Dylan, who had recently broken up with his girlfriend and was on the prowl. With his usual nose for such things, Dylan had discovered a circuit of bars and clubs where the "quality women" could reliably be found. And being the generous guy he was, he'd brought Martin to "the Jack" on a warm spring night.

The two of them pushed through the front door. The Jack London was an old-school, old-time Oregon watering hole. It had high ceilings, cozy booths, and the longest cowboy-style bar west of the Mississippi. The place was humming at 8:30, as Dylan had promised. The crowd was stylish, attractive, eager to have a good time.

"Ha-ha, look at this place," said Dylan, surveying the room. "I told you."

"This looks great," said Martin.

They found stools at the bar and ordered happy-hour drinks. "So that other place I was telling you about," Dylan told him, "the Matador. I was there on Thursday. Their happy hour is even better than this. It's younger though. And a bit snotty. But if you can handle that...."

"If it's too cool for you, it's too cool for me," said Martin.

"No way, dude, you're killing this. Look at you. *Slay-ah!*"

Martin smiled and took his first sip of his vodka tonic. He looked around. He did feel pretty good.

For a few minutes nothing much happened. The two men occasionally scanned the room. They talked about work. Dylan chatted with the bartender.

Then two women in business attire appeared at the bar, standing next to Martin to order drinks. The bartender came and took their orders. When he was gone, Dylan spoke up: "Hey, ladies!" he said.

"Hi, guys," said the nearest. She smiled at Dylan. She was very cute, Martin saw. Makeup, coiffed brown hair, neat business suit, she was even wearing high heels.

"You look like you work in a bank!" said Dylan, over the general noise.

The two girls exchanged surprised looks. The attractive one turned back to Dylan. "How did you know that?"

"What? You *do* work in a bank?" said Dylan. "Ha-ha! I knew it. How smart am I? Now if only I was good looking!"

The girls laughed. "Sounds like someone's wound up tonight," said the cute one.

"Hey, humans are animals," said Dylan. "When springtime comes, animals get crazy!"

The women grinned at each other.

"They wake up from their slumber and search for a mate!" said Dylan.

"If you say so," said the cute one.

"They give birth," said Martin.

All three of them stopped talking at Martin's odd comment. Then they all laughed. "What are you talking about?" said the cute woman.

Dylan slapped his hand onto Martin's back. "Ladies, this is my boss. His name is Martin."

The ladies reluctantly said hi. Their names were Whitney (the cute one), and Erin (the plainer one, behind her).

"What are you the boss of?" said Erin, venturing into the conversation.

"Martin here runs...and *owns*...his own advertising agency," said Dylan. "Which is about to be acquired by Pacifica Sportswear. The reason being he's a fucking genius. And soon to be a *rich* fucking genius."

Whitney's expression changed from amused contempt to a more unsettled discomfort. Erin remained mildly interested. She let her eyes rest on Martin's face.

"So what do you do at the bank?" Dylan asked the two of them.

"I'm a manager," said Erin, quickly.

"I'm a teller," said Whitney.

"So has anybody ever robbed your bank?" asked Dylan. "Do people even do that anymore?"

"They try to hack in now," said Erin. "With computers. They don't come and stick you up."

"Yeah, but sometimes they do," said Whitney. "That guy in Seattle robbed three banks."

"Yeah, but how much money did he get?" Erin said to her. "Like eleven hundred bucks?"

"It's not the *quantity*," said Dylan. "It's the *quality*."

Everyone laughed.

"And anyway," said Dylan, "hackers aren't sexy. But *bank robbers....*"

The bartender brought Erin and Whitney their drinks.

Dylan jumped up and grabbed two empty stools from down the bar and dragged them over so the two women could join them, which they did. The group squeezed together, Martin's knee touching Erin's. She kept looking at him and smiling. He smiled at her too. She was slim, with thin lips. Her face wasn't super memorable, but he liked her general countenance, the way she sat, the way she sipped her drink.

"So when you're standing there," Dylan said to Whitney, "doing the teller thing...like how much money is in the drawer?"

Whitney looked at Erin. "It depends. Sometimes a couple thousand. Sometimes more."

"I love cash," said Dylan. "I like the actual feel of it. One time I took out ten grand and walked around with it all day. I'm serious. It was like this huge bulge in my front pocket...."

The girls smirked.

"What about you?" Dylan asked Whitney. "What's the most cash you've ever had?"

"In my hands or in my drawer?"

"Both. Or either."

"I dunno. Twenty thousand?"

"What did that feel like?"

"It was heavy."

Martin, meanwhile, turned to Erin. "You really manage a bank?" asked Martin.

"Not all of it," she said, smiling.

"That must be fun."

"I don't know if *fun* is the right word."

The four of them talked more. Dylan led the conversation through various bank-related subjects: the cryptic markings on the dollar bill, the psychology of credit cards, if people kept sex toys in their safety deposit boxes. Then the group of them made fun of Martin for his "giving birth" comment.

"It's not that weird of a thing to say," Martin protested. "That's what animals do in the spring. They give birth."

"I think they 'mate' in the spring," said Dylan.

"That's what I've always heard," added Erin.

"Well, when do they give birth then?" asked Martin.

"Jesus, who cares?" Dylan said, laughing.

"In the summer?" said Whitney.

"Not in the fall or they'd die when it got cold," said Erin. She was the smart one, definitely.

"The real question is, do humans get hornier in the spring?" asked Dylan.

"Of course," said Erin.

"Yeah, duh," said Whitney.

"I thought humans were always horny," said Martin.

"That too," said Dylan.

"I definitely feel a different energy in the bank in the springtime," said Erin.

"I feel like dudes hit on you more," said Whitney.

"Yeah? What do they say?" asked Dylan.

"Oh, all sorts of things. Or stupid ways to get your number. Like: 'Can you write your number on my bank statement?'"

"Next to my zero balance!" said Dylan.

"Oh my God!" said Whitney. "Yes! That actually happened once!"

Everyone laughed. Everyone drank. Everyone was having fun.

Twenty minutes later, Dylan looked at his watch. "Actually," he announced, "Martin and I, we gotta roll, but what are you guys doing later?"

Erin shrugged.

Whitney said: "I heard there's a good DJ at K-Club tonight."

"Where are you guys going?" asked Erin, some concern in her face. She glanced at Martin.

"A guy from work, he has a birthday thing," said Dylan, lying. "We just gotta show up for a bit."

The girls both nodded.

Dylan jumped up. "But let's meet up later. Give us your numbers. We'll text you."

With the women's numbers secured, Martin and Dylan left the Jack London.

"Jeez, that was easy," said Martin as they walked back toward their office.

"You cool with the skinny one?" asked Dylan.

"Yeah, sure"

"She seemed into you."

"Yeah, I liked her," said Martin.

"I was thinking we better bounce," said Dylan. "Always leave 'em wanting more."

"Yeah, good move. But what do we do now?"

"We go back to the office and watch the end of the Warriors game."

They stopped at the convenience store in the downstairs of their office building and got beer. Then they went upstairs and made themselves comfortable in the conference room. Dylan turned on the giant HDTV. "Life is sweet," he said.

At 10:40 Dylan started getting texts from Whitney. He read them to Martin. "Where are you guys...? We want to go dancing.... We're at K-Bar and it sucks.... Are you still coming out...?"

Martin got one from Erin. He read it to Dylan: "Are you guys standing us up? We want to hang out."

At 10:50, Dylan checked the clock. "Do you want to go dancing?" he asked Martin.

"Not really. But we told them we would. What do you think?"

"I'm not feeling K-Club," said Dylan keeping his eyes on his phone.

It was thrilling to Martin, the way this was unfolding. "How did you get so good at this?" he asked Dylan.

The younger man shrugged. "I love women."

Martin took a swig of his beer.

"Okay," said Dylan. "I'll tell them that we've had a long week. And we're not up for dancing."

Dylan sent the message. A minute later his phone dinged. "They say they're tired too," reported Dylan. "Do we want to meet them at Erin's place? For a drink? She lives in Northwest."

"Sounds good to me," said Martin.

Dylan texted them back.

"Finally!" said Whitney, when she opened the door to Erin's apartment. Whitney had changed her clothes. She was wearing jeans and a tight T-shirt, which accentuated her full breasts. Erin was behind her, also in jeans, a blouse, and white socks.

"Howdy, ladies," said Dylan going in.

"Hello!" said Martin, loudly. He needed to keep up with Dylan, if he could.

They came in and the four of them stood awkwardly for a moment in the living room. The women, in their nervous excitement, froze in place.

"You got something to drink?" prompted Dylan.

"Yes! Yes, of course!" said Erin, hurrying away.

They all moved into the kitchen, where they crowded together in the small space. Erin had a twelve-pack of Dos Equis cans in the fridge. Dylan opened his, the snap and fizz audible in the excited silence. "To bankers!" said Dylan. Everyone laughed and drank. They were all looking at each other, grinning, relieved to be reunited. The electricity was palpable. Martin tried to stop smiling. But he was having too much fun.

"So, K-Club was no good?" said Dylan.

"Gross people," said Whitney.

"Not as fun as the Jack London," said Erin.

"How was your party?" asked Whitney.

"Oh, you know..." said Dylan.

"It was fun," Martin offered.

"I like your T-shirt," Dylan said to Whitney. Her tight T shirt said MALIBU on it and had a multicolored '70s-style stripe across it. The collar had been cut off, revealing a little more of her shoulders and upper chest than normal. There was also a six-inch slit cut in the top, leading down toward her breasts. "What is this slit for?" said Dylan. "Is this to show cleavage?"

"No, it's just...a thing people do."

"Did you cut that yourself?"

"No, it came like that...."

Dylan inspected the slit. "You *did* cut that yourself."

"No, I didn't."

"You did that on purpose!" he said. He eyed the two of them. "You girls are trying to seduce us!"

"No, we're not!" laughed Whitney, pushing his hand away. For a moment she and Dylan played a little game with their hands, Dylan trying to inspect other parts of Whitney's T-shirt, Whitney fending him off.

They drank more. They talked more. Whitney was blatantly staring at Dylan by this time. Dylan continued to pester her in various ways. Martin and Erin found themselves watching their friends drool over each other.

"Where's the restroom?" said Dylan, finally.

"It's down the hall," said Whitney, her face flushed, her eyes bright with excitement.

"Where down the hall?" said Dylan.

"Come on. I'll show you."

The two of them disappeared down the hall. Martin gripped his beer. He laughed a little, out of nervousness. Erin laughed too. Martin thought about trying to kiss her, right there in the kitchen, but wasn't sure how to do it. Erin seemed to sense the moment too and gave him a questioning look.

"So this is your apartment?" said Martin, since he'd waited too long.

"Yup," said Erin.

Martin looked around the kitchen. He looked at the ceiling.

Erin looked at the ceiling too.

"Yeah," she said quickly. "I've lived here two years. Almost two years. It'll be two years in June."

"It's nice."

"Yeah, I like it," she said, touching the ends of her hair. "Do you want a tour?"

"Sure."

She led him out of the kitchen, into the small dining area, where she pulled up the blinds so he could see the view. It was mostly the apartment building across the alley, but there was a little bit of the street below.

"Nice," said Martin. "It's good you're up a few floors."

"And this is the main room," said Erin, walking three steps to the right, into the small living room. She was wearing white socks on her small feet. It was cute. "And this is the couch, and the coffee table. As you can see...."

"Nice, nice," said Martin.

She approached the hall, where Dylan and Whitney had disappeared. "I'm not sure how far we want to go down *there*..." she said, bashfully.

"I guess they got lost looking for the bathroom," said Martin.

"I guess so," said Erin.

This left them both stranded, standing at the entrance to the hall. Now Martin *had* to do something. So he did. He put his beer down and stepped toward Erin. She immediately turned to face him, her eyes watching his lips. Martin kissed her, tentatively at first, but then with slightly more force. It was a nice kiss. Martin liked the taste of her and how she moved her mouth. They pressed closer together and continued. It was a good fit, the two of them.

This went on for several minutes and eventually included roving hands and the undoing of buttons. Finally, Erin stopped him and took his hand and led him down the dark hallway.

23

On Monday morning, Martin arrived at work with a lot on his mind. This was happening more frequently: he'd arrive at the office on Monday having done something significant over the weekend, something interesting or provocative, something that needed to be mentally reviewed and mulled over on Monday. Previously—pre-Rob and his pickup websites—nothing ever happened to Martin on weekends, least of all anything involving sex or women. Now, after Petra, Angela, and Erin, it was becoming a semi-regular occurrence.

Just before lunch he got a text from Erin. He'd forgotten she had his number. She wrote:

Just wanted to say hi.

And then in the next bubble:

Hi.

Martin studied the text for a moment, then set the phone gently on his desk.

All last week he'd been reading a new blog he'd found, Milfist. One post, "Text Game," had garnered 268 comments.

the red pill

Martin had read every single one. Some of the possible strategies discussed in "Text Game" were: sounding busy, sounding bored, not writing back, the two-thirds rule (however much they write, you write two-thirds of that), the double entendre, the non sequitur, sending random emojis or memes or cat GIFs, pretending to text the wrong person, "flipping the script" (making the woman chase you), and, when the opportunity arose, being bracingly sexually direct.

He wasn't sure which strategy to apply in Erin's case. He picked up his phone again and wrote: "hi back." That sounded bored, non-engaged, funny, brief, aloof...but it sounded almost mean and he didn't want to scare her off. So then he wrote, "Ja Booty" for no reason. He deleted it. "At Work. Wudup?" he tried. That sounded forced. "Hey Girl," he typed, from the popular Ryan Gosling meme...but that was long over.

Since this text was somewhat important, he deleted that too. Then he remembered the most important text game strategy: not to think about it too much. What if you were insanely busy and you got this text? What quick knock off response would you come up with? But, since he'd already thought about it too much, he decided not to do anything. He put his phone away.

For lunch Martin walked to his favorite sushi place. He could hear the bullhorn echoes of a protest at the courthouse. This had been happening almost daily since the election.

He couldn't see the demonstrators, but the police presence downtown was obvious. A large military-style police vehicle rumbled up Broadway, right in front of him.

Four months into Trump's presidency, shit was going down. Bill O'Reilly, a popular conservative TV commentator, had just lost his job for harassing women. This was not an optics firing; it was a real firing, like a "no longer associated in any way" firing. Meanwhile, college campuses were in open revolt. UC Berkeley was having a riot a week, trying to prevent young conservative speeches on campus. The women's march in January, which had numbered in the millions, had morphed into a continual presence of women protesting each new outrage perpetrated by Trump.

Talk about unintended consequences, the assumption had been that Trump winning would move the country slightly to the right. But in fact, Trump's victory had enraged the liberals, energized the Left, and now people were running around in ski masks, throwing things, and lighting trash cans on fire.

At least that's what they were doing in Portland.

Martin called Dylan as he walked.

"Hey," he said. "Erin just texted me."

"Erin? From Friday?"

"Yeah."

"Cool, dude."

"Should I text her back?" asked Martin.

"Should you text her back? I don't know. Do you like her?"

"I guess so."

"Then text her back."

"What if I don't text her back. Can I get in trouble somehow?"

"Like what do you mean?"

"Like…will she get mad?"

"What would she get mad about?"

"I don't know."

"No," said Dylan. "She's not going to get mad."

"Did Whitney text you?"

"Not that I know of."

"Are you gonna text her?"

"I might. I'll see how I feel. Dude, don't sweat this. We partied with them. It was fun. That's it. Nothing else to think about. Okay?"

"Okay."

"I mean, if she texted you, then yes, technically, if you don't want to be an asshole, you should text her back. But if you don't want to hang out with her, just say…you know…I can't hang out right now…or you're busy, or you don't want a relationship, whatever. It's not a big deal. She's a big girl. She can handle it."

"Yeah, okay," said Martin. He stopped to wait for the WALK signal.

"Do you *want* to text her?" asked Dylan.

"Yeah, I think so."

"Then do it."

"Yeah, okay, I will." He hung up. Dylan was right. There was no problem here. He was being paranoid.

Martin had always had this problem. Whatever crises was going on in the larger world, he internalized it. Just because millions of women hated Trump did not mean that Erin hated him.

He ate his sushi by the window. As he chewed a California roll, two Antifa kids, dressed in black masks and hoodies, shot passed the window at a dead sprint. Martin watched them with his chopsticks in midair.

When they were gone, he went back to thinking about Erin. He had, as far as he knew, not made any glaring mistakes so far. Not like with Angela. The Angela situation was astonishing when he thought back on it. He'd done everything wrong you could do with a woman. He'd gushed over her, put her on a pedestal, rearranged his life around her. He'd been sensitive, caring, and understanding. He'd put her needs above his in every way possible. She, in turn, had been repulsed by his neediness, lost all respect for him, and dumped him, just like Rob said she would. Just like *everyone* said she would. And yet at the time, in her presence, he literally couldn't stop himself. Maybe it was a form of self-sabotage, an unconscious desire for total humiliation. Like an alcoholic or a drug addict, he needed to hit rock bottom before he could be reborn.

Martin finished his meal, put on his coat, and went back onto the street. He sighed to himself as he walked. He had genuinely *loved* Angela, that was the real problem. He had loved her with that classic, delusional, unsustainable,

the red pill

Disneyland, make-believe love. The manosphere warned against this constantly. Romantic love was an illusion. It was a spell. It was a chemical reaction that took over your body. Most important to remember: it was men who most often fell victim to it. Not women. Women couldn't afford to be that stupid.

Martin continued to walk, stopping to let two police vehicles speed by. He could hear angry chanting in the distance.

So there is no romantic love, he thought. It seemed too depressing to contemplate. Despite everything, Martin still clung to the idea of a female equal. An intelligent partner. A loving soulmate. He could not imagine a world where that did not exist. But maybe that wasn't even possible anymore.

24

During most of the last month, Martin had avoided Rob and his sister's family. He still felt stupid about Angela, for one thing. And he wasn't super psyched to hang out with Rob, who, as usual, had predicted Martin's failure. But now with his recent Erin triumph, he felt better about things. And so he went to the Carrs' for dinner.

Libby was there. "Oh my God, I never get to do anything! It's driving me crazy!" she was telling Sadie when Martin first entered the house. He had stopped to throw a baseball with Rob and Little Jack in the front yard.

Courtney and Wayne were also there, sitting quietly on stools at the kitchen island. They seemed reluctant to comment on Libby and her life of pain.

Martin said hi to everyone. Ashley appeared. "Where have you been, Uncle Martin?" she asked him, gripping the bottom of his coat.

"I've been here the whole time," Martin said, giving her a squeeze.

"No, you haven't."

"In spirit I have."

"What does that mean?"

"It means I think about you every day and I wonder what you're up to and I think about fun stuff we can do the next time we hang out." All of which sounded unfamiliar coming out of Martin's mouth. He wasn't usually so effusive.

Ashley smiled up at him, her head tilted back. She was missing her two front teeth.

Rob and Jack entered the room. Jack kept slapping the baseball into his mitt. He was a very aggressive young man. Probably Rob had been like that too.

"All right, everyone get a plate and come over and get some of this lasagna. The best frozen lasagna money can buy!"

"Where did you get it?" Libby asked her.

"Whole Foods," said Sadie.

"The guy from Amazon just bought them," said Libby.

"I heard that."

"The Whole Foods in Beaverton is the biggest one in the state," said Rob.

"We've been to that one," said Courtney, who was, as always, round and bunny-like. Her latest hairstyle—a highlighted, sculpted bob—was long on the sides near her face, and then tapered upward as it went behind her head, a geometrical achievement that was hard for Martin to look at.

"It's the new Trader Joe's," said Wayne. His beard was gone. There was apparently a lot of grooming going on at the Wayne-Courtney house.

"Everything changes so fast nowadays," said Libby. "Have you noticed that?"

"The *acceleration*," said Martin, taking his seat.

"Is that a thing now?" said Libby. "Because it's *so* true."

"No, I made it up, but yeah."

"You know Martin..." said Sadie. "We always watch the commercials very closely because of you. Jack's new favorite is Dilly Dilly."

"Dilly Dilly!" shouted Jack.

"Yeah, that's a good one, all right," said Martin. "I wish I'd come up with that."

Everyone was taking their places around the table. Rob sat next to Jack. Everyone else was scattered randomly.

"Did you notice that different ads run at different times?" Martin asked Little Jack, as people began to eat.

Jack wasn't paying attention. Rob said to the boy, "Uncle Martin is talking to you, bub."

Jack looked up. "No," he said.

"Dilly Dilly is an ad for beer, and beer is mostly for men. So that ad runs during sports shows and basketball games."

"Okay," said Jack, cheerfully swinging his legs under his seat.

"Dilly Dilly is something someone had to think up," continued Martin. "That's what we do at my job. We sit around and think up things that people will like and remember."

Jack had lost all interest.

"What does it mean, Uncle Martin?" asked Ashley.

"Dilly Dilly?" said Martin. "It doesn't mean anything. It's just a funny thing that someone might say. It's like a greeting. Or a phrase from olden times. But it's nonsense. So it's funny."

"I like the King," said Jack.

"That's what you do..." Martin told Ashley, who often seemed more capable of understanding complex concepts than Jack was. Or else she was just better at staring at you while you talked. "You try to release your mind and let any odd thing come into it."

"Like a dance," said Ashley.

"Yes, like a dance!" said Martin.

"Very good, Ashley," said Sadie.

"Way to go," said Rob.

"Maybe you could be in advertising someday," said Libby. "Would you like to do that? Make up stuff all day?"

"I don't think so," said Ashley.

"Why not?" asked Libby. She turned to Martin. "Girls work in advertising, don't they?"

"Of course," said Martin.

"It's too hard," said Ashley.

"Dilly Dilly dil dil dil," said Jack.

Everyone ate for a while. Martin very much enjoyed the frozen lasagna. Maybe it *was* the best money could buy.

"What have you been up to?" Libby asked Martin, across the table. "What happened to that teacher you were seeing?"

"She went back to her ex-husband."

"No *way!*" said Libby. "How did that happen?"

"I don't know. She was happily divorced and then the next thing I knew, she wanted to be with her husband again."

"Will they get remarried?"

Martin shrugged.

"People do that," said Libby. "They marry their ex again. It's so insane."

"They marry their old husband?" asked Ashley.

"Yes, they do," said Libby to the child. "They break up with them. And then they decide to go back with them."

Ashley frowned.

Jack was singing loudly to himself. "Dilly dil dil! Doodle do do!"

"All right, Jack," said Rob. "That's enough. We're eating still."

"How did she tell you this?" Libby asked Martin.

"She just did," he replied. "We were watching TV. We were sitting on her couch."

"That is so cold."

Sadie and Rob were listening closely. Martin had mentioned the breakup to Sadie, but neither had heard the whole story.

"I wasn't mad or anything," Martin said to the table. "There was a certain logic to it. I understood."

"Still..." said Wayne.

"But you liked her so much," said Sadie.

"Maybe too much," said Martin, glancing once at Rob.

Rob spoke: "Could be anything, if it's the ex-husband. Finances. Family stuff."

"I think she was worried about her daughter," said Martin. "The daughter's thirteen. She's having some issues. I think things were getting a little chaotic."

"Was she seeing the ex before?" asked Libby. "Like all along?"

"No," said Martin. "I don't think so. I mean, she *saw* him. They dropped the kid back and forth. And they went to some counseling sessions together. With the daughter."

"Uh-oh," said Libby. "There's your problem, right there."

"What?" asked Sadie. "You think they got back together because of counseling?"

"Well, seeing the other person all the time," said Libby. "And having all this drama to deal with? Emotions running high? A certain spark might occur...."

Martin hadn't thought of that.

"Well, I'm sorry for you, Martin," said Sadie, somberly.

"It's over now," said Martin. "The good news is, I went out with Dylan from my office the other night, and we 'cruised for chicks.'"

Everybody chuckled.

"What's that like?" asked Libby. "I mean as an older person?"

"Horrifying," joked Martin. "But no, it was fun. Dylan's very good at it. Seriously, he's like Rob. He's..." Martin stopped himself and reconfigured his sentence. "Dylan's a *charmer.*"

"Ha-ha, I bet he is," said Libby.

"And so what was the result of this *cruising?*" asked Sadie.

"Oh, nothing much," said Martin, blushing slightly.

"What do you mean nothing?" said Sadie. "Look at you! Your face is turning red!"

Martin laughed. "I guess we had some adventures."

After dinner, Martin and Rob sat out on the Carrs' back patio. Rob had made some changes in the backyard. They'd gotten rid of a small shed and in its place was a new black plot of garden soil.

Rob had a Bud Light. Martin had a large gin and tonic, his second of the evening.

"So what's up?" Martin asked, a little drunk.

"Whattaya mean?" said Rob.

"Your guy's president. And it's been a total shit show so far."

"It's been pretty crazy."

"Is he gonna survive?"

"I dunno."

"At Pacifica, people are fucking pissed," said Martin. "They hate him. It's been weird to watch."

"Yup. Things are coming to a head."

"In what way, though?"

"I dunno," said Rob. "Maybe he'll go down. They're coming at him from all sides. And you know he's probably got some sketchy stuff in his past."

"Why did you vote for him then?"

"Who the hell else was I going to vote for?"

"Yeah, I see your point," said Martin, staring into the dark backyard. He sipped his drink. Rob drank his beer.

"So yeah, the other night?" Martin said, in a quieter voice, checking behind him to make sure nobody else could hear. "When Dylan and I went out? We got with these two women! Who worked at a bank!"

"You had sex with them?"

"Yes! Both of them! I mean, not together. You know. In different rooms. He got the cuter one. But he did all the talking. So that seemed fair."

"No kidding," said Rob.

"I know. Can you believe it? Dylan was so funny. He was killing it. Like we meet 'em at this bar, and everything's going great. And then—and this is the genius of Dylan—then he tells them we gotta go to this other thing. So we go back to the office and watch the last half of the basketball game. And I'm telling you, Dylan was so cool. He let the tension build. And then they start texting us! They're worried *we* bailed on *them!* And Dylan, he's never read any manosphere shit. These aren't strategies he read on a website. He just knows. He just feels it. So they invite us back to their apartment! And that was it. Closed the deal!"

Rob couldn't help but laugh. "No shit?"

"No shit! Me! Martin! I got with someone I'd just met four hours before. And not some skanky bar type. The fucking manager of a bank! It was awesome!"

Rob held his beer out. Martin bumped his glass against it.

"Mine was named Erin," continued Martin, in his whisper voice. "She was skinnier than Dylan's girl. But I liked her. I did. And the sex...well...it wasn't great. It was OK for what it was. Actually, it was pretty good. We made out, and then we kinda.... Well, we were both pretty drunk. But it was fun. It was *so fucking fun!*"

"Wow."

"We picked them up in a bar!" said Martin.

"So my efforts were not wasted."

"No, they were not," said Martin. "Dude. Hey, I know you're right about this stuff. Everything you say turns out to be right. I don't want to admit it but that's the truth. With women it's all about your attitude. It's all about inner control.

And then when you actually see this stuff work, in real time, exactly like they said it would...ha-ha...I mean...what can I say?"

"Sounds like you've been red pilled."

"I think I have been red pilled!" said Martin, lifting his glass in acknowledgment.

"So now what are you going to do?"

"I dunno. First, I gotta figure out Erin. I assumed I'd never see her again. But then she texted me. So now it's like...I don't know. Maybe I should ask her out."

"Sure, ask her out, why not?"

"I mean, I liked her. She seemed alright."

"And she works at a bank," said Rob. "So money won't be a problem."

"Exactly!" laughed Martin. He swirled his gin and tonic. "Money will not be a problem!"

25

Martin drove home drunk. He parked in front of his apartment and then strolled down the street to New Seasons.

Inside, he found a basket and began his usual stroll through the large, cold space. What would happen to New Seasons now that Jeff Bezos owned Whole Foods? Would Bezos price them out? Would he buy New Seasons too and establish a monopoly over all the health food supermarkets? Poor New Seasons, with their scattering of Portland locations. They'd got all excited when they opened their first Seattle store. Now they would be overrun by mega-Bezos, swallowed in one gulp.

Martin walked the long aisles. At this late hour, there was hardly anyone in the store. Classical music played on the overhead speakers. Martin had been in a couple of the Whole Foods around town. He doubted the night managers were allowed to pick the music. He'd heard other things about Whole Foods: bad work practices, disgruntled workers. Martin liked to believe that these enlightened, lefty-themed companies were actually as good to their workers as their image suggested. He didn't see why they wouldn't be. The employees at Trader Joe's always appeared healthy, smart, overeducated. Powell's Books workers were the same. Still, you weren't going to get rich working at a supermarket. Not like he and Simon would be, when their Pacifica deal went through. It was taking an awfully long time, though. A year ago Simon had predicted the merger would be done in three months, and here they were, still waiting.

Martin's phone dinged. It was a text from Libby. Martin put down his basket to text her back.

Libby: Hey. Can't sleep. You awake?

Martin: Ya

Libby: Sorry about what I said about that woman you liked.

Martin: No prob.

Libby: It's true tho. Sometimes family drama has that effect on people. I would know.

Martin: Ya

Libby: Where are you?

Martin: New Seasons.

Libby: I love New Seasons. Fuck Whole Foods.

Martin: Ya

Libby: Did you notice Rob and Sadie tonight?

Martin: What about them?

Libby: They were fighting earlier.

Martin: What about?

Libby: Trump

Martin: Really?

Libby: Totally. It's kind of a problem.

the red pill

Martin: I didn't know

Libby: She's your sister. Don't you know how much she hates Trump? He's a rapist.

Martin: Ya

Libby: Ya? Our president is a rapist and that's all you have to say?

Martin: Ya

Libby: You don't care about anything do you?

Martin: I do care

Libby: Lol. You crack me up.

Martin: Why?

When she didn't answer Martin put his phone back in his pocket. But he was getting the hang of this. Text game. Always act like you don't care. Zero Fucks Given. ZFG.

He found a cash register that was open and checked out. The female cashier had a pleasing face and was about Martin's age. He watched her as she ran his six items over the scanner. "That'll be twelve dollars and forty-five cents," she said.

Martin dug out his debit card. "How are you doing tonight?" he asked, as she packed his stuff into a paper bag.

"I'm okay. How about you?"

"I'm doin' pretty good," said Martin. There was no one in line behind him, so he said, "What's up with Whole Foods? Are you guys worried they're gonna mess with your market share?"

"Our market share?" the cashier said.

"You know, take your customers."

She shrugged. "I wouldn't know. I've never been there."

"It's gonna get cheaper supposedly. Now that Bezos bought it."

She didn't seem interested in any of this.

Martin nodded. He wasn't particularly attracted to her, but if he wanted to ask her out, how would he do it?

"I don't recognize you," said Martin. "Are you new?"

"I only work part time. And I work at the Gateway store too."

"I'm Martin."

"Nice to meet you, Martin," she said, handing him his bag and receipt. She then turned away rather abruptly and grabbed her phone out of her back pocket.

Martin did not attempt further conversation. Walking up the street, he drunkenly reviewed the interaction. His opener was weak, for one thing. He had confused the cashier with the "market-share" concept. He had not joked with her, smiled at her, or complimented her on anything. The interaction had not been "light" or "fun." He hadn't "taken her on a journey." The thing *not* to do was bring up Bezos or Whole Foods. No, that was death. A funny anecdote. Something off the wall. Better things to have said would include: "I like your earrings." "Excuse me, I'm a little drunk." "What's up with the Beethoven?" Anything would have been better than "Are you afraid of losing your market share?"

When he got home he checked his texts. There was nothing new. Libby must have gone to bed.

the red pill

The next day at work, Martin texted Erin and asked her out to lunch. She accepted and the lunch was arranged through a series of short, formal messages. Martin was nervous about this date. He began to coach himself several days beforehand: Keep quiet. Don't be needy. Don't be an idiot. But it was always easier to repeat these strategies beforehand than it was to execute them in the moment.

Martin arrived first at the upscale downtown restaurant La Province. Erin had said she could only be an hour; she had a busy schedule that day. Martin unfolded his napkin, put it in his lap, and waited. Erin appeared a few minutes later, looking a bit harried, in her business attire. She seemed surprised they were even doing this. Like this wasn't usually how these things went. But she also looked cautiously excited. Martin was cautiously excited too. He could feel a genuine smile fill his face as he clumsily stood, caught his napkin as it fell, and gave her an awkward, semi-hug.

Both took their seats.

"I really have to be out of here right at one thirty," said Erin.

"No, that's fine," said Martin. "Banking hours. I understand."

She missed his joke or was too nervous to laugh. She let the host scoot her chair in. "I like this place," said Erin. "I come here sometimes with my boss. The steak and fries are good. Do you eat meat?"

"Yeah, I eat everything," said Martin.

"No allergies?"

"Not that I know of."

The waitress appeared and handed them menus. Martin glanced up at Erin as she read. She was younger than he remembered, but also not quite as cute. She was wearing a lot of makeup, and not in a sexually alluring way, more in a covering up your acne way. Her long hair was straight and parted down the middle; she had to tuck it behind her ears whenever she leaned forward.

They ordered and when the waitress was gone, sat awkwardly, staring into the center of the table.

"So your advertising company," said Erin. "You said you mostly work with Pacifica?"

"Yes," said Martin. "At first, we had a few other clients but at this point, it's all Pacifica, all the time." Martin paused for a moment and then added, "There's been talk of merging us into their marketing department. They'd effectively buy us out. I don't know all the details. My partner deals with that stuff. I make up the catchy phrases."

"Have you made up any catchy phrases I might know?"

"Probably nothing you'd know lately," said Martin. "A lot of our recent stuff is for overseas markets."

"That makes sense."

Martin straightened the knife beside his plate. "And you... you really work at a bank?"

"Yup, Capital West, right down the street. Not as interesting as your job, I'm sure. But it pays the bills."

"And you get to wear those suits."

"Yes, the suits."

"That was fun the other night," said Martin, grinning slightly, and rotating his water glass.

the red pill

"It was," said Erin, letting the tiniest possible smile show on her face.

They ate and talked and after the meal Martin gulped down a cappuccino. Then he walked her down the street to her bank. The conversation remained mostly superficial but Martin got a general feel for Erin's life. She hadn't finished college, but was finishing now with online classes and community college. She was from Forest Grove, which was a small farm town about twenty miles outside Portland. She wasn't privileged like he was. But she also had a certain solidity he liked. He had noticed that solidity when they were drunkenly grinding against each other in the dark the night they met. She seemed like she would be a dependable friend. But of course, she hung out at the Jack London and banged random dudes, so maybe she wasn't quite the model citizen she seemed.

In any event, it seemed unclear what their status was. When he'd walked her back to the bank, Martin decided to find out. In the large open area, in front of the bank's main entrance, with people walking by and probably some of her coworkers in sight, he slid one hand around her waist, pulled her close, and gave her a short kiss on the lips.

She was surprised, shocked even, but didn't resist. "Oh!" she said, when he let her go.

"Thanks for meeting up," he said.

"Yeah...thanks for lunch," said Erin.

They studied each other. Erin pulled her hair behind one ear. There was a hard quality to her face, Martin saw, in the daylight. But it seemed possible that the hardness was only there to cover up a lack of hardness.

"All right," said Erin. "Gotta go." She turned and marched across the open area, clacking on her high heels, her business suit moving with the motion of her slim figure.

Martin walked back toward his own office six blocks away. His head was spinning slightly, in a pleasant way. But he needed to be careful with this. Being physically aggressive—"escalating," as the bloggers called it—was obviously an effective strategy to get sex. But it was also a fast track to the unknown. He would give Rob a call when he got back to the office and see what he had to say.

But at the office there were other things happening.

26

MARTIN COULD FEEL the tension the moment he stepped off the elevator. Simon was in his office. His door was wide open. He was talking loudly on the phone, almost shouting. Dylan was not there. The new college kid intern was running around, an oppressed look on his face.

"Martin, is that you?" shouted Simon.

"Hey, wudup?" said Martin from the hallway.

"Can you come in here for a minute?"

"Let me dump my coat."

Martin continued to his own office, ditched his coat, grabbed a water, and went into his partner's office.

Simon was putting down his phone. "Hey," he said to Martin, avoiding eye contact. "Come in, come in," he said. "Shut the door."

Martin shut the door. He moved slowly to the chair across from Simon's desk and sat. Simon was still not looking at him.

"What's up?" said Martin.

Simon had a pen behind his ear, which he grabbed and threw on the desk. He stretched backward, straining his ergonomic office chair to its limit. He covered his tired, red eyes with his hands for a moment before springing forward again. "I'm getting sued," he told Martin. "Fucking Regan is suing me for sexual harassment. I'm sorry, 'sexual assault.' Or some fucking thing. I need you to write me a character assessment, or whattaya call it, a character reference. You know, to tell them I'm a good guy and that I don't 'sexually assault' people."

Martin sat blinking at him. "What...what happened?"

"Oh, Jesus, I don't fucking know. Honestly? Nothing happened. But by the definitions of whatever...since she works here...." He shook his head. "I was drunk and I grabbed her in my car...which she was in, by the way, because she'd been fucking me for two months, and enjoying it a great deal, and letting me fly her to Sun Valley...."

"What part was the assault?" asked Martin.

"I can't even think right now.... I just know...since I'm her boss...so that's part of it. And we were having a 'sexual relationship.' So that's another part. And there was the thing in the car. She was trying to break up with me, according to her lawyer, which was news to me...."

For a moment Martin thought Simon was drunk. But no, he was just tired, and stressed out of his mind.

"So will you write it?" said Simon, a look of genuine desperation and pathos on his face. "I kind of need it. I'm going to need a bunch of them."

"Sure. Of course. Absolutely," said Martin.

"I have it here," said Simon, reaching for his leather bag on the floor. He pulled out a bunch of mangled papers, paged through them, then pulled one out and slid it across the desk. Martin had to scoot forward to take it. It was a template of some kind, but with Simon's full name, Simon J. Howard, handwritten on top.

"It should be self-explanatory. They'll email you some other stuff. And use your own words of course. Can you fucking believe this?"

"I had a weird interaction with her once myself."

"Yeah?" said Simon, looking up.

"I mean...I found myself chatting her up. Flirting, I guess. Nothing happened...it was before you guys...."

Simon stared at him. "You knew about me and her?"

"No, no," said Martin. "Not at first. But then I kinda suspected...."

"What made you suspect?"

"The time we were at Kelly's. She had this look on her face."

"What kinda look?"

"Like...I dunno...like she was sleeping with you. It was a smug look."

"A smug look," said Simon. "I bet it was. I bet it fucking was."

"Is it a money thing? Is she looking to get paid?"

"I have no idea. My guy's been talking to her guy. How the fuck does a girl that age even know how to do this? What the fuck is the world coming to? I come back from New York and I open some fucking email and here's this whole fucking...*case*, against me. Pages and fucking pages. They do that on purpose, you know. They pound the shit out of you. Scare tactics. Fucking lawyers."

Martin sat back in his chair and began reading the template.

"She was thinking of this the whole time," said Simon. "They claim she wasn't of course...."

Martin skimmed through the character reference sheet. "Just out of curiosity," he asked Simon, "has this ever happened before?"

"What?"

"You get sued like this? Or some other harassment thing?"

"Jesus, Martin, fuck no it hasn't happened to me before. You've known me my whole life. Do I do shit like this?"

"Well, it seems like, these days, some of the definitions might have changed."

"Yes! That's exactly what I told my lawyer. Why do *they* get to define what all these terms mean? Sexual assault? What the fuck is that? I'm serious. I asked my lawyer. He didn't know."

"Are you going to fight it?"

"My guy is telling me to settle. It's cheaper. Less publicity. *No* publicity hopefully, but who knows nowadays."

Martin said nothing.

Simon sat back in his seat and rocked back and forth. Martin had been watching him do that since they were sixteen.

"Is this gonna affect the Pacifica deal?" asked Martin in a quiet voice.

Simon took a moment to answer. "That's why we settle," he said, softly. "So we don't fuck up the Pacifica deal. She signs a nondisclosure agreement. She gets the fuck out of town. Far, far away. And we go ahead with the Pacifica deal. If we can."

"What do you mean by that?"

"What I mean by that," he said with an edge in his voice "is it's still not a done deal. You know as well as I do. They delay and delay. You gotta wonder how interested they are at this point. If we can't get the thing done. And that fuckwit Raj Taheed. He's the one stopping it. Oh, I'm sorry, was that racist of me? Am I not allowed to criticize him? Fuck these people. Fuck all of them."

Simon leaned forward again. He looked around at the mess of papers on his desk. "I'm sorry, man. I'm really sorry about this."

"No," said Martin. "It's not your fault. It could have happened to anyone."

"What the fuck is wrong with women nowadays? It's like they're trying to fuck us every way they possibly can."

Martin nodded. Though his life experience with women was vastly different from Simon's, he felt compelled to agree with his business partner. "There does seem to be something in the air," he said.

That night at home, Martin found another character reference template in his email, with detailed notes from Simon's attorney and three examples of how to approach it. He wished he'd asked Simon for more details. He couldn't call him now and ask what happened exactly. And technically, it made no difference. Martin was not writing his opinions about the case.

He began to type. He started by describing Simon in high school, reflecting on his character in the most positive light he could. He tried to maintain a certain distance in his tone, to sound as objective and believable as possible. But he also had to make it abundantly clear that Simon was not a person who sexually assaulted women.

It made him think, though. Simon did have a temper. And he was a physically reactive person. Martin remembered Simon getting in a fight at a party in high school. Nothing much happened; nobody was hurt. Martin only remembered it because of what it did to Simon's reputation. People had buzzed about it for weeks. It was considered uncouth by some, but in a deeper more fundamental way, it had elevated him. You didn't fuck around with Simon. It wasn't about his fighting ability or his physical strength; it was about his refusal to back down. Within a month of the incident, Simon had a new girlfriend, Jessica Pearlman, who at that time was considered the most desirable high school girl in all of Portland.

Martin wasn't going to write that, of course. What he did write was a dry, dull accounting of how responsible, kind, rational, and decent a person Simon Howard was. When he'd finished it, Martin read it over. It was terrible. Unreadable. And it sounded like a lie. He created a new folder on his laptop called Simon's Lawsuit and put the Word document inside it. He would have to think about this. And try again. The letter would need to be perfect.

He then turned on the late local news and got a beer from his fridge. On his couch he checked his phone for messages. Maybe Erin had texted. But she hadn't. He looked over the previous messages between them. There weren't many, mostly the arrangement of their recent lunch. He wondered what she would think of the Simon situation. She probably had a good grasp of contemporary workplace culture.

After the news, he put on *Jimmy Fallon* and returned to his laptop. Thank God for the internet. He googled "how to write a character reference" and found a couple articles that were somewhat helpful. Then he went to Middle Aged Dad, his favorite new manosphere blog. Middle Aged Dad was written by a forty-five-year-old father of three and featured the same kind of humorous life and relationship advice the other guys did, except that MAD was forty-five, and therefore more relatable to Martin. Tonight, he was talking about the inevitable battles between a father and his adolescent daughter. According to MAD it was essential that the father "maintain hand." To give in to a daughter's whims and demands would ruin her forever. To be an immovable object in her life, to lay down the law and ruthlessly maintain it, that was the best gift a father could give any of his children, but most crucially a daughter.

After he'd read some of the comments to the post, Martin checked Erin's message thread again. Could he send her a short note, thanking her for coming to lunch? He tried writing one and then deleted it. He wrote another, and then deleted that. No, the thank-you note was a bad idea. Better to say nothing. Better to remain aloof.

27

And then Libby called. Martin was home on his couch with his laptop. It was 9:30.

"Hey," said Libby. "What are you doing?"

"Nothing. Watching videos. What are you doing?"

"I'm driving around with Delilah. I'm sorta near you. Do you want to ride around with us?"

"Right now?"

"Yeah. Delilah fell asleep in her car seat. So I'm driving around."

"Won't she wake up if I get in?"

"Not if you're quiet."

Martin went downstairs and stood outside his apartment building. Libby drove up in her Toyota Highlander and Martin got in.

She turned left and they headed east on Burnside, on smooth freshly paved asphalt.

Martin put his seat belt on. He was glad to be riding in a car, in the passenger seat, to relax. "My business partner just got accused of sexual assault by one of our interns," he told Libby. "I've been working on a character statement."

"Jesus. That's terrible."

"I know."

"Did he do it?"

"I guess so," said Martin. "He wasn't denying it."

"That seems to be happening a lot," said Libby.

"Yeah."

"I mean, not to me. But Kevin says people are getting so paranoid at work. Now they have rules for all these things, at these sales conferences he goes to. You can't go into someone's room. You can't buy someone a drink...."

"My partner's kind of a womanizer," said Martin. "Not kind of. He is. He's always been."

"He better change his ways."

"It might be too late. It might affect our company."

"Oh, right."

Martin sunk into silence. He was glad to be with Libby, though. She was an easy person to talk to, even easier than Rob, who he'd come to depend on in certain ways, as a confidant, despite their political differences.

Martin looked in the back to see Delilah. Her chubby face hung forward as she slept. "How old is she again?" said Martin.

"Seventeen months."

"Yeah, she's gotten bigger."

"You know, I sometimes think I'm the worst parent."

"Don't be ridiculous."

"No seriously. I'm not suited to it. There are people like that. My mother was a terrible mom. She forgot we were there half the time."

"I'm sure a lot of people think they're bad parents."

"Sadie's a great mom. I feel like whatever good things I know, I learned from her."

"Yeah. Rob too. They do seem to have the parent thing figured out."

Libby had pulled onto the narrow road that led up to the Mount Tabor Park. "Do you mind if we go up here?" she asked, steering her way through the tall trees.

"No."

They pulled into the viewpoint parking lot and Libby quietly turned the car off. Then she thought about it and turned it back on. "Do you mind if I leave it on? I think the engine sound is what makes her sleep."

"It's fine with me."

"Not good for the environment, I know," said Libby.

They sat for a moment, looking out over the eastern suburbs below and, beyond that, the city. It was June now and warm enough for Martin to lower his window and put his arm on the door. "We used to come up here in high school," he said. "It was one of the make-out spots."

"Really?" said Libby, hopefully. "Do you want to make out?"

Martin looked at her.

"I'm kidding," said Libby. "I didn't mean that. I'm having a little trouble lately. I wish I still smoked."

"You used to smoke?"

"Yeah, but I quit," said Libby. "I just get restless sometimes and then I don't know what to do with myself."

"Yeah," said Martin. He stared out at the city lights. The air smelled good. The large fir and cedar trees that populated the park had a tangy bark smell.

the red pill

"So I talked to Sadie the other night," said Libby. "She was really upset."

"What about?"

"The usual marriage crap. But still, it was not like her."

"Huh."

"She has this friend who's doing these fund-raisers to stop Trump. Sadie wants to do it, but she doesn't want to tell Rob."

"He wouldn't care, would he? If that's what she wants to do. He would never...."

"He might not say anything. But he wouldn't like it. He *loves* Trump. If he wasn't married to Sadie he'd have signs on his lawn."

Martin looked out his open window. Some other cars were parked at the viewpoint but no high school kids seemed to be in any of them. There was an older couple though, in their fifties probably, standing by the railing. They had a dog on a leash and appeared to be deep in conversation. *People still love each other*, Martin thought to himself. He turned and looked at Libby. She was staring straight ahead, thinking. She looked fidgety, anxious, distracted. She drummed her fingers on the steering wheel.

Martin was sitting in his office a few days later when he got a text from Erin. Did he want to go to a bluegrass concert her bank was sponsoring? It was part of Capital West's "Roots by the River" series. A famous bluegrass band from Kentucky was playing. Martin said yes.

The night of the concert he showed up at the park with a blanket and a bottle of wine. Erin was there with another blanket and some snacks from Trader Joe's: grapes, crackers, European cheese.

They set up fairly far back, but as it got dark, so many people showed up, they became squeezed in the middle of a sea of blanket sitters.

They chatted, without saying too much. Martin opened the bottle of wine he'd grabbed from his office closet where they often stashed alcohol, paper plates, and other leftover supplies from office parties. Martin watched the tiny cars moving along the freeway across the river. He remained a little perplexed at what to talk to Erin about, and found himself saying very little. Erin didn't speak either but that seemed okay. Wasn't it good to not talk? "Laconic" was the word Milfist used. "The power of silence is infinite." It was such a sound concept, Martin envisioned a TV spot: *A man who is a real man is a man of few words* and then some goofy millennial, naked, standing in the woods, with a toothbrush and a fishing pole. Like the Old Spice ads that everybody loved that made no sense. Absurdist masculinity.

The bluegrass band made their way onto the stage. When they were introduced, the crowd went nuts. The bluegrass songs were surprisingly fast and intricately played. But after twenty minutes it all sounded the same to Martin's ears. He drank his wine. At one point a small girl appeared in front of them. She was wandering among the blankets.

the red pill

"My niece is four," Martin told Erin. "Her favorite ad is the Captain Obvious spot."

"Oh yeah?" said Erin holding her wine glass. "What does she like about it?"

"Just how goofy it is. Now though, she likes Dilly Dilly. You know, the beer ad?"

"So you discuss these things with her? Is she like a test market?"

"Yeah, in some ways. She's pretty sharp."

Martin, who was laying on his side, his head supported by one hand, leaned over and kissed Erin on the side of the head. She smiled approvingly and then leaned toward him and kissed him once on the lips. Then they went back to watching the boring bluegrass. Martin wondered if it was possible to have a purely sexual relationship with Erin. Just meet occasionally and have sex. Or do stuff like this and have sex. But never really talk.

After the concert, they went back to Martin's. He got two beers for them from the refrigerator. Erin went to the bathroom. Martin sat on his couch and opened his beer. It occurred to him that whatever might happen with Erin was based on momentum Dylan had created. He hadn't really done this himself; that's why he and Erin barely spoke. But no sooner had this thought flickered through his brain then he dismissed it. He got up, went into the kitchen, rinsed out some dirty dishes, and stuck them in his dishwasher. No. This wasn't about Dylan. This was between him and Erin. There was real attraction there. It was okay that they didn't have much to say. So they didn't talk? So what? What mattered was sex. The talking follows the sex.

When Erin came out of the bathroom, she'd refreshed her lipstick. Martin took the hint and went right for her, intercepting her at the kitchen entrance and holding her by the waist. He pulled her tight and kissed her deeply. She reciprocated. Then he pulled back and went for smaller kisses, lighter touching. He kissed her neck, her shoulder, the back of her neck, until he was standing behind her, where he squeezed her breasts through her shirt and bra. She was into it, quietly gasping and humming and letting her head hang backward as he found new places to touch and caress: the inside of her forearms, her hands, her fingertips.

In the bedroom, despite their excitement, both of them were careful to maintain the pace they had set in the kitchen. They undressed quickly but calmly, and then found each other, in the darkness, slowly immersing themselves in the other's soft skin. The initial penetration, when it finally came, seemed to alter Martin's consciousness. Erin also seemed transformed by the moment. Locked inside her, Martin pressed himself hard against her soft body, holding her, gripping her tightly in his hands, maximizing the sensation.

They didn't prolong the act or attempt any unusual variations. The rhythm that had been set was followed through on. Still, it was possibly the most intense sex Martin had ever had and afterward he was seeing stars, breathing hard, his heart thudding in his chest. He moved enough to get his weight off her, then dropped into a state of semiconsciousness, and a few moments later, into a deep sleep.

Erin was still there when he woke up the next morning. The sun was out. Birds chirped outside the window. Erin was asleep. He watched the slight movement of her body as she breathed. Would they spend the morning together?

He quietly slipped out of the bed, grabbing a clean pair of underwear, a fresh T-shirt, and his pants. He went into the bathroom, where he peed, brushed his teeth, and got dressed. Then he padded softly to the kitchen and opened the shades, to a sharp blue sky. He looked around his kitchen. Making coffee seemed like the first order of business. He put the required scoops in the basket and filled the machine with water. He then checked the refrigerator for breakfast possibilities. There wasn't much there. Should he run down to New Seasons and get stuff? Orange juice would be good since his mouth was dry from all the wine last night. She would probably want that too. And what to eat? Eggs. Toast. He could get some Dave's Killer Bread, if they had it. Some cheese in the eggs, a tomato, chives, what else did people put in eggs? Mushrooms? And what would she want to do? Maybe she'd rather go out. He looked at the bedroom door from where he was. Should he ask her?

No. What he needed to do was chill. And not worry about it. He closed the refrigerator and sighed to himself. He was thinking about this all wrong. No, the thing to do in this situation was go back into the bedroom and have sex with her some more.

28

AND SO IT went with Erin. Dates here and there. Solid sex. Awkward mornings. In July, Erin went on a two-week vacation with her parents to a lake in Idaho. Martin was relieved the day she left. A kind of bond was forming between them that he felt vaguely uncomfortable with. She was definitely becoming his girlfriend—if she wasn't already—and he wasn't sure how he felt about that. The solution, according to the manosphere, was to continue seeing other people. But Martin, now forty-two, didn't have the time or the energy to juggle multiple romantic scenarios.

He and Erin were further separated when at the end of July he flew to Los Angeles for the big LA ADFEST conference. This particular event was usually a four-day blowout for ad people. Its alcoholic, narcotic, and sexual escapades were legendary. Martin had been especially looking forward to it as an opportunity to put his new pickup skills to the test.

But from the moment he arrived in the hotel lobby, Martin could feel a change of mood. Checking in, there were new security protocols and a general air of suspicion and paranoia. On the first day, Martin appeared on a panel on "memology," which instantly degenerated into a bitch-fest about the Trump election. Martin, the only straight white male on the panel, kept his mouth shut. Every panel or presentation was like that. Suddenly, politics was king. The pose of casual amorality that had always been the default attitude of the advertising profession was unthinkable now. People suddenly had very strong views and ideological positions, positions they were ready to fight over. The people from New York and LA seemed especially rageful. Unfortunately for them there was nobody to rage against. If there were any actual conservatives present they would have left immediately, lest they ruin their careers forever.

Martin wished people could control themselves a little more. If everyone was on the same side, why did they have to kill the party vibe by shrieking about Trump? But even this opinion was probably unacceptable and so Martin kept it to himself. The conference was ruined anyway. The parties sucked. The women were furious. The guys all stood around, looking at their phones. Nobody was snorting coke in the stairwell or waking up in the wrong room.

Martin spent the majority of the festival dozing by the pool and getting quietly drunk with a few male colleagues from GGI in New York. He found himself missing small-town Erin at odd moments, like when he got stuck eating breakfast at a table of Brooklyn millennials complaining about catcalling in full uptalk mode. He almost called Erin on Saturday night, while he sat bored at a rooftop party. He was greatly relieved on Monday to be back on a plane home.

the red pill

It was a week or so later, in August, that Martin got a frantic phone call from Dylan. "Dude! Are you watching the news?"

"No."

"Dude, there's *Nazis* marching through the streets of Charlottesville, Virginia!"

"Right now?"

"Yes, right now!"

Martin got up from his desk and dug through the couch cushions until he found the remote. He turned on the TV.

"It's the alt-right!" said Dylan. "That's what the Nazis call themselves."

Martin knew about the alt-right. Since Trump's election, the term was all over the manosphere. Some people made fun of it. Others embraced it. The most interesting thing to Martin was that the alt-right was effectively a youth movement. They had their own hairstyle ('80s undercuts), fashion (fitted suits and ties), and music (synthwave). Fittingly, they referred to themselves as the "punk rock of politics."

Martin had not yet seen an actual alt-right person live on camera and so began clicking urgently back and forth among the news stations. It was hard to tell what was happening. He didn't see any marching. What he did see were hysterical reporters, commentators, and bystanders at the scene. The horror on the faces of even the most hardened broadcasters was very real. But he didn't see any Nazis. "Where are the Nazis?" he asked Dylan.

"They marched last night. Like thousands of them. It's unbelievable!"

"What do they look like?"

"They're marching. They have torches."

Torches? Martin's pulse quickened. He continued to flip back and forth until he found a local station that was replaying the footage from the night before. The caption read: "Neo-Nazis, white supremacists, march in Charlottesville." The video showed what looked like several hundred young white men, frat bros it appeared, walking with tiki torches. They looked fairly ordinary. Some of them wore khakis and button-down shirts.

"Wait," said Martin. "The guys in the khakis? Those are the Nazis?"

"Go on YouTube," said Dylan. "You can see the whole thing."

"Where are they going?"

"They're protesting the statue of Robert E. Lee. The locals want to tear it down, and these guys are trying to stop it."

Martin didn't see any statues. The young men on TV marched around an old building, up one set of stairs and down the other with their tiki torches. It was a dramatic and alarming sight.

He clicked back to the cable stations. Commentators were weighing in: "Ever since Trump got elected we've been waiting for this moment...."

"These are definitely neo-Nazis and white supremacists," another newsman said.

"Can you believe this fucking shit?" said Dylan through the phone. "Can you believe this is happening *in our lifetime?*"

"This is because of Trump," said a female analyst on another channel. "This is Trump's army. These are the people we are going to war with."

One male commentator was apoplectic: "These bigots will stop at nothing to get their filthy, disgusting agenda across! These people literally worship Hitler. Look at them. Look at how they're marching!"

"Dude this is just.... This has to stop...! They have to do something!" It was Dylan, still on his phone. "These people are psychos. This is *serious*. And it's all fucking Trump. He did this! He started this on purpose!"

"Yeah?" said Martin, as he stared blankly at the screen. Was it true? Were these kids really Nazis? Were there more of them? Could there be some kind of war? Martin stared helplessly at the TV screen. Everything was changing. The language was changing. Everything was being redefined. And nobody knew where it would lead.

The next day, Sunday, Sadie and Rob were having one of their summer barbecues. Martin arrived late and walked through the open front door and out to the backyard. Wayne was there, in shorts and a Hawaiian shirt, a beer cradled against his belly. Courtney and their boy, Guthrie, were farther out in the backyard, throwing a baseball with Jack. Rob had the grill going. Several pink patties of hamburger sizzled over the heat.

Sadie was inside, on her phone somewhere. She was very upset according to everyone. Martin assumed it was the aftershocks of Charlottesville and the new firestorm over Trump's refusal to denounce the alt-right. Martin got a beer from the cooler and then wandered the house in search of Sadie. He found her in her bedroom, on her phone, commiserating with a friend.

Sadie gave him a cursory hug without making eye contact. She seemed distant. Was she pissed at him? Would the new culture war become a boys versus girls conflict as well? The world was getting complicated. She made a gesture to Martin that she'd be done in a second. He left the room.

Back in the kitchen, his mother and Ashley were baking cookies. Wayne had settled on a stool at the kitchen island. Some other neighbors arrived with children, creating a small commotion. Rob remained outside, attending to the grill. Martin eventually joined him, sipping his beer and making small talk.

At one point, when they were alone, Martin said to Rob, "You saw the Nazi stuff?"

"Yeah. Pretty crazy."

"The TV coverage," said Martin. "I mean, wow. And Trump's comments...."

"Trump didn't organize that march."

Martin drank his beer. "Well, they're blaming him for it."

Rob didn't answer.

"Aren't you afraid of being accused of something?" Martin quietly asked his brother-in-law.

"What would I be accused of?"

"I don't know. Being a racist? Being a Nazi?"

"Why would anyone accuse me of that?"

the red pill

Martin shrugged. "Because they're accusing everyone of everything?"

Rob sipped his own beer. "Last time I checked, I'm not a Nazi. Are you?"

"No," said Martin.

"So who cares?"

"It just seems dangerous..." reasoned Martin. "And the manosphere guys, they support this stuff. Are all of them Nazis? And what if they can track those blogs? What if they can find out who reads them?"

"They probably can. They'll probably show up at your house tonight."

"I'm serious."

"If you're so worried, stop reading them."

"Even the pickup guys," said Martin. "Now they've turned political. Even P-Crusher had a thing about immigration the other day."

"P-Crusher did?" said Rob. "What does he think about immigration?"

"He's against it. He's a racist like the rest of them."

"He's entitled to his opinion," said Rob.

"I'm not sure he is. Not the way they're talking on TV."

"Well, if you don't want any trouble, keep your mouth shut, and don't look at weird shit on the internet."

Martin pondered that thought. Rob rotated his hot dogs.

"What's going on with Sadie?" said Martin.

Now it was Rob who became uneasy. He took a tight sip of his Bud Light. "She doesn't like it. She hates Trump."

"What do the kids think about it?"

"My kids? Nothing. They're kids."

"Yeah."

"But Sadie..." said Rob, in a low voice. "It's weird. It's never been like this before."

Martin squinted at his brother-in-law. "What do you mean?"

"Just what I said. We don't talk. She hasn't said one word to me since Friday night."

Martin nodded seriously. Rob and Sadie not talking seemed like a genuine problem. Not like the surreal hysteria on the TV.

Martin also felt a surge of self-pity for his own lack of a family. Why didn't he have kids? Why didn't he have a wife to worry about and get into ideological arguments with?

"And she's constantly on the phone with her friends," Rob quietly continued. "And you know the bullshit they're all feeding each other on Facebook. God only knows what she's thinking. And fucking Trump. I mean, he's not doing married guys any favors, mouthing off like he does. Guys on my crew say that too. Women get pissed off at Trump, and then it's the husband who gets it. He's not putting us in a good position."

Martin could see how that would go. He nodded. He drank his beer.

As the barbecue wound down, Martin checked his messages. He'd been in sporadic contact with Erin since he got back from LA. She hadn't messaged him. Perhaps she was the one having second thoughts now. He missed her though. He texted her.

Hey, wudup? What are you doing?

She typed back:

Nothing much

Then she wrote:

I'm doing my nails and watching the news. Come over if you want.

Martin immediately excused himself and drove back into town, to Erin's apartment. She was wearing sweatpants when she opened the door. Martin came in. She turned the sound down on the TV while Martin got himself a Dos Equis from her fridge. Erin was still working on her toenails. Surrounding her on the coffee table were cotton balls, brushes, a small tray of different colored toenail polish.

"Where have you been?" she asked him.

"My sister's house. They had a barbecue."

"How was that?"

"Not so good," said Martin. "My sister's freaking out about Charlottesville. And Rob, her husband, he's a Trump guy."

"Uh-oh."

"Yeah, it's getting ugly."

"People were already on edge at the bank," said Erin. "I can't imagine how they'll be tomorrow."

"What do the bank people say, in general? What do they think?"

"Honestly, it kinda breaks down male-female. I mean, a lot of the guys say they don't like Trump. But it's hard to tell if they mean it."

"My office isn't too bad," said Martin. "There's not that many of us. We're all on the same page, more or less."

Martin sat down beside Erin on the couch. He began scratching her back, through her hoodie, which he knew she liked.

"What about you?" he asked. "Are you afraid of the Nazis?"

"Yeah," she said, dabbing the paint brush on her toenails. "A little. Are you?"

"A little," said Martin, watching the TV.

They said nothing for several minutes. Martin continued to rub her back.

"It's the millennials," said Martin. "They're coming of age. The left-wing millennials are all at college, driving everyone crazy with their safe space bullshit. And now the right-wing millennials have shown up with their Hitler haircuts, to piss them off. It's really between them. It's not even about us."

"I think I might be a millennial," said Erin.

"How old are you?"

"Thirty-four."

Martin sipped his beer. "Yeah, you're right on the cusp."

the red pill

When her toes had dried, Erin moved closer to Martin on the couch and they began kissing. Things progressed quickly. Erin slipped off her sweatpants and crawled on top of him on the couch. Joined together, they did their usual: not much eye contact, no talking. As Erin began to move on top of him, Martin felt a sense of peace came over him, peace and ease, so much so that he broke tradition and grinned up at Erin, who also smiled, a funny girlish expression that Martin had never seen before.

Martin spent the night. He woke up the next morning at 8:30 in Erin's empty bed. She had gone to work. Alone for the first time in her apartment, he walked around in his underwear scratching himself. He started the coffee maker and looked at the pictures on her refrigerator as it brewed. Erin was cute as a kid. She was the oldest, she'd told him, and you could tell by the pictures. She was the responsible one. You could see it in her ten-year-old face.

He looked at other things in the kitchen. She had good knives, he noticed. And kept her pots and pans organized in a coherent manner. The coffee maker began to gurgle, and he poured himself a cup. He drank it, sitting at the small table, looking out her window at the building across the street. It felt profound, this moment, being in her place, though he wasn't thinking about anything in particular as he sat there.

When he was done, he rinsed the cup in the sink and set it upside down in the drying rack. Then he dressed and walked down the street toward his office.

29

"THE PROBLEM WITH feminists," said Martin, "is they don't take into account anything about being male. They refuse to acknowledge what it's like to be in our skin. And if they won't even consider the male side, our different psychology, our different brain chemistry, what kind of negotiation is that? We do all the changing, and they do nothing? How is that right? How is that even possible?"

Kristi, 36, whose favorite things included laughter, fish tacos, and social justice, stared at him in amazement. "My housemates would hate you," she said.

They were in a café, and it was dark outside. "It doesn't matter what anyone thinks," continued Martin. "You can't sustain that position. You can't vilify one gender, or one race, and have that be your ideology. That's not a platform; that's prejudice from the other side."

"What about white male privilege?" said Kristi.

"What about it? I'm not denying it. I'm just saying, the sexes are different. They think different. They have different strategies." Martin had never done this before, just blatantly start arguing with a woman like this. And Kristi was cute!

"So you're going to destroy the system?" pressed Martin. "And then what happens? It's gonna go backward, that's what. That's how you end up with *The Handmaid's Tale*. Is that what you want? Because if you burn this society down, what's gonna grow back in its place? You have no idea."

"I can't even listen to this," said Kristi. She put her hands over her ears.

Martin laughed. He shook his head and stared out the window. Was he losing his mind? None of these ideas were even his. He was repeating stuff he'd read online. His newest favorite blogger, a midwestern Christian named SuperDuper, had made this exact argument in a post Martin had read that morning.

"Okay, Okay," he said to Kristi. Martin reached over and gently gripped her wrists, pulling them away from her ears.

"I hope you're done," said Kristi.

"I am done," said Martin. "I apologize. I get worked up sometimes."

He smiled and leaned back in his own chair. Kristi did a funny eye-rolling thing. "I'm never going to tell anyone about this date," she said.

"I'm glad I amuse you," he said back.

They both sat looking around at the other café patrons. Martin began talking about the recent season of *Game of Thrones* and the date was salvaged somewhat. Leaving the coffee shop, Martin walked her back to her car. Then, for the hell of it, he went for the kiss. She kissed him back. They ended up making out, leaning against the car. Eventually, they got *in* the car, in the back seat. Things got pretty involved.

Afterward, Martin walked back to his Audi, vibrating slightly, from the not-quite-consummated make-out session. He got in and took a moment to collect himself. He checked his phone. There was a message from Libby. What was he doing? Did he want to come over?

There'd been a lot of texts from Libby lately. Summer was ending. Kevin was away on business again. Martin decided he'd had enough fun for one night and pulled up SuperDuper's blog on his phone. He'd already read the most recent post but the comments were good, so he scrolled down to where he'd left off. The original post was about how contemporary churches, which had already become bastions of Leftism, had doubled down after the election of Trump. Now, in 2017, when you entered a typical American church, you got lesbian priests, sermons on diversity, "rainbow retreats," and, most importantly, the reworking of the Bible so that instead of wives submitting to their husbands, wives were to be strong, empowered, and independent. It was pretty interesting to Martin, who had been in a church maybe a dozen times in his entire life. And yet he could totally picture the situation described. And of course, woe to the poor white male who ventured into such a place. Why would he? The contemporary church was not a place for him. It was a place to help others recover from him.

Martin looked up suddenly from his phone and understood that he had to stop doing this. He had to stop reading these blogs. If he didn't, it was only a matter of time until he said the wrong thing to the wrong person. What if he'd done at work what he'd just done with Kristi—start throwing around arguments that were completely inappropriate? He'd get shunned. He'd ruin his career. They'd lose the Pacifica deal. Martin didn't have the self-control to fill himself with controversial ideas. Some of them might leak out.

But he still read more comments anyway. They were too funny and too accurate to resist. This was the problem: reading these blogs gave him a hit of something—dopamine, adrenaline, laughter chemicals, whatever. He was already acting like a drug addict with this stuff, sneaking secret hits of it at work, pretending to others he knew nothing about it. And worst of all: he was starting to agree with some of it. Like this church business. Wasn't church supposed to be for old people? Or people who never drank and got embarrassed if you mentioned sex? And now they'd turned it into *this?* It wasn't right. It wasn't fair to boring people. Where were they supposed to go?

Martin stuffed his phone into his pocket and started his car. He drove to Libby's. This was probably another bad idea, but he did it anyway. He pulled into her driveway and rang the bell. Libby let him in. She was glad to see him, of course. She cinched her bathrobe closed and pushed up onto her tiptoes to kiss his cheek.

Delilah was sleeping, Libby told him, as he followed her inside. They entered her kitchen and she smiled suggestively at him over her shoulder. "Thanks for coming over," she said.

"No problem."

In the kitchen she busied herself looking for snacks to offer Martin. "I've been getting a lot better with my alone time," she told him. "I have a new therapist. He wants me to study Spanish, which I've always wanted to learn. So I listen to these Spanish lessons on my laptop. Delilah and I listen to them together. She'll probably learn Spanish faster than I will. Little kids pick up languages better than anyone. They literally absorb it."

Martin sat down on one of her kitchen island stools.

"Want something to drink?" continued Libby, opening the refrigerator door. "Better yet, wanna get drunk?"

Martin shook his head.

"No? Okay. Do you want a beer at least?"

"Sure."

"I don't know what we have.... Here's a dark lager. Is that okay?"

Martin took it.

"What have you been up to tonight?" asked Libby, refilling her wine glass at the kitchen counter.

"Went on a date."

"Yeah? With who?"

"A Tinder person."

"And?"

Martin shrugged. "It was fine."

"Will you see her again?"

"Probably not."

"Oh, to be on a date..." mused Libby. "That sounds *so fun*. The mystery. The anticipation. Will you get lucky?" She sipped her wine and smiled at him. "I mean, that's if they're cute. Which you are. I don't know why you aren't hooking up more on these dating sites. Isn't that the point of Tinder?"

"Not really, not in your forties," said Martin. Libby drank more wine and leaned her back against the counter. Martin took a deep sip of his lager, and then got up and walked the six steps it took to get to Libby. He pushed her long black hair away from the side of her face and tucked it behind her shoulder. Then he leaned down and kissed the side of her neck.

Libby lowered her head slightly, and turned it to the side, to give him better access. "Ummm," she murmured, as he kissed her more.

Martin found her breasts inside the folds of her robe. She was completely naked beneath it.

"Are you really doing this," she whispered. "After all this time?"

Martin nodded that he was. Two minutes later they were in her and Kevin's bedroom, on the huge soft bed. Martin hadn't planned for things to happen so quickly. His condoms were back in the Audi. Libby had to stop him and go find some of her own.

Things proceeded after that. One problem: Libby didn't smell very good. She had drunk a lot of wine and her breath was bad, which forced Martin to keep his head away from her face. Also, he couldn't seem to get the two of them into a mutually satisfying position. She kept squirming around, trying to pleasure herself while he tried to do what he was doing. Finally, when she had loudly finished, Martin tried to come but couldn't. After a few minutes, Martin gave up and rolled off her. He let his sweaty head sink into the pillow and dozed off for a moment.

He was woken up by Libby kicking him. "Hey! Hey, Martin!" she hissed. "It's almost two a.m.! Our neighbor comes home from work then. He's friends with Kevin. You have to go!"

Martin hauled himself out of the bed. Libby turned on the harsh overhead light. The whole scene was deeply depressing. Martin tore through the bedding to find his pants and underwear, pulling them on and jamming his feet into his shoes. At 1:52, he slipped out the front door, still buttoning his shirt. He hurried to his car, swung it backward out of the driveway, and quickly drove away.

30

MARTIN WAS AT the YMCA, at his Tuesday basketball game, when he got the fateful call. He was sitting in the bleachers when his phone lit up.

"Martin, it's Simon." There was a lot of background noise on Simon's end.

"Hey, what's up?" said Martin.

"Hey...listen...there's some shit I gotta tell you."

Martin braced himself. He was pretty sure he knew what was coming.

"First of all, I'm really sorry I have to make this call."

Martin looked down at his bare knees, his athletic socks, his basketball shoes.

"I had a talk with Kate Thompson at Pacifica this morning. They've decided not to bring us in. The acquisition is not happening."

Martin lowered his head and closed his eyes. "Okay," he said.

"We had a long conversation about it. They love us. They wanted us there. But too much has happened over the last six months. There's a lot of factors involved. Stuff we can't control, obviously. The current climate. That kinda thing. You know the drill."

"Right, right," said Martin. His voice felt thin when he spoke.

"So they don't want to bring us in. And, in fact, they're letting us go. They're terminating our contract."

Martin stared across the gym as Simon's words registered in his brain.

"Part of this is my situation with Regan," said Simon. "That's on me. And I take full responsibility for it. And part of it is a perception thing. They see us a certain way. The humor. The bro culture. You know. That's what we do. That's what we're known for. But that's not the direction they want to go right now, for obvious reasons."

"What did they say the reasons were?" Martin asked.

"What?"

"The obvious reasons? What were they?"

"You know. They want a different vibe. The current climate. The usual."

"Okay..." said Martin.

"Yeah..." breathed Simon.

"So that's it?" said Martin. "We're fired?"

"Yeah, we're basically fired."

"As of when?"

"As of Friday."

"*This* Friday?"

"Yes."

"Like move our shit out by *this* Friday? Are you serious? Like in three days?"

"Yeah. And I'd be careful with that. I mean Kate's being super cool about everything, but if I were you, I'd be totally cleared out by Friday at six."

the red pill

"What the fuck?" said Martin. Tears had sprung to his eyes. Not that he loved his office, or Pacifica, or the executives at Pacifica. It was just such a violent end. "So they hate us now."

"They don't hate us," said Simon. "They do not hate us. All of this goes in the file as amicable. Parted ways. They still love us. We're still gold, if we want to continue. Which is something you and I...well...I don't know about you but I want to step back. Take a break. Clear my head. Maybe this isn't the best business to be in right now."

"Yeah," said Martin.

Both men remained silent for a moment.

"So yeah, your personal belongings, out by Friday at six..." said Simon.

Another silence came between them.

"And part of this is Regan?" said Martin.

"Yes. Part of it. I mean. Like I said. That's on me. I'm very sorry that happened. The one thing I can say in my defense is that, how could I have possibly known? You meet people, you have fun with them, everything seems perfectly okay. And then suddenly it's not. I got conned. She made me fall in love with her."

"Yeah."

"It's hard not to fall in love with someone if they're coming at you like that."

"Yeah, I can imagine."

"I fell for it. I'm stupid. What can I say? But I'm not the first guy to go down like this. This is what happens. Maybe I'll learn something. I'll definitely never dip my pen in the company ink again, I'll tell you that. But whatever. I can't blame anyone but myself. It happened. I fucked myself. And I hurt you. And I'm sorry."

Another odd noise rang in the background.

"Where are you?" asked Martin.

"At the airport."

"Where are you going?"

"Mexico. My parents still have their house there."

"Are you running from the law?"

"No. Fuck no. I just want to get the fuck out of here. This country. I mean, it's too dangerous. And I don't want to see all the shit on TV anymore. I'm done. I'm getting the fuck out."

"What happened with her, anyway?"

"What do you mean?"

"The sexual assault thing. With Regan. What did you actually do to her? I'm curious."

"I hit her."

"Like how?"

"Like with the back of my hand, while we were driving. It cut her lip. She took pictures of it."

"Why'd you do that?"

"She was winding me up about some shit. In the car. Totally provoking me. She wanted me to hit her. I wonder if that wasn't the plan all along. Who knows. It doesn't matter."

Martin thought about this. "And that's considered sexual assault?"

"No, that's just assault."

"But weren't they calling it sexual assault?"

"No, it was plain assault."

"But what happened to the sexual assault charges?"

"The other charges are for sexual misconduct."

Martin felt dizzy and unbalanced for a moment. He tried to stay focused on Simon and what he was saying but his brain was overloaded. He couldn't take in any more information.

"All right, well, so...is there anything else?" asked Martin.

"I think that's it, my friend. My guy is dissolving the company as well. You'll get a little something. I hope you saved some money."

"I did."

"Of course you did, you're a smart guy."

"I can't believe it's over," said Martin, his voice faltering slightly. "Just like that."

"I know. Neither can I. That's how it goes sometimes. Welcome to the big leagues."

"I guess so."

"All right, Martin. I gotta get on this plane."

"All right, Simon."

"I'll catch you later."

Martin cleaned out his office the next day. He didn't want to see anyone, so he went late, 10 p.m. The building was leased by Pacifica, that's how tight EKO was with their only client: Pacifica paid their rent. It was amazing how fast things had fallen apart. Just a year ago, the love between Pacifica and EKO had seemed infinite.

Martin got off the elevator and turned on the lights. Simon's office had been emptied already. There were papers on the floor, cabinets left open. Martin went into his own office with two big moving boxes and his backpack.

He turned on the little Bose radio on the windowsill. He went through his desk drawers, his cabinets. In the closet he found a tennis racquet, an unopened bag of Kettle Chips, a pair of dress shoes he'd been looking for. He went through the portfolio drawers, the kitchenette, the half-fridge. He made a preliminary trip to his car in the parking garage, where he spotted a dumpster. He'd assumed he'd take home a whole carload of stuff, but once he thought about it, he realized most of his stuff could go directly there. Some of it, in fact, he could just leave where it was. Let Pacifica clean it up.

So that's what happened. What he thought would be an evening's project took about thirty minutes. He drove back to his apartment and carried the one box he did want upstairs. He set it on the floor, in the living room. Then he locked his front door and collapsed on his couch. He sat there for a long time, in the quiet darkness. He stared at the box. He'd saved a lot of money over the years. And he still had his Pacifica stock options. That was the good news. And he didn't have a family or any other real expenses except for the modest rent he was paying here. He could live on his savings indefinitely, if need be.

Still, he was only forty-two years old. He had half a lifetime ahead of him.

the red pill

He'd kept Erin updated on this situation and the next day he called her to tell her it was done. He was officially unemployed. She immediately made reservations for the two of them, at La Provence.

In a personal finance class, at community college, Erin had studied techniques for dealing with getting fired. Now she shared what she'd learned with Martin. "First, you have to think about the freedom you have," she said, after they'd cut into their steaks. "It's a gift. You can do anything you want. You're free. After that you think about things you've always wanted to do. What have you always wanted to *try?*"

Martin sipped his water and pondered this. What had he always wanted to try? Hang gliding, bird watching, a threesome? He'd studied English literature in college. He thought about teaching. He thought about Angela and the rich social world of a big public high school, the other teachers, the kids, the parents, a huge community....

Or maybe he could write a novel. Or a nonfiction book. *The Idiot's Guide to Advertising.* Or maybe a biography of someone. Or a history...the French Revolution.... There'd been a lot of revolution talk on the manosphere lately. Martin had read a long post about the Cultural Revolution in China, where rabid young people had been unleashed upon the old. This was Mao's clever way of destroying the institutions that had turned against him. He incited generational warfare, and in the chaos reclaimed his power.

"And also, to think about people you look up to," said Erin. "What kind of lives do they lead?"

The first person Martin thought of was Rob. What did he do? He fished. He played poker one night a week with his construction buddies. What else did he care about? Nothing much really. He came straight home most nights. His kids. His job. Mostly his kids though. If you thought about Rob's life, the kids were it.

"What's Simon going to do?" asked Erin.

"Simon?" sighed Martin. "I don't know. He'll do something eventually. He can't sit still."

Erin smeared some butter on a piece of bread. "Do you like advertising?" she asked him.

"Yeah, I do," he admitted.

"Do you *love* advertising?"

Martin thought about it. He looked down at his plate. "Yeah. I do."

"What do you love about it?"

"It's fun. It's the most fun thing I've ever done. It's looking at the world and seeing things, seeing patterns...." Martin felt a sadness welling up inside him. "What do people like? What do people relate to? And making them laugh. Being funny. And seeing something in the culture a half-second before everyone else sees it...." Martin was getting choked up. He cut into his steak.

"That's good you feel that way," she said. "That's important. You're lucky. So now you have to think, what other ways could you use that passion, and use those same skills which you obviously have...?"

31

OCTOBER WAS PROBABLY the best time to visit New York City. Everyone looked great: new clothes, new fashions, everyone renewed and refreshed, a cool crisp *readiness* in the air.

Martin had flown in for an interview at Aronofsky & Krell and was staying with his old friend and advertising colleague Adam Weissman. Adam lived in Park Slope, Brooklyn, and was married and had twin boys, sixteen months.

"It's the fertility drugs," he told Martin, about his sons. "That's why there's so many twins nowadays." Adam was pushing the two boys in an ingenious and probably very expensive two-person baby stroller. Like the Portland car seat, the Park Slope stroller had its various types and designs and status levels. Martin walked alongside Adam, or tried to, on busy Seventh Avenue.

"So what's the game plan?" asked Adam. "You wanna move back here?"

"I think I do. I think I might have to."

"Nothing going on in Portland?"

"There is stuff. But it's so small. Portland's tiny. There just aren't many options."

"Yeah, it's tough here too. But it's advertising, people move around. You'll find something."

Martin was staring into the shops along the avenue, watching the people. New York was such a feast for the senses. Even Park Slope, in far-off Brooklyn, had that pleasing human density. All the faces, the different nationalities, the peaceful anonymity of being one among millions. "Do you know the guys who did Dilly Dilly by any chance?" Martin asked his friend.

Adam smiled widely. "No, I don't but I've heard things."

"Like what?"

"They're young guys, so let's just say they're enjoying their success *a great deal.*"

"Like what? Coke and hookers?"

"I don't know about that. But it was a huge hit. An instant classic."

Martin stopped to look in the window of an upscale toy store. "I've got these nieces and nephews, back in Portland," he said. "They give me the lowdown on what's up."

"How old are they?"

"Seven and five. They loved Dilly Dilly."

"That's why it's such a hit," said Adam. "Everybody loves it. Four-year-olds love it."

The executive at Aronofsky & Krell, who Martin was going to interview with, was unexpectedly unavailable on the day they'd agreed on. Rescheduling was also not a possibility, for reasons not explained. And so Martin would meet with another person, a VP, Ellen Rainey. Martin had never heard of her, but A&K was a great company; just last year they'd come up with a series of psychedelic chewing gum spots that won awards all over the world. He had almost worked there himself at one point, back in his New York days. A&K knew what they were doing. Martin felt comfortable they would recognize his talent and experience.

He arrived comfortably early in the very slick reception area. Since he had a few minutes, he made himself a peppermint tea at a well-stocked coffee bar. He returned to his seat and breathed and tried to prepare himself. Contrary to what he'd said to Adam, Martin had not decided to relocate. To him this was more of a fact-finding mission. Could he reestablish himself in New York at forty-two? Would he want to? "It's important that you feel comfortable in your surroundings," Erin had counseled.

He was having trouble getting comfortable in the reception area. For starters, the receptionist was fashion-model gorgeous, a stone cold ten, and easily the most beautiful woman Martin had spoken to in years, maybe in his life. The room itself—the leather couches, the futuristic furniture, the super-slick A&K logo—was something to behold. You inevitably lost your sense of such things living in Oregon. Nothing within a thousand miles of Portland was as chic or sophisticated as this twenty by thirty-foot reception area. It sucked the confidence right out of you. Martin tried not to worry too much. "Fact-finding mission," he murmured under his breath.

"Mr. Harris?" said a voice, coming out of a hallway. This was Ellen Rainey. She too was unusually attractive, though older. Martin jumped up and shook hands with her, taking in her lipstick smile, her bright blue eyes, but also the prim professionalism that instantly established her authority over the situation.

"Come this way. There's a conference room where we can talk."

Martin followed her down the hall. As he walked he tried to summon that clarity of mind, that singleness of purpose that was necessary in any interview situation in New York City. This was not an easy place to stand out. How had he acted when he interviewed for his first ad job at twenty-four? He didn't remember. It probably hadn't mattered. They needed bright, funny kids, so they hired you.

Martin followed Ellen Rainey into a cold, blank-walled room. They both took seats at the near end of a long, elegant conference table. Martin tried to make himself comfortable. He still had his tea, which he sipped daintily one last time, before setting it aside for good.

"So I looked over your résumé and I've talked to Michael," Ellen Rainey began. "You're presently located in Portland, Oregon?"

"Yes," said Martin. "I'm looking to make a move back to the city."

"Do you miss New York?"

"Yes, very much."

She opened a folder and perused the top sheet of paper. "And in Portland, you were a partner, I see...at EKO...and you worked mostly with Pacifica?"

"Pretty much exclusively the last couple years."

"I love Pacifica. My daughter has the cutest little puffer jacket of theirs."

"They make a quality product," said Martin, smiling. "It was a great pleasure to work with them."

"Yes, I'm sure," she said, her eyes working their way down the paper. "Yes…all right…this is all very impressive."

Ellen Rainey read a little more and then checked the other pages.

Then, with a noticeable change in her expression, she placed her hands on the table and said, "Let me give you an idea of where we currently stand."

She gave Martin a short description of Aronofsky & Krell in terms of their goals, their brand, their overall vision. Martin was a little surprised this was necessary but listened carefully as she spoke. Aronosky & Krell "was committed to diversity and inclusiveness," he was told. They believed in "the empowerment of those who had not previously enjoyed privilege and opportunity." She talked about "implicit bias," "critical self-awareness," and referred to something called "a gender lens," which Martin had never heard of. Still, he did his best to absorb this information, nodding along, smiling, doing his best to appear pleased with the current corporate culture at A&K.

After that, Ellen Rainey began to straighten the papers in front of her. She paused meaningfully for several seconds and then said: "Just so you know, we are aware of the nature of the breakup at EKO."

"Oh," said Martin. This was a surprise. He'd asked Adam if it was possible that Simon's mistakes would taint Martin in any way. Adam had promised him they would not. If they looked into it at all, they would see that Martin had nothing to do with it.

"There were sexual harassment charges?" asked Ellen. "And other issues?"

"That's right," Martin said, carefully. "Sexual misconduct, I think it was. My partner, Simon Howard, unbeknownst to me, was..." He searched for the right words. "...breaking the law."

"Was there a culture of this at EKO?"

"No. No, there was not."

"Because that happens. I know. I've experienced it myself."

"No. We were actually..." but Martin didn't want to praise his old company. "I guess the best thing to say is, it was not common. I mean, really, to be honest, never. We were a small group, we were tight-knit, and when this happened we were literally blindsided. It was a terrible shock. Especially for me. I've personally known Simon for years...." But Martin didn't want to go in that direction either. He shifted: "It's terrible when something like that happens. When I was here in New York, over at GGI, everyone got along great. We had a lot of fun. It was a very productive working environment."

"Unfortunately, having a lot of fun is sometimes the problem."

"Right. Yes," said Martin. "What I mean is *creatively*. That creative energy you need. That's what I mean. That's what we had. That's what I'm good at creating and fostering in the people I work with."

the red pill

The meeting ended soon after and Ellen marched Martin back to the reception area. They'd been in the conference room for exactly nine minutes, Martin noted, as he rode the elevator down to the lobby. Outside, he wanted to kick the metal-meshed trash can on the corner, but restrained himself, so as not to shred his new shoes on the jagged steel.

Fuck, he muttered to himself as he walked. *Fuck fuck fuck.* And *Simon*, that fucking piece of shit! *Simon* gets laid and Martin gets fucked! It seemed possible that he might never get another gig in advertising again.

Martin stormed up Fifth Avenue and into Central Park. He found a bench and plopped down on it. He breathed and tried to calm himself. But then he'd remember Ellen Rainey. Her face. Her tone of voice. *What the fuck was wrong with people?*

He sat back on the bench, stretching his arms along the top of it. Despite his anger, the perfect autumnal air felt good on his face and hands. The leaves were turning. It was a beautiful day. And what did he expect? This was New York. This was what happens. *Welcome to the big leagues*, as Simon had said.

He took a moment to contemplate the grass, the stones, the tree branches moving slightly in the breeze. An attractive couple—the man in a suit, the woman in a professional skirt and blouse—strode confidently passed him. He got out his phone and called Erin.

"Hey," he said to her. "I just got out of my interview."

"What happened?"

Martin sat forward, lowering his head and gripping his temples with his thumb and finger. "Nothing good," he said. "According to them, I'm literally the last person they need. Like literally. The head guy wasn't there. And then this VP lectured me about my white male privilege. I couldn't believe it. It was like, why was I even there? It lasted nine minutes. I flew three thousand miles for nine minutes."

"What did she say?"

"Nothing. She told me about their principles. She told me what superior people they are. And then she reminded me that my partner is a rapist, and by the way, *fuck my toxic masculinity*. That was it. That was literally her tone. I spent the whole time defending myself. And to this fucking woman who has done what? Weaseled her way up to some bullshit position as vice president of political correctness?"

"That sounds bad."

"It was awful. It was fucking humiliating. I was, like, who the fuck are you? I built a fucking agency out of nothing. Fucking *nothing*. I actually had to do shit. There's a reason we were on the cover of *Influence Magazine*, you dumb twit. What have you done? Let's see your portfolio. And think of the money she probably makes. And it's probably the same everywhere. The whole industry's probably like this now. One huge tangle of HR political bullshit. I've been lucky. I didn't have to deal with this stuff back in Portland. And I'll tell you what. I'm not going to deal with it here. Fuck this shit. Fuck Aronofsky & Krell. If they don't want me, they're not going to get me. They don't fucking deserve me!"

the red pill

When he was done he took a breath. He sat back. He pondered the tall buildings in the distance. "Can you do me a favor?" he asked Erin.

"What?"

"Forget everything I just said?"

"Yes."

Martin felt his body relax. He looked at his fingernails. "It doesn't matter. I don't have to come back here. New York is probably over for me. It sure is beautiful though."

"Where are you now?" asked Erin.

"Central Park," said Martin. He watched two businessmen in suits walk by. How did they still have jobs?

"Have you ever been here?" he asked Erin.

"No."

"But you've seen it in movies."

"I have," said Erin.

"Yeah, it's nice. It's tough, but it's nice."

"I'd love to go there sometime."

"Yeah, maybe someday..." said Martin. But he stopped himself. "Yeah, you'd probably like it."

"I think so."

"Listen, I better get going. Thanks for listening to my rant."

"No problem."

That night, Martin had dinner with Adam and his wife at their brownstone in Park Slope. Adam's wife, Susan, was a producer at Netflix Films. She looked like a serious person, a successful person. Martin didn't want to discuss his fruitless interview at A&K in front of her.

After dinner, Martin went for a walk by himself along Seventh Ave. It wasn't helping his mood that Harvey Weinstein's face was everywhere. On his phone. On pizza parlor TVs. On the many newspapers that surprisingly still existed in the Big Apple. The Weinstein allegations had broken a couple weeks before, and now, in the thirty-six hours Martin had been in New York, the story had surged again. New accusers. New charges. Thank God Simon Howard was a nobody from Portland, Oregon. Still, Martin wondered if shopping himself in the current job market would do more harm than good. Maybe he should take some time off. Go on vacation. Bali. Or Thailand. Or Mexico. Go sit on a beach for a year. Let the EKO situation fade into history a bit.

Or maybe he needed a total change, go teach poetry to disadvantaged kids somewhere, get out of the business altogether. Or would Simon Howard's disgrace somehow follow him there too? Maybe do the year on the beach and *then* try for the teaching gig. Thank God the Regan debacle had never got reported anywhere. That must have been in the settlement, a nondisclosure agreement, but even those didn't always work. What a clusterfuck. And fucking Simon, banging an intern and then hitting her in the face! What fucking idiot would *ever do that?* Martin should sue him too. He probably could. He would look into it. Fuck Simon and his white male privilege.

32

THE OTHER THING Martin wanted to do in New York was see his ex-wife. He had trouble giving her a concrete reason for the reunion, just that it would be nice "to catch up." His own secret motivation was the thought that he had changed significantly in the last year and he wanted to see what this new self looked like, reflected in the last woman he'd been seriously involved with. She had hesitated at first but then agreed to a late-morning coffee in Cobble Hill.

They met at a café and hugged awkwardly. They sat at a booth by the window. She had her own name again, Rachel Cohen. She looked okay, pretty much the same. She was unmarried too, but had a steady boyfriend, a "partner" as people liked to say now, as if it was only a matter of time before heterosexuality would be eliminated altogether. She was still teaching art at the same private school in Brooklyn Heights, which she disliked but couldn't seem to detach from. Her bohemian mother had taught there as well.

Still, it was fun and somehow comforting to sit across from her again as they recounted their current life situations. There was even a faint tinge of excitement, not sexual but familial, like long-lost cousins meeting for the first time as adults.

"So, you like Oregon?" she said.

"It's all right," said Martin. "The terrain is nice. Mild weather. Great for hiking. If you like hiking."

"I always thought we'd end up there," she said, touching the rim of her coffee cup. "I would try to picture it. Me, walking around in the woods."

"You don't actually walk in the woods very much. I mean, you can, if you want to."

"Are you going to move back to New York?"

"I'm thinking about it," said Martin. "I need a new job. I'm kind of adrift at the moment."

"So you call me."

"No. It wasn't like that. I just wanted to see how you're doing."

She accepted this explanation, smiling and wiggling her head slightly in a familiar gesture.

"So this partner, David, what's his deal?" said Martin. "And why hasn't he married you?"

She shrugged. "I guess he's thinking about it."

"He's weighing his options."

"And I'm weighing mine."

"Naturally," said Martin. "You can't be too careful."

"He's funny. So that's good. He makes me laugh."

"Yeah. That's crucial, I think."

"I'm really the one holding things up," said Rachel. "I think he would do it, if I pushed him. We have these conversations, you know, to figure it out. Which we never do. And then another six months goes by...."

"It's more of a common-law marriage."

"Something like that."

the red pill

This was the kind of banter that had brought them together, all those years ago. Light. Pleasing. A certain ease that they weren't quite achieving now, but that was fun to remember.

Martin drank from his coffee. Rachel drank from hers. Martin watched out the window at the steady stream of young Brooklynites walking by.

"This Harvey Weinstein thing is crazy," he said.

"It's so disgusting."

"I remember when I first moved here. He was the king of this town. Just his name: *Harvey Weinstein*. He was like a mafia don."

"Ugh. I can't even think about it. I hope he goes to prison."

"Movies are over now anyway," said Martin, sipping his coffee. "It's all TV. Everything is TV."

"It's been like that for years."

"It's good for my business anyway," said Martin. "Lots of commercials. You wonder about TV though. People watching for hours at a time. Watching whole seasons of TV shows, in a weekend."

"David and I do that sometimes."

"In Portland, you can see the giant screens from the street."

"My students are all addicted to their phones," said Rachel.

"They probably have nice stuff."

"The best stuff. Always. Whatever it is, they have the best of it."

"Rich people rule the world."

"It sure seems like it."

Afterward, Martin walked back to Park Slope through the Gowanus Canal area. He found that he had no thoughts regarding the question of had he changed or not. Instead, he felt vaguely sad, and a little nostalgic, but mostly he was happy to be by himself again. Honestly, he was surprised how little connection he felt to Rachel Cohen. *Nothing really mattered* was the true lesson of life. You could go on this track. You could go on that track. You could change. Or not change. You ended up the same person anyway, no matter what you did.

He stopped at the Gowanus Whole Foods for a slice of their pizza and to check out the scene. The pizza crust was excellent, as Dylan had once mentioned. As he studied the texture, Martin had a moment of panic as he contemplated a life outside of advertising. Everything he did was about products: how good they were, *why* they were good, *how* to explain to someone else what was good about them. If he didn't sell things for a living, what would he even think about?

He sipped from his three-dollar, locally crafted root beer and watched the other lunchtime customers. Whole Foods. They had yet to run any TV spots, at least none that Martin was aware of. Jeff Bezos didn't bother with advertising, at least not in the traditional sense. He didn't have to. He was the Harvey Weinstein of the current time, the ten-ton gorilla. Everyone knew who he was. Everyone was aware of his immense power.

But back to the pizza: what kind of TV spot would you run for Whole Foods? People used to call it "Whole Paycheck" because it cost so much. Could you do something contrary to that? Two broke skateboarder bros, standing in line, their long hair sticking out of their trucker hats. When they get to the checker, they have to count out pennies to buy their healthy snacks.

The only problem: skater bros were passé. It would have to be girls. One white, one black. No, one Asian and one black. And would they have skateboards? They could. But it wouldn't look the same. The fun of broke skater bros was they actually existed. Two broke different-raced skater girls, that wouldn't be charming, that would be weird. And you couldn't portray girls as dumb on TV. Only boys could be dumb.

Adam was still at work when Martin returned to the apartment. Susan was in her home office, with her two small children. Martin could hear her talking on the phone in a producer's voice. He caught bits of her conversation as he reclined on the guest bed, where he was surfing job sites online.

From the tone of Susan's voice, it sounded like someone at Netflix had messed up. Martin wondered if he could ever work under a real boss again. He supposed he might have to at some point. Or he could start something new himself. That was the other possibility Erin had brought up: starting another agency of his own.

At 3:30 the nanny appeared. She was from Ecuador, Adam had told him. She loaded the infants into the fancy stroller and set out for their afternoon walk. The house went very quiet once they were gone. Adam's wife shut her office door and continued her terse conversation.

Martin took the opportunity to make a sandwich in the kitchen and then ate it standing at the window, looking down into the narrow backyard. There were still toys in the grass from the summer. Or maybe they belonged to the family upstairs, who also had young children. Martin tried to imagine growing up in Park Slope, your formative years spent in the pressure cooker of New York City, how it might warp or stunt a fragile personality. On the other hand, think of the nourishment you'd receive, the extraordinary glow of human achievement all around you, inspiring you, educating you. What heights you might achieve....

33

It was the morning of his last full day in New York that Martin came across a posting by his old friend Brian Walden on Facebook. Brian helped him get his first job at GGI, a job Martin, at twenty-four, had not taken very seriously at first but that subsequently changed his life. In a way, he owed Brian everything he had. Which might have been why they'd drifted apart once they were both ensconced at GGI. Martin had been more successful there than his friend. Martin was funnier, snarkier, a little better suited to the politics of the place. Though he certainly would have done anything to help Brian as payback, the way things worked out, he'd never been able to.

Brian had eventually left GGI for a lifestyle startup, and then married a secretive woman from Bulgaria a year or two later. That was the last Martin had heard of him. But now, here he was, sharing *New York* magazine articles about the evils of Trump.

Martin did a quick study of his old friend's presence on Facebook. It was hard to tell what he was actually doing from his sparse postings. *Fuck it*, thought Martin. He sent Brian a Facebook message. Was he around? Did he want to get a beer? It turned out he was, and he did.

❖

Martin rode the subway to the Upper West Side to meet him. Brian was already at the bar at 7:30 when Martin arrived, already with a pint of something half finished. They greeted each other awkwardly. Brian had a distinctly sour aspect to his face. He appeared self-conscious and not terribly happy to see his old friend, despite his enthusiastic FB message.

Once seated, Martin tried to make Brian feel better by recounting his recent troubles: the implosion of his company, his unemployment, his disastrous interview at A&K.

None of this seemed to improve Brian's mood, so Martin tried a different tack: "How are you doing?" he asked. "How's your wife, and your…daughter, was it?"

"Oh, you know…" said Brian, as if there was nothing to tell. In fact, there was a great deal to tell. Brian was divorced and had been further separated from his ex-wife and his now seven-year-old daughter by a restraining order. There was an ongoing legal battle over money and custody. Brian saw his child once a week, for three hours, and always with a third person present in the room. This was because of an outrageous and untrue story the Bulgarian ex had told the judge. She had a nasty lawyer, it turned out, who might have also been her boyfriend. There was also some petty thievery and bank fraud involved. As the story unfolded, Martin found it hard to adjust his facial expression to match each new gruesome twist to the story.

Despite all this, Brian was philosophical about his ex-wife. It was the separation from his daughter that was killing him.

The look on his face when he said his daughter's name, Hanna, was so disturbing Martin could no longer make eye contact. Sneaking glances at his old friend in the bar mirror, Martin had to wonder if Brian hadn't somehow cracked, or literally lost his sanity in some way. It was possible he was suffering from actual, genuine PTSD.

"Have you ever thought about just walking away from all this?" asked Martin.

"No," said Brian, defiantly. He drank his beer.

"But, dude, she sounds like a psychopath."

"One of my friends told me to get her deported," he said. "She's only a US citizen because of me. But then I might never see my daughter again."

"Yeah, but is it worth it?" said Martin. He was sounding like Rob now. "I mean seriously, a couple hours a week? With a chaperone? And the kid's going to hate you anyway. Go find someone else and have some other kids."

Martin understood he was crossing a line here, but there seemed no point in not speaking his mind. And it didn't matter anyway; nothing Martin said was affecting his friend. Brian appeared to enjoy Martin's frustration. *See? See what it's like?* was Brian's attitude.

Martin backed off his "walk-away" suggestion and apologized. He admitted he had no experience with children. He was then able to steer the conversation back to remembering the old days back at GGI. That was actually fun. For about three minutes. Then they sunk into silence again. At that point, Martin checked his watch and slid off his barstool. He needed to go. He had an early flight the next morning. On the sidewalk outside, he gave Brian a quick hug but when he tried to say good-bye he found himself speechless. He couldn't come up with a single word of encouragement to share with his friend.

Descending into the bright lights of the subway revived Martin's spirits. Once he was inside the A train again, with the doors safely shut, Martin forgot Brian's problems *en masse* and focused instead on his own relative freedom and prosperity. He was still sane, still unencumbered, still capable of total if momentary happiness whenever he cared to indulge in it. He sat back on the A train's hard plastic bench and breathed a deep sigh of relief.

Later, when he transferred to the F train, he found himself sitting next to a serious young woman reading a paperback copy of Roxanne Gay's *Bad Feminist*. The woman, probably about thirty, had a wide face, small round lips.

"That has to be the most popular book in the country right now," Martin said to her, despite her deep absorption in the text. It took her several seconds to realize she was being spoken to. She looked up at Martin and stared at him for a moment.

"That book," he repeated. "I see it everywhere. It's ubiquitous."

"Yeah?" she said.

"What's she saying, anyway? Is it good to be a bad feminist?"

the red pill

"I don't know. I just started it. But I think it's about the pressures of it. And the expectations."

She blinked at him several times, almost like a tic.

"That makes sense," said Martin. "Lotta peer pressure, being the best feminist you can be."

She looked at him as they both swayed slightly with the motion of the subway.

"How about you?" said Martin. "Do you feel pressured?"

"No. But I think it's a good thing to think about. You have to think for yourself. But you also want to do what's right."

"I always thought I was a good feminist," Martin told her. "But now I don't know. I kinda want a family. But that doesn't seem right. Make some poor woman have a bunch of kids with me and then have to take care of them while I'm just hanging out at the office. Not that I have an office. But you know what I mean. Subjugate her or whatever."

"You don't have to subjugate her."

"Well, that's kind of what happens."

"You can make it work if you want to."

"Really? Can you, though?"

"Of course. You just have to communicate."

Her name was Liz. She and Martin both got off at Seventh Avenue. Liz wore a knit hat that looked homemade and black tights and a wool skirt. She worked at a website about food.

They continued talking as they walked.

"I'm finding I'm turning against all the stuff I used to believe," he told her. "I don't want to have a feminist relationship. I don't want to live a progressive life."

"But what's the alternative?"

"I don't know exactly. I don't think anyone knows. Obviously, we can't go back to the fifties. But what we're doing now isn't working either."

"But don't you want things to be fair?"

"I don't know. What does 'fair' even mean?"

"It means equal."

"But people aren't equal," said Martin. "And the world isn't fair. And I'm sick of pretending it is. That's what I'm saying. I don't want to live someone else's idea of a relationship. It's not organic. I don't want a 'partner.' I want a wife."

This seemed to silence Liz. She looked up at him in an odd way. Her whole demeanor changed.

Martin asked her if she wanted to get a beer but she said she couldn't. She had to work the next day. He ended up walking her to her building. They stopped outside.

"I hope I didn't freak you out," Martin told her.

"No. This has been an interesting conversation."

"It has. Thanks for talking."

They both stood there. Liz still had that same reluctance in her face, and yet, she remained where she was. She was not quite ready to leave. She looked up into his face. Her small lips seemed to glisten in the dark.

Martin went for the kiss. Why not? *Always go for the kiss.*

But she shied away. So he stepped back.

"Sorry," he said.

the red pill

"It's okay. I just don't usually...."

"No, of course not."

They both stood there in the dark. "And you're leaving tomorrow," she said.

"Yeah," Martin said. "Unfortunately."

She continued to stand there. Martin considered trying to kiss her again, but something about the quiet Brooklyn street, the austerity of the great metropolis. He decided not to. "I guess I'll go," he said. "But can you give me your number? In case I stay? In case I come back?"

She hesitated for a moment, then typed her number into his phone. "I really have to go," she said.

"Okay. Bye. Have a nice night."

She walked up the steps of her building and Martin continued to Adam's, his body surging with a strange and unexpected hopefulness.

TWO DAYS LATER, still a little jet-lagged, Martin found himself at the Space Room Lounge in Southeast Portland. With its seediness and retro jukebox, the Space Room was the perfect place to be getting drunk with Alice, 32, an associate professor, whose interests included wandering aimlessly, thinking about society, and Popsicles.

"I never date women who work at pet stores," blabbered Martin, as he swirled his third vodka tonic. "They're affections are too diverse. Or no, *diffuse*...or whatever that word is."

"Diffuse," said Alice. She was sipping on her third vodka cranberry.

"*Diffuse*," said Martin. "Like, if she's giving love to all these pets all day, what's left for me?"

"Right," said Alice. "All those puppies. All those goldfish."

"Exactly. And kittens too. Kittens are the worst. They suck the love right out of people."

They were sitting at the bar. Martin had turned his stool so he was facing Alice, who was facing straight ahead. She had short, bluntly cut hair and a plain, doughy face. She wore an old, mustard-colored Shetland sweater, old Levi's, and black Converse low tops.

"That's selfish though," said Alice. "To want all the love for yourself."

the red pill

"Yes, but love is selfish," said Martin. "I can't share my love with a bunch of cats. Or a fish. Or your bird or whatever."

"Oh my God, a bird!" said Alice. "I'd love to have a bird."

"Yeah?" said Martin. "What kind would you get?"

"A goldfinch."

"Yeah, birds are cool," agreed Martin. "I was in this café in Morocco once and there were bird cages everywhere. Like on the walls and hanging off the ceiling. You'd go in there in the morning and they'd be chirping away."

"That sounds heavenly."

"It was great. The sun's just up. The coffee's brewing. The desert sky. And all these birds chirping. It actually got pretty loud. It was kind of a problem, to be perfectly honest. You're, like, trying to drink your coffee, and there's all this bird conversation."

"Discussing their different issues," said Alice.

"Oh my God, *yes!*" said Martin, laughing. "Birds coming at you with their different bird concerns! So annoying."

"That's what I like about cats," said Alice. "They keep that shit to themselves."

"I mean, no offense, but I'm paying for a coffee," said Martin. "Not to listen to some bird complain about normative gender binary whatever."

"Maybe they're gossiping," said Alice.

"Oh, you know they are. 'Oh my God, did you see Tiffany's plumage yesterday?'"

Alice began to laugh.

Martin laughed too. He kept going. "'Who's *that* fucking bird? Who does *that* fucking bird think he is?'"

They both laughed, and in the joviality of the moment, Martin leaned over and kissed Alice on the ear. Then on the cheek. Then on the mouth, right there at the bar. Alice kissed him back. They made out for about six seconds, then they both withdrew, sipping their drinks and grinning to themselves.

From there it was on to another place, the Back Door, which was a divey metal bar, across the street from Alice's apartment.

At the dimly lit Back Door, which was rocking hard to Scorpions and Judas Priest classics, they sat at the end of the bar and began to fool around, kissing, nibbling, rubbing each other under the bar. Alice was not only smart and funny, she apparently had an exhibitionist streak. Martin was cool with that. He'd learned to always push forward. *Escalate.* And if your date wanted to go even further, all the better.

After one beer, they crossed the street to her apartment and immediately had rough, aggressive sex. Afterward, they both lay in Alice's red-painted bedroom, panting upward at the ceiling. When Alice went to the bathroom, Martin turned enough to see the spines of the books on her bedside table. On the top of the pile was something called *Toxic Parents: Overcoming Their Hurtful Legacy and Reclaiming Your Life.* Under that was *We Should All Be Feminists*, by Chimamanda Ngozi Adichie. Below that were some academic books he didn't recognize. *Wild*, by Cheryl Strayed, was at the bottom.

the red pill

Alice came into the room in a robe, with two tall glasses of water. She climbed in next to him and they both sat up, their backs against the pillows, and drank their waters.

"I actually have to get up tomorrow," said Alice. "I'm teaching a class."

"What sort of class?"

"It's called The Crimes of Capitalism."

"I should have known," said Martin.

"It's not as bad as it sounds."

"You know I'm in advertising, don't you?"

Alice nodded that she did.

"I sell potato chips to people who shouldn't be eating them."

"I know."

"So who takes a class called The Crimes of Capitalism?" asked Martin.

"It's part of the women's studies curriculum," said Alice.

"So, no guys."

"There've been a few guys."

Martin took another long drink of water and then got up and began to gather his clothes. He located the squishy condom in the sheets and discreetly removed it, slipping it into the small coin pocket of his jeans. He sat on the bed and put on his socks and shoes. He had the idea that Alice might try to kiss him again, or crawl over the bed to give him a hug before he left. But who was he kidding? Alice was not that kind of person. He glanced back at her. She was holding her water glass and thinking about her class.

"That was fun," he said, as he stood to go.

Alice nodded her agreement and drank more water.

"I'll call you," said Martin.

"Okay," said Alice.

Martin woke up the next morning, at 10:30, tired and hung over. He was glad to be in his own apartment, in his own bed. His night with Alice seemed far away, like a distant dream. He lay there quietly for a moment, and then did what had become his habit in his unemployment: he reached over, turned his radio on, then snuggled back under his covers and listened to it with his eyes closed.

Today they were talking about #MeToo, as they had been every day for the last week. Which new prominent men had been exposed as predators. Such men were going down at a rate of two or three a day. People had become addicted to it. They needed new harassment narratives daily. They wanted the details: Where did he touch her? What did he say to her? What videos did he make her watch? The news outlets couldn't get enough.

This particular morning there were two new potential predators, as well as updates on the pending ones. Martin had initially thought that some of the accused might turn out to be innocent but so far none had. If you were accused, you went down. That was the pattern so far.

Even in sleepy Portland, they were uncovering cases. At the stodgy Oregon Society for the Arts there had been accusations and denials, leading finally to an elderly executive director being removed from his position. Another high-profile administrator had been fired from a health-care advocacy group. And a locally famous ex-NFL football player who owned several car dealerships suddenly resigned from his own company, under a cloud of shame and disgrace.

Martin, unemployed and with nothing better to do, lay listening to the news for a full hour. When the AM news station went back to their cheerful national talk show, he switched over to NPR, which in grave tones went into far greater detail about the same stories, including interviews with women's rights advocates, experts on sexual abuse, and survivors of rape and incest.

Martin rolled over again and lay there for another hour. He'd been doing this a lot lately. Letting most of a day slip by in a sleepy haze, hidden and protected under the covers. Other people were doing it too. He'd read an article about it on Facebook. People were freaked out. They were traumatized. So they stayed in bed. For hours. For the whole day. Why wouldn't you? Why would you want to go out there?

35

THEN ONE RAINY night in November, Rob called. He was in his truck, at a work site, in an outlying suburb.

"Rob! Hey, what's up?" said Martin, surprised to get a call from his brother-in-law. Martin was always glad to hear from someone—anyone—these days. It was 8 p.m., he was sitting at home, reading stuff on the internet. At that moment it was Middle Aged Dad's nostalgic memories of his high school prom in Minnesota (everyone was white, everyone got along, nobody got stabbed).

Martin had decided during his trip to New York that he would no longer read Middle Aged Dad, or any of the other blogs. While he fully acknowledged that these websites had helped him with his dating life, the political direction they had taken, or had perhaps been aimed in all along, were not helping his career prospects. It was brainwashing him in the wrong direction. For most of his life he'd been "center left" politically and he needed to be like that again. Diversity, inclusion, acknowledgment of privilege. What was wrong with any of that? Nothing. He needed to get on board. If he couldn't get back to thinking like a normie, he'd never get another job.

Meanwhile, Rob was on the phone. "Where are you?" Martin asked his brother-in-law. "What's going on?"

"I'm having a little problem."

"What's that?"

"Sadie would rather I didn't stay at the house at the moment."

"What? Are you serious?"

"We're going through a rough patch."

"What happened?"

Rob sighed. "I can't really get into it. It's marriage stuff."

"Okay..." said Martin. "So what are you gonna do?"

"I'm not sure long term. I stayed at a Motel 6 last night."

"Jesus," said Martin. "A Motel 6?"

"Like I said...."

"Listen. Don't do that again. You can always come here. I've got a whole office I don't use."

"Yeah?"

"Absolutely. Definitely. Come on over."

Rob arrived a half hour later. He had a small, neatly arranged backpack, with some clothes and toiletries. Martin felt a little nervous letting him inside. Rob had never seen his place. Not that that there was anything to see. Martin had nice furniture, a few pictures on the wall, a few posters he'd picked up from various ad campaigns he'd either worked on or admired.

Rob looked around.

"Wanna beer?" Martin asked him. "Or I might have some real liquor somewhere...."

"Beer's fine," said Rob. He sat down on Martin's couch, took off his baseball cap and set it on the cushion beside him. Martin brought him a Sierra Nevada ESP. "This okay?" he asked.

Rob didn't look at it. He took a sip.

Martin sat down across from him with a beer of his own. Rob didn't look good. He was pale, unshaven. A dull pain showed in his face.

"I think there's some college football on," said Martin. He clicked the TV on and then joined Rob on the couch so he could see the TV.

They'd sat there for about twenty minutes when Rob finally spoke: "Women..." he said, sipping his beer. "They really hate Trump."

"They do," said Martin, lowering the sound.

Rob stared at the TV. "Did you hate Obama?"

"I voted for Obama. Twice."

"Oh, right," remembered Rob. "Well, you know what I mean. Obviously, some people didn't like Obama. Conservatives didn't. But they weren't breaking up families over it."

"No."

"I don't like being away from my kids."

"No, that's not good."

They both said nothing for a long while.

"Do you want to tell me what happened?" Martin asked.

What happened was Little Jack hit another kid at his school and had been in other ways disruptive. This led to a call from the principal, which Sadie had dealt with. Then Jack pushed another kid off one of the playground structures and the boy hit his head, and possibly had a concussion. This resulted in Sadie and Rob meeting with the principal and a psychologist from the school district. Jack had been evaluated and it was the psychologist's opinion that they try putting Jack on a new medication, designed for children, to calm them and help them focus. Rob was against this. Sadie thought it might be a good idea.

"The psychologist was a woman," said Rob.

"Yeah?" said Martin. "Is that significant?"

"I thought it was. I mean, no, it wouldn't normally be. But in this case...."

"What about her?"

"Just the vibe of her."

"Like what?"

"She was insisting. She was like, 'You have to do this. This is the only option.' I was like, 'I don't think it is.'"

"Huh."

"So what am I supposed to do?" said Rob. "They want to tranquilize my son. I'm not going to let them."

"Sadie wants to do it?"

"Sadie, in a normal situation, would *not* want to do it. But because Sadie is under the influence of all this bullshit. People like this psychologist, who looked like she was bat shit crazy herself...but no, Sadie would not want to do this. We kind of already decided this, knowing how Jack is. But now she's thinking about it, and, of course, I'm the asshole. And her friends all think I'm the asshole, since I had a Trump sticker on my truck for a week, which I removed, at Sadie's request."

"I don't think her friends dislike you. Really. I don't."

"Not her friends around here. She has college friends. People I barely know. I see her Facebook. They're deep into all this."

Martin nodded. It was true. Sadie's college friends—East Coasters mostly—were much more political than the suburban "mom friends" she had now.

As for the situation with Jack, Martin had never had to think about such things. "They put first graders on medication?" he said.

"They do."

"That's so weird."

"And now...with Sadie and I...since we're barely speaking, I don't know what the plan is."

"That doesn't sound like her."

"I'm telling you. The women...all of them...they're digging their heels in."

Martin nodded his understanding.

"Has this ever happened before?" Rob looked at Martin. He was seriously asking him. "Have women said fuck you to guys on this level before? Like in history?"

Martin shrugged and thought about it. "Maybe during Prohibition?"

"Yeah?"

"I mean, that was started by women. I think it was. The suffragettes. They got the vote and the first thing they did was outlaw liquor."

"No shit, *women* did that?"

"I guess so. One of the commentators on Middle Aged Dad was talking about it. Like how the entire male population was basically alcoholics, the working class anyway, so when the women got the vote, they banned alcohol."

"And how long did that go on for?"

"Thirteen years," said Martin.

"Thirteen years?"

At this point in the conversation Martin remembered it was Tuesday. He had an OKCupid date that night. "Oh shit, I got a date! I gotta go!" he told Rob.

He had twelve minutes to get across town. He ran into his room, changed his clothes, doused himself with Old Spice.

"Good luck," said Rob dryly as Martin hurried to the door.

"Make yourself at home," said Martin. "There's food... beer...there's a couch in the office. New Seasons is down the street."

Martin hurried downstairs and drove speedily to the bar across the river. He was ten minutes late walking in. He spotted Bridget by herself in a booth and slid in across from her.

Bridget was 38, a web designer. Her interests included the psychology of colors, kindness, learning new things, and her nine-year-old son. Martin had messaged her because she'd gone to undergrad at the Rhode Island School of Design, which sounded interesting.

Bridget *was* interesting, except for the small problem of her oversized, oddly shaped, red-colored eyeglasses. From the moment he sat down Martin had difficulty looking directly into her face. Her glasses were like something you'd see in a cartoon. Or in a *Saturday Night Live* skit about a pretentious art professor.

Martin tried to ignore them. He ordered a drink. He talked to her about web design, wondering if she might have ideas about work prospects. When she brought up her young son, all Martin could think was how did the poor kid deal with his mother's awful glasses? What did he tell his friends? Did he get teased about them? Did he get bullied?

"Your son," he asked, "does he go to a private school?"

The boy did. Thankfully. An alternative school, Bridget told him, where they gardened and purified their own water. Martin nodded along. The kid was probably as weird as his mother.

Martin got a little drunk. Bridget was slender, at least. And she was clean and had nice skin. But when she went to the restroom, he saw that her high-fashion, high-waisted slacks were cut strangely and hung off her hips in an odd way. She either had no ass or it was hidden inside the flat-lined pants somehow.

While she was gone, Martin checked his phone. Alice had texted. She wanted Martin to come over for "a snuggle." Martin texted back he'd be right over and when Bridget returned he made an excuse, a family emergency had come up, he needed to leave, he was terribly sorry....

the red pill

Sixty seconds later, he was in his Audi, revving the engine. He was relieved to be out of sight of Bridget's glasses. They were giving him a headache.

At Alice's apartment there was no messing around. They tore off each other's clothes and were doing it with barely a word spoken between them. This was how Alice preferred it, apparently.

Martin was fine with that. It was definitely a bracing experience to walk into a young woman's apartment and go straight for the aggro bang. Martin had never done anything like it before.

But then, halfway through the actual sex, something went wrong. Something in Martin's consciousness shifted, or altered—something in his soul even. Alice's grimacing face, as she clawed at his shoulders and struggled to climax. It was monstrous to him. The whole scenario: the room, the floor, the red-painted walls. This was not what he wanted. He was hurting himself by even being here. He was killing himself.

36

DID WOMEN EVER really love you? Martin pondered this question as he drove to his sister's on a cold, gray afternoon. *No, they did not. Not like you want to be loved. Not unconditionally. Not like your mother did.*

This was another common refrain in the manosphere. It was considered one of the fundamental truths. What kept women attached to you was power, status, wealth. You want to show your soft side, your vulnerability? Express your fears and insecurities? Lean on your wife or girlfriend during moments of indecision? Go ahead. See what happens.

Martin did not actually believe this. Of course, women really loved you, to whatever extent anyone loved anyone. He'd been vulnerable around girlfriends. Nothing terrible had happened. They didn't drop him and run off with some stronger, more invincible guy. And it wasn't like there were so many strong, invincible guys walking around. Everyone was a mess. It was the human condition.

Martin arrived at Rob and Sadie's and knocked on the door. He hadn't been invited; he was just dropping by, bored in his unemployment. His excuse was he'd been at the nearby Westview Tennis Center, where he'd signed up for a weekly "singles friendly" mixed doubles night.

There was an unfamiliar car in the driveway, Martin noticed. When nobody answered, Martin let himself in. Jed was sitting on the floor by himself in the main room, surrounded by toys. The faucet in the kitchen was running. Sadie was there, doing something. And then Lauren Ackerman came out of the hall bathroom. "So what did you say to him?" she said to Sadie, as she tucked in her shirt. Then she saw Martin.

"Oh, hi, Martin," she said. She then called out loudly, "Hey, Sadie! Martin's here!"

Sadie shut off the faucet. "Martin?" she came into the main room. "What are you doing here? Why didn't you call?"

"I did. It went to voice mail. I was in the neighborhood, anyway." The two women were flustered but quickly composed themselves. The three of them moved into the kitchen.

"Want some coffee?" Sadie asked him. "What's going on? Did you ever hear back from that agency in New York?"

"No. That's not happening," said Martin, accepting a cup of coffee.

"Mom's coming over too," said Sadie. "She's picking up Ashley from day care."

Martin was glad to hear that. He hadn't seen Ashley, or any of the kids, in too long. Rob had stayed two nights in his apartment and then moved into the guest house of a friend. The Rob-Sadie separation, now in its second week, had been very disruptive, even for Martin, who had the least stake in it of anyone.

"How are you doing, Martin?" asked Lauren. She had been one of Sadie's best friends in high school and had also gone back east to college.

"Fine. Fine," he said.

"I heard about your company," she said. "I'm sorry things didn't work out."

"Yeah well, you know..."

"And I heard about Simon too," continued Lauren. "That's too bad. I sort of knew him in high school. Or I knew *of* him."

"He was always trouble, I thought," said Sadie.

"Yeah, but still," said Lauren. "It wasn't Martin's fault."

"No, that's true."

The conversation ended there. Jed came into the kitchen area and Sadie got him a juice box. Martin wondered what they'd been talking about when he walked in.

Then he heard car doors slamming outside. His mother had arrived with Ashley. Martin could hear his little niece's voice. His heart leapt at the sound of it.

His mom came in first, then Ashley squeezed in behind her.

"Uncle Martin! Uncle Martin!" she cried, running to him. "Where have you been?"

"I've been in New York City. Doing very important things."

The girl ran up to him and gave him a hug. "What important things?" she asked.

"Well, like riding on the subway," said Martin.

"What's a subway?"

"It's a train that goes underground. And all different kinds of people ride it. People from every country in the world."

Martin's mother also gave him a hug. He suspected some sort of female meeting of the minds was in the works, and he was interrupting it.

the red pill

"Do you want to get an ice cream?" Martin asked Ashley, thinking this might be helpful.

"I just had ice cream with Nana!" said Ashley.

"No more ice cream," said Sadie.

"Another time then," Martin told his niece. Martin looked around at the group. They all stood looking at Ashley.

"Well," said Martin. "I just wanted to say hi. And get my Ashley hug. I'll head out."

"Why don't you come for dinner tomorrow?" asked Sadie. "We're having tuna casserole."

"Come to dinner, Uncle Martin!" said Ashley. "Please?"

"That sounds like a great idea," said Martin. "I will definitely come for dinner tomorrow." He reached down and picked up Ashley, who was surprisingly heavy. Still, to hold her for a moment, it did him good. He bounced her a couple times and then set her back down again.

Martin drove around, aimlessly. He ended up downtown again. He'd been thinking about buying an electric guitar for some reason. He checked music store locations on his phone at a stoplight. Then he thought of Erin, who he'd neglected in all the recent excitement. They'd texted a bit when he first got back from New York, but he hadn't followed up. He called her and asked her to have dinner.

"I have plans," she said.

"To do what?"

"Just plans."

"Like real plans or made-up plans because you don't want to?"

There was a long pause. "You know, women aren't supposed to accept dates that start in two hours," she said.

"It's not a date; it's dinner. It's food. I'm asking you to come eat food with me."

"Why?"

"Because I want to. I haven't seen you." Martin sighed into his phone. "Come on. I've been super busy. My sister and her husband are having a huge fight. He had to stay with me. It's a big mess."

There was another long pause. "All right," said Erin. "I get off at five thirty."

"I'll pick you up."

There was an open parking space right outside Erin's bank, and since he was a few minutes early, Martin parked and went in. He pushed through the heavy glass doors. He'd never been in Capital West before; this branch was pretty nice, as you'd expect, being their flagship downtown Portland location. There were tall ceilings, marble floors, and then a separate, carpeted area of desks and work spaces. Everything was humming along bank style, the tellers crisply working their computers and cash-counting machines, the customers helpfully prepared when it was their turn in line. In the carpeted area, Martin saw a young, ordinary looking couple, anxious expressions on both their faces, sitting across from a bank executive. And then Erin appeared from a back office. She didn't see him and Martin moved slightly, so as to remain hidden behind some other customers.

Erin's hair was pulled back, manager style. She wore a gray suit coat, a matching skirt, a white blouse, and white tights, which looked odd, but were probably standard female wear in the banking world. She pulled a beige raincoat down from a hook and put it on, shrugging her shoulders inside it and pulling her hair clear of the collar. She was definitely a manager. You could see it in the ease and directness of her movements and gestures. She said something to one of her female colleagues; the two women smiled and chatted for a moment, then began walking together toward the front. Martin raised a hand to indicate his presence. Erin saw him and her smile faded slightly.

"Thanks for coming out," he said, as they got in his car. She put on her seat belt as he pulled out of the parking space and they rode in silence for a few minutes. Then Martin began to talk. "I was at my sister's earlier. It's not looking good over there. My brother-in-law is staying in his friend's guest house."

Erin said nothing. They drove over the river; the Willamette River spread beneath them for a moment. Martin kept talking: "They're so different. She's a lefty, all the way. Rob's a suburban jock sorta guy. Loves Trump. Well, *likes* him. That's the thing, you marry someone and you think politics isn't going to matter that much. But then the world goes bonkers and suddenly it matters a lot...."

Erin lowered Martin's visor and touched up her makeup in the mirror. "Where are we going?"

They went to Romano, a new Italian restaurant in the Irvington neighborhood. Martin hadn't been there. It looked a bit trendy for Martin's taste but all the restaurants were like that now. Erin was still not speaking.

They were seated. Martin put his napkin in his lap. The water was brought. Some odd gelatinous food items appeared on a tiny plate.

"So what happened with New York?" Erin finally asked.

"Nothing. I sent a courtesy email to that woman. I haven't heard back. I had zero chance, was my impression."

Erin didn't respond.

"It's probably for the best," said Martin. "I didn't get a great feeling about New York."

Erin read her menu.

Faced with her continued silence, Martin felt obligated to say something. "Listen," he said. "I'm sorry I didn't get back to you sooner. Things got a little crazy."

"That's all right. You don't owe me anything."

"Yes, I do. You talked me through some hard stuff. You helped me. I appreciate it."

She didn't respond. The waitress came and they ordered. They sat and watched the people around them. Finally, the food came.

"Yeah, this thing with my sister," said Martin. "The thing that started it is the school wants to medicate their son. He's being disruptive in first grade."

"Oh, Jesus," said Erin.

"That's crazy, right?"

"I think it is."

"But that's what they do now," said Martin.

Erin drank some of her water. The soup came. Erin often ordered soup in restaurants. Martin never did.

"How's the bank?" Martin asked her.

She told him. They talked about other things. She told him about her female cousin who'd gotten divorced. Her husband had been a salesman of heavy equipment, bulldozers and backhoes. They had two kids. He was living in someone's garage now. It was all very Forest Grove, very lower middle class, which always made Martin uneasy. And yet it also interested him in a way. His advertising brain sifted through Erin's story, trying to picture the garage, the sales job, the hair gel. Sitcoms still tried to do that occasionally: portray the American working class. The main characters were always overweight.

After dinner, Martin talked his way into Erin's apartment. He sat on her couch while she made tea. It felt good to be there; he liked the smell of it. And the layout. And the general neatness.

It also reminded him of having sex with her. He wondered if he could have sex with her tonight. Probably not, judging from the tone so far. But that was his own fault. He'd disappeared on her after New York.

She brought out the tea. They sat sipping their respective cups on the couch. It was too quiet though, so she got up and turned on the radio. It was tuned to NPR when she turned it on and she changed it to a music station. Sadie also listened to NPR in the morning. As did Martin's mother. Probably every person he knew listened to NPR, if they listened to the radio at all. Rob, of course, listened to Rush Limbaugh.

Erin came back and sat on the couch again, a full three feet away from him.

"Hey, I'm sorry I didn't call you earlier," Martin said.

"It's all right."

"No, I mean like..." said Martin. He tried to organize his thoughts. "You gave me good advice for that trip. And I took it."

"It's fine," she said.

"It meant a lot to me," he said. "That you helped me...."

"I'm not going to sleep with you tonight," she said, staring forward.

"Okay," said Martin, looking over at her. "But I'm not saying this to get you to sleep with me."

She said nothing.

Martin turned away. "Now you're pissed."

"I'm not pissed."

"You seem pissed."

"I'm not," said Erin. "I just...I was hoping this wouldn't turn into a flaky sex thing."

"I don't think of it as a flaky sex thing."

"What do you think of it as then?"

Martin thought about it. "Well...to be completely honest....can I be completely honest?"

"Please."

"Well..." Martin thought more. "I guess if I had to define the relationship, I think...to me...it's kinda like a friends thing."

"Okay."

"I mean, but also with sex. The sex was great, wasn't it? It seemed to me like it was."

"I enjoyed it."

"Okay, so that's what it feels like to me. We hooked up. And it was super fun. And now we're getting to know each other. And you seem like...well, like a solid person. At the same time, I just lost everything: my career, my business, my income.... I might be even more fucked than I realize...."

"Okay."

"Jesus, I don't know," blurted Martin. "I'm sorry, okay? I wasn't avoiding you. I wasn't trying to hurt you. This isn't a 'people getting hurt' situation. It's more of an easy thing, a comfortable thing."

"I'm not complaining," said Erin. "I agree with you."

"Okay. Good. Then we agree."

"I'm still not going to sleep with you."

"Fine. Good. I don't want to sleep with you either."

37

As promised, Martin was at the Carrs' the next night for dinner. It felt strained, the group of them, without Rob's presence. Also, Libby wasn't there, being funny and outrageous. Instead, there was Martin, as the lone adult male; his mother, the symbolic matriarch; Lauren Ackerman, the dutiful friend; and Sadie herself at the head of the table. This was her house now, it seemed. Though that didn't seem to put anyone at ease.

Sadie looked pretty good, considering. She had her hair tied back. She was wearing a loose peasant blouse, probably from South America, the kind popular when Martin and she were in college. The kids appeared subdued and oblivious, though they were obviously aware of their father's absence. It was an excellent acting job on their part.

Little Jack was on his right and Martin found himself studying the boy. He was behaving himself tonight. He sat quietly, ate most of his food, went into reveries occasionally, staring off into space. Ashley, meanwhile, was talking mostly to her grandmother. Jed was making a mess as he tended to do, but doing it in his slow careful way, so as not to attract attention.

Then Ashley decided to speak up. "Mommy, when is Daddy coming back?"

"I don't know, Ashley. We're talking about it. Like I told you."

"He was supposed to help me with my project," said Little Jack, in an exaggerated whine.

"Maybe Uncle Martin can help you," said Sadie.

Martin couldn't imagine what kind of a project a seven-year-old would be doing, but leaned toward the child. "What's your project, Jack?"

But the boy didn't answer. He frowned, leaned his head on his hand, and dug his spoon into his mashed potatoes, which he declined to put in his mouth.

"Sometimes in a family," Martin's mother told Ashley, "people need a little break from each other. Don't you sometimes need a break from Jack?"

"Yes," said Ashley.

"I never did anything to you," said Jack.

"You've done a lot of things to me," said Ashley. "You hit me with a stick!"

"That was a long time ago," said Jack, rubbing one eye with his fist. He settled his head on his hand again.

"Jack's not nice," said Ashley.

"You've done things to me!" said Jack.

"Okay, that's enough," said Sadie.

"So, Martin," said Lauren Ackerman, "are you looking for work now? Or just taking a break?"

"Both," said Martin.

"My husband got laid off from Adidas last year," said Lauren. "It was very stressful for him. For both of us. But he found something even better in the end."

Martin wondered why Lauren was here again today. Emotional support? Or something more specific? She and Sadie had been close in high school. But not after, not that Martin could remember. He ate his tuna casserole and watched Lauren eat across from him. She still had that overanxious alertness he remembered from when she was a teenager. She was the "hide the weed!" person in her group. But she'd also dated a notorious guy senior year. Martin just now remembered this. Drake was his name. She and Sadie were a couple grades younger than Martin, but he remembered Drake, a weaselly scammer type. Sold dope. Could get you an iPod for fifty bucks. You kinda wanted to punch him. Maybe that's when Sadie and Lauren stopped being so close. In any event, after college, Lauren did the smart thing and married dull Richard Ackerman, who then had an affair with a coworker, or something like that. They were still together though.

The kids all disappeared once the meal was completed. Little Jack went down to the basement. Ashley went to her room. Jed went to play in the living room. Without the kids around, a gloom fell over the adults. Martin had questions but he couldn't figure out how to ask them.

He decided to say nothing and leave as soon as possible, though to leave Ashley and Little Jack in this predicament seemed cruel and neglectful. This was what it was to have a family, Martin saw. Constant change. Periods of calm and then periods of disaster. And yet painful as it could be, it was the only thing that gave real meaning to people's lives. For humans, having a family was life itself.

the red pill

Sadie made coffee. People got up and moved around. Lauren had to go, and then Martin's mother went to read the kids a bedtime story. This left Martin alone at the table. His sister joined him, with a glass of wine.

"How are you doing?" Martin asked her.

"I'm okay," she said, adjusting her voice to the quiet of the dining room.

"So, I talked to Rob," said Martin. "He's staying with one of his construction buddies."

"Yeah, I know."

Martin rotated his coffee cup. "And this is still about Little Jack? And not the election, right?"

Sadie drank a little wine. "It's not about either," she said. "It's about Libby."

Martin looked at her. "It's about *Libby*?"

"Yes."

"What did she do?"

"She and Rob...hooked up," said Sadie.

Martin's mouth dropped open. He looked at his sister. "Are you sure? How is that possible?"

Sadie said nothing.

Martin thought about it. "Jesus. Rob and *Libby*? How did you...?"

"I don't know the details."

"Did you say something?" Martin asked.

"Of course I said something. I kicked him out."

"For fuck's sake," said Martin. He sat back in his chair.

"The part about Jack. That's also true," said Sadie. "We're still dealing with that."

"Jesus," said Martin.

"Yeah," said his sister.

Martin continued to process this. He drank some of his coffee. "Wow."

"That's what I said," whispered Sadie to herself.

"So what are you going to do?"

"I don't know."

"Did you talk to Mom?"

"Yeah," said Sadie. "She doesn't know either. It's just so… out of nowhere."

"What the fuck?"

"I'm afraid to do anything right away because I don't want to make a mistake. Not so much for myself but for the kids...obviously."

"Of course."

"According to various people, this happens. It happened to Lauren. I guess I was living with my head in the sand...."

"No," said Martin. "You shouldn't think that. This is surprising. It is. I know Rob and it surprises me. It really does."

Sadie stared at Jed, who was stacking blocks in the living room.

"And anyway, it's not right to think it's your fault," said Martin. "It's not your fault. It's his fault. And her fault. And Jesus...*Libby?* She hit on *me.*"

"She hits on everybody. It's a joke."

Martin touched his coffee cup. He noticed the small desk near the wall was empty. This was where Rob's work stuff usually was. "Did Rob take his stuff?"

the red pill

"He took everything."

Martin stared at the desk. "That's not good."

"People are telling me to talk to a lawyer…." said Sadie.

"A lawyer?"

"I know," said Sadie, her eyes moistening. "Can you imagine explaining that to Ashley?"

"No, and I don't want to," said Martin. "Is there anything I can do? Have you talked to him?"

"No. Not for a couple days."

"You do want to get back together though, right?"

She didn't answer. Tears now filled her eyes. But in a few seconds she was under control again. "If I get back together with him…then what? Wait until it happens again? That's the thing. I don't even know the rules of this stuff. I never planned any of this. Living out here, in the dumbfuck suburbs. With people like Libby running around. And Courtney and Wayne. I don't know this world. If I get back together with him, then what? He'll do it again. Of course, he will. And I'm stuck here, sitting around, waiting for what? And meanwhile he's driving around in his stupid pickup truck with his stupid fucking Trump sticker."

"Yeah," said Martin.

"I know you see him a certain way. Everybody does. He's this great guy. Great dad. But he's not that great. I see it. Nobody else sees it."

"Nobody's that great."

"No, they're not," said Sadie, lowering her head. "And then there's the kids…the fucking kids…."

A bedroom door opened in the hallway. Children's voices could be heard, and then footsteps coming toward them.

It was Ashley. She was thirsty. Sadie got her a juice box.

Martin eventually let himself out, saying good-bye to his mother and giving each of the children a hug. They seemed to cling to him in a new way tonight. "Jeez, Jack," said Martin. "You're getting so strong."

"I know," said the boy.

"Will you come back?" said Ashley.

"Of course," he told her.

"No, but really, Uncle Martin," said Ashley. "Will you come back a lot and keep us company?"

"I will, Ashley. I will."

On the freeway, Martin found he couldn't quite face his empty apartment and took the downtown exit. He parked outside Powell's Books and then texted Erin. Was she around? He waited five, ten minutes in his car. She didn't answer. She had to work in the morning anyway.

There were other people he could text. Alice had suggested that she was available for "a snuggle" whenever. Martin considered it.

But no. He went into the bookstore instead.

38

Later in the week, Martin called Erin and made a proper date with her. He took her to a movie in Southeast. They stopped at the Buddhist tea shop across the street before. Martin was on his best behavior, keeping quiet, holding doors open. But once seated in the tea shop he couldn't help but spill the latest news about his sister, Rob, and Libby.

"I'll need to talk to Rob at some point," concluded Martin, sipping a tea that tasted like burnt wood.

"Yeah, you could do that," said Erin. "Or you could stay out of it completely."

"I can't do that," said Martin.

"Why not?"

"I'm part of the family. I might be able to help."

"How though?"

"I don't know. Communicate between them. Or help the kids."

Erin said nothing. Ambient music played in the background.

"You don't think I should do *anything*?"

"Not unless you're asked. I mean, isn't that usually the best strategy? You don't want to screw something up."

Martin considered this. Erin was probably right. Rob hadn't confided in him about Libby. In a way, he'd lied to him. And Sadie wouldn't want him representing her point of view.

"Yeah," he said. "Maybe so. Anyway, she's got this old friend who's been hanging around. Her husband cheated on her and she's still with the guy...."

"Shit happens," said Erin.

"Yeah, but how *much* shit happens? That's the question. Or maybe I'm naive. Maybe all human existence is just constant fuckery from birth to death. Like Shakespeare...." Martin imagined a thirty-second TV spot where a young man is faced with the infinity of the universe, which at first is a vast empty space. Then the universe inverts itself to reveal that it is actually a giant party, filled to the brim with bikini girls, parties, water slides, and Sun Chips. The tag line: "Feel the Real with Sun Chips!"

"Anyway," said Martin, checking his watch. "We should go. The movie's starting."

Afterward, the two of them climbed the steps to her apartment where they drank half glasses of wine in the kitchen. They stood facing each other, leaning on opposite counters. Martin held his wine glass close to his face and took small sips. Erin had some fancy cheese from Trader Joe's and they amused themselves trying to spread the hard cheese on some fragile Italian crackers.

After that, Martin massaged Erin's neck. Then he worked on her finance-weary shoulders, finding a knot on the right side, which he worked on. There was no hurry tonight. With the two of them in this close space, a slow but inevitable attraction was building. She had forgiven him, it appeared.

Finally, they proceeded to the bedroom, where they had slow intense sex, which left Martin dizzy and not completely himself afterward. When he'd recovered, he began to talk. He had a lot to say, now that he had no office or coworkers in his life. Stuff had built up over recent weeks: a subpar Pacifica spot he'd seen on TV, his worries about employment, his opinions and observations on the evolving political scene.

When he finally got up to go, he wondered if he'd said too much. Babbling to women was not recommended by the manosphere. Always, it was better to remain silent, aloof, in control. But how could you do that, realistically? Life happened. You had to tell your troubles to someone.

Outside, in his car, Martin checked his phone as he let his car warm up. There was a message from Libby. When he opened it he found a long string of texts, piled one on top of another, like an elongated snowman.

Martin, I need to talk to you

Whatever Sadie is saying about Rob and me is not true. We were not having a relationship.

And we are not having one now

The stuff she's doing. To make it seem like I am a home-wrecker and telling everyone that.

It's not fair. She shouldn't say that.

Rob helped me out. He helped me during a very difficult time. It wasn't his fault.

She's overreacting, is what I'm trying to say. Even though she is a longtime friend.

Kevin hates me now. He's going to leave me.

I never should have got married. I never should have had a kid.

I feel like I've fucked up my own life but I didn't do that to Rob.

I feel like everyone's going to hate me and turn against me and I have nobody to ask for help.

Martin shook his head. What a shit-show. He turned off his phone.

the red pill

A couple days passed. Martin heard nothing more from Libby. He heard nothing from Rob. Sadie and the Carr household remained functioning, with help from Lauren Ackerman and his mother.

And so on Friday, with nothing else to do, Martin went out drinking with Dylan. They hit a couple happy hours after work, and then went to K-Club. Martin, without his company and the status it gave him, had to drink more than usual to bolster his confidence. By eleven he was solidly drunk and, thanks to Dylan, having fun. He somehow became attached to a woman named Marianne, who was clearly in her midforties, if not older, but kept claiming she was thirty-five. Martin teased her mercilessly about her age. "I don't think a *thirty-five-year-old* would wear pants like that," he told her, hooking a finger inside the top of her black leather pants and turning her from side to side.

It was '80s night at K-Club, and everyone was goofing around to the Cure, Depeche Mode, the Clash. Marianne could dance at least; she had a few genuinely sexy moves in her suburban divorcée dance repertoire. After working up a sweat, the two of them went outside while Marianne smoked a cigarette. It was raining and cold and Martin stood close beside her, eventually sliding a hand around her waist.

"We should go out to my car," he said to Marianne.

"Yeah? What's in your car?"

"A roof, for one thing. A heater."

"You just want to get me alone," said Marianne, flicking an ash.

"Normally, I would want that. But you're too young for me, being *thirty-five*."

"I *am* thirty-five!" Marianne maintained, as she had all night.

"Let me see your driver's license."

"I'm not showing you my driver's license!"

"You could be jailbait, for all I know. And anyway, I don't like younger women. They don't understand me."

"Oh, *gawd*," she protested, though she liked it, he could tell.

Back inside, Dylan had found a different group of women and Martin joined them, ignoring Marianne, who promptly disappeared. With this new group, Martin kept in the background, letting Dylan lead. His younger friend had already corralled the most attractive woman in the group. Probably nothing was happening for Martin tonight.

But then outside, at closing time, Marianne reappeared, coming down the sidewalk with a cigarette. Martin went for a different approach. "You're still here?" he said, with concern. "I thought you left."

"No...."

Martin went up to her, put his arms around her in a concerned embrace. "Are you okay? Do you need a ride home?"

"No, I have my car."

"Did you go somewhere?"

"No..." she said. But she probably had. Maybe to someone's car to do coke.

"Okay," said Martin. "And you know I didn't mean that stuff about how old you are. I was teasing you because I like you."

"Yeah? What exactly do you like about me?"

"Lots of things. You're game, for one," he said, smiling. "I love that."

She smiled slightly.

"And you're sexy for another, and you can dance...." He was talking in a low voice now, his arm still around her waist. He moved closer and managed to steal a small peck on her cheek.

"Yeah," she said, resisting him. "Even with these pants that you hate?"

"Are you kidding, those pants are smokin' hot!" he said. He stepped back and turned her slightly, so he could better see her pants. She was drunk and did a sexy modeling move, rotating ninety degrees so he could get a good view.

"Come sit in my car for a second," Martin said.

"What for?"

"So we can talk."

"Can I smoke?"

"Sure."

They went to Martin's car. Inside, Martin went for the kiss right away. He couldn't remember any advice about drunken older women you met on the sidewalk at closing time, but it seemed like immediate escalation was probably the best strategy.

"I thought you said I could smoke," said Marianne.

"You can," said Martin. "After."

Marianne reluctantly kissed him back. Her breath was a mix of cigarettes and alcohol and a general dankness. But Martin pressed forward. He got a hand inside her coat and felt her breast. But then someone called out "*Marianne!?*" from behind them in the parking lot.

"Oh, shit," she said, pushing him away. "I have to drive those guys home."

Martin tried to see who they were through his back window. "Can I meet you somewhere?" he asked her. "After you drop them off?"

"No. I gotta go. Do you want my number?"

Martin said he did.

"Here, I have a card." She dug through her purse for a moment, spilling her keys at one point, and handed him a card. He looked at it: she was a "stylist" of some kind. More stuff fell out of her purse as she drunkenly reached for her keys on the floor. "Shit!" She began feeling around, grabbing at the spilled items. She wasn't sure she'd found everything, so she opened the door and got out of the car so she could feel under the seat. "My phone," she said. "That's all that matters. And my cigarettes."

Martin dug out his own phone and turned on the flashlight. He shined it on the floor just as Marianne bent forward.

This was when he saw Marianne's face for the first time that night, up close and in clear white light. She looked like a ghoul. Her eyes were sunken, her face wrinkled, her cheekbones prominent but not in a good way.

At the sight of her, Martin had to suppress a gasp. He immediately refocused on the floor and kept his eyes there.

"I think I got it. I think I have everything," said Marianne.

"Good, good," said Martin, switching off his light.

the red pill

"But seriously. Call me. What are you doing tomorrow? We could get brunch."

"I don't know," said Martin, avoiding eye contact. "But yeah, I'll call you. Totally."

"Okay. Bye," she said, giving him a flirty wave.

When she was gone, Martin sat stunned by what he had just seen, what he had just *kissed*. When she was safely gone, he rolled down his window and threw her card out, quickly, drawing his hand back, as if it were on fire.

39

Two DAYS LATER, Martin was sitting with his laptop in his kitchen when Libby texted him. She was in her car, with Delilah. They were in Martin's neighborhood. When he didn't answer this text, she called him, leaving a voice mail that she could see him through his window, she knew he was there, and to please come down. When he didn't respond to that, she stopped her car in the middle of his street, stood on the sidewalk, and yelled loudly up at his window.

Martin went down to talk to her.

"Jesus, Libby," he hissed, in the drizzly darkness. "Get your car out of the street!"

"Will you talk to me if I do?"

"Yes."

"How do I know you will?"

"Because I will!" he snapped.

She looked back at the car. "Will you ride around with me?"

"No. I'm not riding around with you."

"Just for a few minutes. I can't leave Delilah. And she'll wake up if the car's not moving."

Martin scowled at her. "Okay, okay," he said. He went around to the passenger side and opened the door. "But drive slow!" he commanded.

the red pill

"Of course, I'll drive slow. My daughter's in the car. I'm not crazy!"

Martin got in. Libby got in too and began to drive. At first, she said nothing. Martin stared straight ahead, considering which would be safer: seat belt *on*, in case Libby decided to drive into a tree; or seat belt *off*, in case she decided to drive off a cliff.

He looked behind him into the back seat. Delilah was there, asleep in her car seat, her chubby round face leaning to the side this time. She had a little knit hat that had fallen into her lap. Martin reached back and replaced it on her head.

Libby meanwhile, had begun to cry. Not audibly, but her eyes appeared damp and she wiped them with a finger.

Here we go, thought Martin.

He faced forward again. "So what do you want to talk about?"

"Why are you being such an asshole!?" she said.

"I'm not being an asshole," he said.

"Yes, you are."

"No, I'm not."

"What are you being then?"

"I'm not being anything," said Martin. "You came to my house and stood in the street to force me to talk to you. So now I'm here, what do you want to talk about?"

"God, what happened to nice Martin? You used to be nice."

"I'm still nice. And that's not why you're here anyway. So what's this about you and Rob? You were sleeping with him?"

Libby wasn't ready to get into that yet. She turned and gave him a panicked look. Then she turned her head forward, tears flowing freely from her fluttering eyes. "Look at you. Look at the way you're looking at me! Now you hate me too. Everyone hates me!"

She stopped the car, in the middle of the street, and began to sob. "Everyone hates me. I don't know what I'm going to do. I can't kill myself because what would happen to Delilah?"

Martin looked back at Delilah, who was happily asleep.

He looked at Libby, who was genuinely, deeply crying. He looked ahead at where the headlights lit up the wet street. He looked out the side mirror. No one was behind them, thankfully.

"Where's Kevin?"

"Kevin hates me. He's always hated me. I don't know why we had a child. I don't know why we got married."

Martin sighed and looked straight ahead. "So what happened with Rob?"

Libby couldn't talk yet. She was still crying and sniffling and now there was snot involved.

Martin had seen a Kleenex box on the floor of the back seat. He reached down and grabbed it and handed it to Libby, who slowly cleared her eyes and gathered herself.

"It wasn't Rob's fault," she said, dramatically.

Martin was glad to hear that, though it didn't change anything.

"You know what my life is like. He was trying to help me. He didn't want to hurt anyone. And I didn't want to either.

That's what nobody understands. I was not trying to cause any problems."

"So you slept together? Like a lot? Once? How many times?"

"It wasn't some big *affair*. And he doesn't love me. I mean, maybe in some way. But I'm trapped! That's the problem. And at least Rob tried to understand that. If I could just get through this part of it. If I could get through the next year until Delilah gets old enough to go to day care, and maybe then, I could figure things out. Kevin and I could. Because Kevin's not a bad person. He doesn't want to be miserable either. That's what nobody understands...." She began to cry again. And then to sob.

Martin stared straight ahead.

"And if *you* had been nicer," said Libby, between sobs, "maybe Rob wouldn't even be involved...but nooooo, you're too busy. You're Martin Harris with your own company, nobody can bother you!"

Martin started to laugh.

"What?" said Libby.

"There's no way on Earth you're blaming this on me."

"I'm not blaming it on you!"

Martin looked back at Delilah, who was beginning to stir.

Libby cried some more. Martin checked the street again. They were still not obstructing anybody. People talked about how insanely crowded Portland had become. And yet you could stop your car in the middle of the street and have a meltdown and nobody pulled up behind you and honked. They could sit there all night, if need be.

"So what happens next?" asked Martin.

"Nothing!" said Libby. "I'm sorry. Okay? I tried to apologize to Sadie, but she won't talk to me."

"Send her an email."

"See? That's what I mean. You used to be nice. We used to be friends. You used to talk to me like I was a human being. Now it's...*do this...do that*. You're kind of horrible, you know that? And you didn't used to be. Something happened to you. It was a mistake to come here, to try to get some understanding from you. Or some advice. You just used me like Rob did. All guys just use women."

Martin quietly absorbed this speech. Then Delilah made a noise. Martin looked back at her. "I think Delilah is waking up," said Martin. "You should probably go home."

When he woke up the next morning, Martin made coffee and called Rob several times. He wasn't answering, and so Martin left a message. "Listen," he said into his phone. "I know about Libby. And then last night she came over to my house. She's not doing too well. Would you mind calling me back?"

He hung up. He'd barely put down his phone when it lit up with Rob's name and number.

"Dude," said his brother-in-law. "What are you doing? Why are you getting involved in this?"

"I got involved in this because fucking Libby showed up at my apartment in the middle of the night with her fucking kid in the back seat of her car."

"Oh, Jesus," said Rob.

"She's done it to me before."

"What did you do?"

"I gave in, naturally, and drove around with her and listened to her. As it turns out, you and her hooking up is *my* fault because I wouldn't get with her."

"Yeah?"

"The funny thing is, I *did* get with her, but it was so weird and fucked up, I avoided her afterward."

"Wait, *you* got with her?"

"Yes, I did."

"Why?"

"Because I'm a fucking idiot! What was your excuse?"

"Same."

Neither spoke for a moment.

"Why didn't you tell me about her?" Martin asked.

"Because you're Sadie's brother. Which means you are not the person I'm gonna tell that shit to, okay?"

Martin understood the logic of that.

"So what did Libby say about me?" asked Rob.

"She said you were trying to help her."

"Well, that's true, at least," said Rob. "I definitely never had any intention of...well...I don't know what my intentions were. I thought I was trying to help her. Who knows."

"We're all helpless," said Martin. "That's what's so funny. They can't control themselves and we can't control ourselves. We're all a bunch of chimpanzees."

"What's going on with Sadie?" Rob asked.

"I don't know. I was over there the other night. She's all fucked up. She's not happy."

"What did she say?"

"Nothing really. Just that she doesn't know what to do. That was mostly it. She's undecided."

"Well, I don't know what to do either."

"You've apologized?"

"Yes, I've apologized. I apologized my ass off. And I fucking meant it."

"Yeah...?"

"And what's that Lauren hanging around for? Who's she?"

"They're old friends."

"I don't like the looks of that."

"Lauren's husband had an affair. So I think she's advising her. Lauren's all right."

"What did she do when her husband had an affair?"

"I don't know exactly. They're still together though."

"They are?" said Rob. "Well, like I said, Sadie should be talking to her wise and knowledgeable friends...."

Martin chuckled.

"*I just wanna see my fucking kids,*" blurted Rob suddenly, with a force that startled Martin.

"I know you do," said Martin. "And they want to see you too."

"What are they doing for Thanksgiving?"

"I couldn't tell. Probably they'll go to my mom's."

"Jesus. Ashley loves Thanksgiving."

"Yeah."

the red pill

"This is so fucked up."

"I gotta tell you," said Martin. "I don't understand why you did it. For Libby, of all people. For that, you risk this other stuff? You have everything."

"I don't have everything. Nobody has everything. And even if you do, you fuck it up. I think we're programmed like that. To self-destruct. I really believe that. Look around you."

"Yeah but you love your kids. That's programmed too. Hell, they're designed so you'll love them. So obviously you're *not* supposed to self-destruct."

"No, what really happens is you're programmed to go make more kids. As far as nature's concerned, there's never enough kids. So you self-destruct that way. When the guy next door catches you banging his wife or his daughter and comes at you with an ax. That's what it really comes down to. Whatever we get, we gotta have more...*and that's every single male walking the earth.* How is that gonna end, I wonder...."

"That's your red pill," said Martin.

"That's your *black* pill."

40

It was an unsettled Thanksgiving holiday for the Harris-Carr clan that year. At first, as Martin predicted, the plan was to do Thanksgiving dinner at his mother's. Arrangements were made, though it never made sense, as Sadie was a much better cook and had a better kitchen and dining room for it. Their mother—who, like Martin, favored a minimalist lifestyle—lived in a condo apartment and didn't have many of the necessary supplies. As the situation was discussed further, Sadie finally gave in and agreed to do the holiday meal at her house, which was a great relief to everyone—except Sadie.

Martin came to the house early, to help out. He felt bad for his sister, but when he saw how completely occupied and in her element she was, he saw they'd made the right decision. Lauren was there, also helping. Her husband would be by later. Courtney and Wayne would be there too, with Guthrie. Martin's mom was on her way.

"Hi, Uncle Martin!" said Little Jack, as Martin stood at the kitchen island with a beer. He'd brought the beer, a twelve-pack of Baxter's Amber Ale, not Bud Light.

"Hey, Little Jack," said Martin.

"Wanna come down in the basement and see my Lego city?"

"You have a Lego city? That you made yourself?"

the red pill

"Yes," he said, tugging on Martin's coat. "Come on! I'll show you!"

Martin followed his nephew down the narrow stairway to the basement. As they descended into the cool, musky space, Martin understood that this house, these stairs, the basement, the backyard, it would all be forever implanted in the brain of the little boy. It was his paradise, his Eden, his beginning. He would be recalling these places, these people, until the end of his life.

"What's your Lego city called?" Martin asked, as Little Jack stomped down hard on the last two steps, with both of his feet together.

"What do you mean?" asked Jack.

"Like, does it have a name? You know, like Portland or Seattle or New York?"

"It doesn't have a name," said Jack. He pulled Martin by the coat sleeve. They knelt on the carpet between the couch and the TV and considered Jack's handiwork.

The unnamed city Jack had built was fairly impressive for a seven-year-old. Or maybe not. It turned out that a Lego city was mostly toys that were already fully assembled. Vehicles, bridges, trees: you didn't build these objects out of square Lego bricks like people did when Martin was a child. You just took them out of the package and stuck them where you wanted. They looked better premade, Martin had to admit. A Lego city was more like a model-train city.

Jack's concept of how a city would be organized was a little unusual: lined up on the main street was a dump truck, a Star Wars fighter jet, and a large gas pump that was out of scale and was probably not a Lego product at all. A beige-colored tank, stationed outside the city, had a baker, complete with puffy white hat and rolling pin, standing on top of it. "This is great, Jack," said Martin. "Is this baker driving the tank?"

"I don't know," said Jack.

"Is he going to bake something? Maybe the tank is actually a giant cake."

"No. It's a tank. It's going to blow up the city."

"Oh yeah?"

"I'm going to bomb it later and destroy the whole thing."

"What are you going to bomb it with?"

"Golf balls."

"Oh," said Martin. "That'll be fun."

"I have to build it up more first. So it explodes."

"Okay."

"Do you want to help me build it up? I have more Legos."

Jack did have more Legos. He had a large plastic tub of them. Martin put down his beer and dug around inside it. It wasn't just Lego stuff; there were other toys as well. He pulled out a cow, a crane, a school bus, an old plastic army man that might have been Martin's when he was a boy.

"Is my dad going to come tonight?" asked Jack as he moved the tank and rearranged his one intersection.

"I don't know. What did your mom say?"

"She said he might," said Jack.

"Oh?" said Martin. "I didn't know that. He might come over?"

"That's what she said."

"Okay. Well, maybe he will then."

"I don't like it when he's not here because then there's no one...there's no one to help me."

"What do you need help with?"

"Just everything. And anyway, it's not as fun with just girls around. And everyone cries all the time."

"At least you have Jed," said Martin.

"Yeah, but he's a baby."

"He can't play with Legos yet?"

"No. He doesn't know how."

"How about bombing, can he do that?"

"He can't throw. Or if he does, the ball goes all over the place."

"Yeah?"

"Do you want to play catch later?" asked Little Jack.

"Sure, I mean, I might need to help your mom too though. In fact, I better get up there and see how it's going...."

Upstairs, Martin's mother had arrived with two freshly baked pies from Country Village Bakery.

"Isn't Miriam the best?" said everyone.

Courtney and Wayne showed up soon after with Guthrie and two side dishes.

Martin gripped Guthrie by the shoulder and informed him that there was a Lego city down in the basement, waiting to be bombed by golf balls. Guthrie immediately ran down the stairs.

Richard Ackerman, Lauren's adulterous husband, had arrived and stood by himself next to the dining room table. He wore a tie under a burgundy V-neck sweater. Martin felt compelled to chat with him and Wayne about sports or whatever else he could think of. Richard Ackerman literally said not one word, and opened his mouth only to pour small amounts of Baxter's Amber Ale into it. Martin and Wayne carefully avoided the obvious topics of conversation: the latest #MeToo allegations, Trump's radical tax cut, a just-announced policy change at the Boy Scouts, that they would now admit girls.

But then Courtney, with her suburban helmet hair, brought up the scouting controversy. "So then what happens to the Girl Scouts?" she said. "And Girl Scout cookies?"

"Girl Scout cookies are sexist," said Martin, attempting a joke. "They're banning them."

"Guthrie isn't interested in Boy Scouts," said Wayne. "Kids today don't care about that stuff."

"It seems pretty antiquated," said Martin.

"I don't understand why girls would want to be in Boy Scouts," said Courtney.

"But shouldn't they have a choice at least?" said Lauren.

"Boys don't get a choice," said Martin. "But who cares about them, right?"

"Single-sex schools are still legal," said Courtney.

"But it wasn't a case of legality," said Wayne. "The Boy Scouts just decided to do it."

"But why would they?" said Courtney.

"Pressure," said Wayne. "Political pressure. And people being afraid to stand up and defend themselves from this stuff."

"Don't get Wayne started on politics," Courtney warned the others. "Everything is a controversy to him."

"What? I'm just saying...."

Nobody spoke after that. The group, realizing they were on dangerous ground, dissipated.

Martin moved casually into the kitchen. He saw Sadie was alone and moved closer. "Is Rob coming over?" he whispered.

Sadie was washing her hands. She looked up at him.

"Who told you that?"

"Jack."

She went back to her washing. "Rob begged me to come," she said.

"And what did you say?"

"I said no...at first."

"And...?"

"I said he could come later. After we'd eaten. I had to, the kids would kill me."

Martin thought about this.

"Just for coffee," said Sadie. "And he can't bring anything, and he can't make a big show of it. We're telling the kids he's working on something and he needs to be away right now."

"Which is sort of true," said Martin.

"I hate this, Martin. I'm being forced into it and there's nothing I can do."

"Maybe forgive him?"

She shut off the water. "You know, a lot of people say that," she said, struggling to control her emotions. "And I say okay, but what if I can't actually do that? What if I can't override how I feel with what I'm supposed to do?"

Martin nodded his understanding.

"And what is he going to do?" she continued. "What price is he going to pay? None, basically. He gets away with it. Like everything else in this world. And then not only do I have to feel like I got fucked over, but I have to drive around in my fucking minivan and watch the same thing happen to every other woman. It's so fucking depressing...."

Martin made a quiet *shhh*, sound.

Sadie lowered her voice: "I mean, maybe I should give him the kids and move to California and start over. That's all he wants, is the kids. He doesn't care about me. If he cared about me, he wouldn't be fucking around with Libby."

Martin nodded more. "It's a bad situation."

Sadie looked up at her brother then. "What do you think I should do?"

"Me?" said Martin. "I don't know. I just hate to not see you guys together."

"But what is he thinking? What the fuck is he thinking?"

"He's thinking he fucked up and he has to make it up to you."

"Yeah. I know. It sounds good. But does Trump think like that? Do the kind of men who support Trump think like that? Because it doesn't seem like they do. What it seems like is *fuck women*. That's what they seem to be saying. That's how they act. *Fuck women*. You know Trump was asked once, how to deal with women. You know what he said? 'Treat 'em like shit.' He actually said that, on the record. That's how you deal with women. That's how you make them obey you and do what you want. You think that sounds like a good life for me?

You think I'm gonna live that life?" Her face was hardening; a deep fury was building in her eyes. "Because I'm not. I'm not gonna live that life. I can't. Maybe some women can, but I can't."

"Yeah," muttered Martin. "It's bad. You're right. It's a bad situation."

"Yeah, it is. And even letting him come by, it's ruined this for me. My Thanksgiving is ruined. And why am I doing it? For the kids? For him? For his feelings? My own feelings are nothing. My own feelings count for shit."

Martin absorbed all this. He remained standing close to Sadie, as she spoke, to help muffle her words. Sadie dried her hands and tucked her hair behind one ear.

"When is he coming?" asked Martin.

"Six."

Martin looked at his watch. It was 4:45.

"Does everyone else know?"

"Pretty much."

Sadie turned away from Martin. "Ashley!" she called out. "Can you start setting the table? Maybe Uncle Martin will help you."

41

MOST OF THE feasting was done by 5:40. Martin kept an eye on the clock in the kitchen as Lauren and Courtney helped Sadie clear the table. Martin got up too, to stretch his legs and use the restroom.

After dinner there was coffee. Lauren and her husband, Richard, were in charge of that. Everyone got a cup and then Lauren came around with the coffeepot. There was a last-minute attempt to make hot chocolate for the kids—at Little Jack's request—but Sadie nixed that. The Carr children, subdued and not in the mood to argue, let it go.

As he sipped his coffee, Martin watched the clock. The dinner had not been a success. It lacked leadership. He felt uncomfortable thinking of it that way, but the truth was the truth: without Rob's presence the room had felt ungrounded. People couldn't relax or have fun. Sure, in some families a mother might play that role but not in this one. Martin hadn't been much help either. Despite the improvements he'd made in his life, he was still who he was: an observer, a guest, an uncle, not a central figure. At least not in this house.

The doorbell rang at 6:07. "Daddy!" shrieked Little Jack, jumping off his chair and running for the door.

the red pill

The adults at the table, stunned by this reaction, remained seated, staring after the boy.

Martin glanced once at Sadie, who lowered her head, closed her eyes, and seemed to be saying a silent prayer to herself.

Jack yanked open the door. There he was, Rob, all six feet of him, with his black hair and dark eyebrows. He looked pale though, and nervous, and drawn in his face. He set down what appeared to be two small tubs of ice cream in a plastic bag to pick up little Jack and hold him in his arms.

Ashley was up too, but she was more cautious. She got halfway across the living room and stopped. Perhaps she blamed herself for her father's disappearance. Even without seeing her face, Martin could feel the conflict inside her.

Rob put down his son and beckoned to Ashley. Slowly, cautiously, she moved forward a few steps, then moved faster, then skipped into his arms as he swept her up to his face. He had tears in his eyes, Martin could see.

"Where did you go, Daddy?" she asked him.

"I didn't go anywhere, sweetie," said Rob.

People were getting to their feet. Lauren retreated to the kitchen. Richard went with her. Baby Jed was heading toward his father too, though he seemed not to grasp the significance of the moment. Since no other adults were welcoming Rob, Martin did. He approached his brother-in-law. Not wanting to interrupt this moment with his children, he offered a low-key "Hey, Rob," and discretely picked up the plastic bag with the ice cream.

With all three of his children hanging off him, Rob slowly—very slowly—began to make his way toward the dining area. Martin's mother came forward to greet her son-in-law. When he got closer to the table, Courtney said hi and Wayne wished him a happy Thanksgiving. Sadie was in the kitchen furiously rinsing out coffee cups.

"Daddy, are you going to eat with us?" Ashley said.

"It looks like you guys already ate," said Rob.

"But we didn't eat with you!" said Ashley.

"Can you come see my Lego city?" asked Little Jack. "We're going to bomb it!"

"I would love to see your Lego city," said Rob.

"What did you bring us?" asked Ashley, looking around for the ice cream tubs.

"Just a little dessert."

Martin had brought the ice cream into the kitchen. He caught Sadie's eye. "I'll just stick these in here," he said, opening the freezer.

"No, no," said Sadie, in defeat. "What's the point? Just serve it. The kids will want it. She opened a cabinet and pulled out a stack of plastic bowls. She slapped them down on the counter in front of Martin.

Martin passed out the bowls and distributed the ice cream. The children were ecstatic. The grownups did their best to maintain a calm front. Rob sat at the end of the table closest to the front door. Martin was to his left. The ice cream was

Häagen-Dazs, which gave Martin something to talk about. "Do you guys know what 'Häagen-Dazs' means?" Martin asked the children, as they took their first bites.

"No," said Ashley.

"Fruit Loops!" said Little Jack.

"Fruit Loops?" said Martin's mother. "What gave you that idea?"

"It's Swedish for something...." said Courtney. "Isn't it?"

"I think I know this one," said Wayne.

"What do you think it means, Guthrie?" Martin asked Wayne's son.

"Uh...good ice cream?" said the boy.

"Good guess," said Courtney.

"Excellent guess," said Martin. "Anybody else?" The kids were all stumped.

"What does it mean?" asked Martin's mother.

"It doesn't mean anything," said Martin. "It's a made-up word."

"Why did they make it up?" asked Ashley.

"Because sometimes, when a company makes something like ice cream, they try to think of a name that sounds like what it is."

"Häagen-Dazs," said Jack.

"Doesn't 'Häagen-Dazs' sound like something delicious?" asked Martin.

"Häagen-Dazs," said Jack.

"Häagen-Dazs," said Ashley.

"Haaaaa-gun dazs dazs," said Jack.

"Haaaaa-gun dazs dazs dazs," said Guthrie, imitating Jack.

"Sometimes in advertising the best thing is to make up a word," explained Martin. "You make up something that's fun to say. Or that looks good when it's printed. Häagen-Dazs ice cream was invented in New York. But it sounds like it's from Sweden or Denmark or someplace snowy and fun. Which makes you want to buy it."

"They lied," said Ashley.

"Yes, they did but it's not really a lie, because you can name things whatever you want, right? You can name your cat Randy or Paper Plate or anything you want. Or your dog. You can make up a word."

"Dog dog dog," said Jack.

"Doggie dog daaawwwwg," said Guthrie, spooning ice cream into his mouth. The boys exchanged mischievous looks.

"Daddy!" shrieked Jack, suddenly. "Will you come and bomb my Lego city now!?"

"Shhhhh, indoor voices," said his grandmother.

"Not right this second," said Rob. Baby Jed, who wasn't actually a baby anymore but still had a disconnected expression on his face most of the time, had crawled into his father's lap. Rob was holding him. Silence again descended on the table. Wayne then asked Richard a question and Richard began to talk finally. Lauren and Martin's mother began to talk. And then Courtney and Sadie both got up to clear the dishes and check on another pot of coffee. Lauren made sure to take Rob's bowl, so Sadie wouldn't have to.

Martin, sitting closest to Rob and Jed, leaned over and poked Jed in the belly. Martin glanced up into Rob's face. He was smiling at his youngest son, but Martin could see the underlying stress. When Rob glanced over at Sadie, his misery was obvious. When Sadie came back out of the kitchen, Rob dropped his eyes.

"How you doin'?" Martin whispered quietly to his brother-in-law.

"I'm all right," he said.

"You look like shit."

"Yeah, well...."

Rob began to make excuses for why he had to go. He had not bombed Jack's Lego city with golf balls yet. Or read Ashley and Jed a bedtime story. Sadie had not spoken to him, or even looked at him as far as Martin could tell. But Rob was sticking to the deal.

There were some quick hugs. And some difficult questions. And then Ashley started to cry. Little Jack began stomping up and down on both feet. He climbed onto one arm of the couch and then threw himself off, almost hurting himself.

"I'm going to come back very soon," he told Ashley. "And I love you no matter what, wherever I am, whatever is happening, I love you. So don't you worry, honey."

"*Who's going to destroy my city!?*" raged Little Jack when nobody would talk to him.

Baby Jed stood silently in the middle of it all. Sadie picked him up at one point and distracted herself talking to him.

"But I don't want you to go!" pleaded Ashley, as Rob straightened up, leaving his daughter with her head bent back, staring up at him.

{❁}

When Rob was gone, Lauren quickly shut the front door, turned to the kids, and said, "Who wants to play a game!?"

No one did. Ashley had begun to cry. Sadie set down Jed and went to her.

Jack and Guthrie ran down the stairs to the basement, their footsteps pounding as loudly as possible.

Wayne, Courtney, and Martin made their way awkwardly back to the dining room table. Lauren went into the kitchen and opened a bottle of wine.

"Well, that was something," said Martin, to Courtney and Wayne.

"The kids will be okay," said Wayne.

"These things can be hard," said Courtney. Martin looked toward the kitchen. Sadie was holding Ashley, who was still crying, her head laid sideways against her mother's shoulder. Martin, watching them, checked the clock. It was 7:25. Martin had told Erin he would swing by her family gathering later. Maybe this would be a good time.

42

MARTIN LET HIS iPhone direct him to Erin's sister's neighborhood. This was the younger sister who Erin didn't say much about. She was married, had kids. She sounded a little more prosperous than the Forest Grove members of Erin's family. Martin suspected there might be some sibling rivalry going on.

Following the directions, Martin found himself in an area that had been an untamed forest when he was in high school. Sylvan Glen was the name of it now, or at least the particular development Erin's sister lived in. Sylvan Glen had its own European style. The homes, which looked like boxes stacked atop one another, were oddly spaced and brightly colored.

Martin followed a slowly curving street through the woods, which left him feeling directionally disoriented. The developers had taken pains to preserve as many trees as possible, to maintain a deep forest atmosphere. In some cases it looked unsafe: giant, fully grown Douglas firs sticking up between the toy-like houses, which were themselves only thirty or forty feet apart in some places.

Martin found the address and parked across the street. It was just above freezing according to his car's external thermometer. He got out and pulled his coat closed. The air was still, the street ghostly quiet and dark. Crossing the asphalt, every sound, every footstep reverberated through the night.

He found the front door and rang the bell. It would be a relief, after his sister's dinner, to be in a completely different environment. There'd be no tensions here, at least none that concerned him.

A young, attractive, suburban woman opened the door. She wore a festive white sweater, which matched her perfect teeth. "Hello," she said. "You must be Martin. I'm Kaitlyn, Erin's sister. Come on in."

Martin wasn't sure what Erin had told her family about him. He got his answer when Kaitlyn introduced him to an older couple, on their way out. "Aunt Myrna, this is Martin. He's Erin's friend? Who I told you about?"

"Ohhh," said Aunt Myrna. She was quite old, eighty-plus, as was her male companion. They were country folk, it appeared, a little out of their element in the futuristic subdivision. They stopped, though. They wanted to look Martin over.

"And where do you live?" asked Aunt Myrna.

"Downtown," said Martin.

"And you're the advertising person?"

"Yes, I am," said Martin, with a smile. He appreciated the way Aunt Myrna went right for the pertinent info. That's what Martin did when he met a person of interest.

"And what do you advertise?"

"Tennis shoes mostly," said Martin. "And other things."

"And what do you have to say about tennis shoes?"

the red pill

"Well..." said Martin, thinking about it, "mainly, that if you wear the right kind you'll accept yourself and love yourself and be happy."

"Is that what really happens?" asked Aunt Myrna.

"Yes, it is," said Martin. "But it doesn't last very long."

"Sounds like I should get me some of those shoes," joked her companion. He was also quite old. He had a small round belly and wore a blue flannel shirt with red suspenders. Suspenders were an interesting fashion accessory, Martin observed. The hipsters had ruined them, of course, but they looked great on older people. This guy was killing it.

Aunt Myrna studied him a moment more, then said, "Well, good luck to you. And you be careful with Erin. She's pretty tough, you know. She doesn't suffer fools."

"Yes, I know," said Martin, smiling.

Aunt Myrna tried to pat her hand against his left shoulder. It was actually more of a flop, her old bony hand not being completely under her control.

Kaitlyn led him forward into a spacious living room, with high ceilings and large windows. The walls were a comfy wood grain. It was a genuinely nice house. There were a lot of people too. Fifteen, twenty, that Martin could see. All generations seemed to be represented.

Kaitlyn introduced him to Michael, her husband, and then a child appeared, their daughter, about Ashley's age, pulling on Michael's shirt. Michael himself was a fit, normal looking guy, in a pressed shirt and jeans. He and Martin had a brief conversation.

Then Erin appeared. She wore a black turtleneck, her brown hair lying smooth and shiny along her shoulders. Erin's look was more dramatic than her sister's, or anyone else's in the house at that moment. But Erin lived and worked downtown, so this was her chance to express her urban chic to her semi-rural family.

Michael excused himself and for a moment it was just Martin and the two sisters. The three of them talked easily: smiling, laughing, interrupting each other. It was fun. Martin saw that Erin's family considered him a person of consequence. It was nice to be appreciated. Martin felt himself puff up a little. His smile deepened. He was glad he had come.

Kaitlyn eventually wandered away and Erin took Martin into the kitchen to get him some food. She was efficient and helpful with him, finding a plate and utensils, though he didn't need to eat any more. She did not speak to him as she performed these tasks. But that was often the case when they were together; she existed in tandem with him, without excess verbal communication. Martin understood this behavior as one of the limits to their relationship. Erin was a "friend with benefits," a person you like and respect and could take on a trip, with the add-on of sex. According to Middle Aged Dad, "friends with benefits" was the preferred relationship to have with the contemporary businesswoman. They were tough and driven and could become touchy when things got too intimate. But they liked to travel, and they liked sex, so if you could maintain the proper balance there was uncomplicated pleasure to be had. Also, they tended to be intelligent and good company. You could often keep such a "friendship" going for years.

Whatever. It didn't matter. Martin was happy to be free of his own troubled family for the moment. While Erin talked to another woman, he put aside the overstuffed plate she had given him and helped himself to a narrow slice of pumpkin pie, eating it in tiny bites, dipping each morsel into a dollop of whipped cream.

Later, while sitting on the couch with Michael, Kaitlyn, and some other people, a teenaged boy came over to Martin and introduced himself.

"I'm Kyle," he said.

"Hi, Kyle," said Martin.

The skinny boy wore Vans, jeans, a button-down shirt. "My aunt said you work in advertising?"

"Yeah, I do," said Martin.

"What sort of things? Like stuff on TV?"

"I do that. TV, online, radio...."

"Have you ever done movies?"

"Movie advertising?" said Martin. "No. They have their own people, I think."

"Because I like making my own movie posters."

"Yeah? Like what?"

"Just whatever movies I like. I do them on my computer. I can show you if you want."

The kid got out his phone and showed Martin his own poster for *Blade Runner 2049.* It was pretty good. The colors were good. And the font. It was possibly better than the real one.

"Huh," said Martin. "Yeah, that's nice."

"Really?" said Kyle. "You like it?"

Martin nodded. "Yeah. It's good. It's simple."

"Do you think I could...like.... How do you do that? How do you get a job doing that?"

"Making movie posters?" said Martin. "I don't know. You could probably study design. Or marketing. What grade are you in?"

"I'm a junior. In high school."

"Well, going to college would probably be the best thing. Or art school."

"Yeah, I don't know exactly what I want to do," said Kyle. "Movie posters are my favorite. But I sorta like car commercials too. I watch them online."

"Yeah?" said Martin, watching the kid's face.

"I just like stuff that looks cool," admitted Kyle.

"Well, there you go. You're halfway there."

"So, like, how did you get your job?"

"I had a friend from college who worked at an ad agency. In New York. And they needed people. So I got an interview and they hired me."

"And when you got there, you just started doing it?"

"Yeah. You work on the crappy stuff first. I was a writer mostly. Bro humor was my thing."

"Bro humor?"

"You know...*hey dude*...that sort of stuff. Beer commercials. Doritos. Taco Bell. Being from the West Coast, they figured I could speak that language."

Kyle's eyes widened. He became visibly excited, almost agitated. But he seemed aware that he shouldn't bother Martin with too many questions.

"I'm a friend of Erin's," Martin told the kid. "She has my email. Check in with me, as you go along. I'm around. I'm currently unemployed myself."

"You lost your job?"

"I lost my company. But that's advertising. You make a lot of money and then you don't."

Kyle swallowed. He stared at Martin like he was seeing his own destiny.

"Go to college. That's the best thing. And have fun. But pay attention. Not just in school, everywhere."

When Kyle was gone, Martin went back to the kitchen and poured himself a cup of coffee. He felt pleased with himself, having imparted some wisdom to the young. Now where had Erin run off to? Biting into a piece of celery, he wondered if he could sleep over at her apartment that night.

Martin walked around and eventually found Erin again. She proposed giving him a tour of the house. It was deceptively big. There was a large TV room and an elaborate home office in the basement. "What does Michael do?" Martin asked Erin.

"Commercial real estate."

That sounded boring. But he was obviously doing well. On the second floor, Erin showed him the two small bedrooms for the kids, and the master bedroom with its large bed, covered in coats. Martin, standing behind Erin, took the opportunity to put his arms around her and kiss her neck.

She closed her eyes and sighed. "Martin?" she said.

"Yeah?"

"I have to tell you something."

"Okay," said Martin, releasing her.

Erin turned around and faced him. "It's kind of important."

"Yeah? What is it?"

She pulled him over to the bed and made a space among the coats for them to sit.

"Uh..." she said, looking nervously into her lap. "The thing is...well...."

"What?" said Martin, smiling at her. "It can't be that bad."

"It's not bad."

"What is it?

"I'm pregnant."

"You're what?" said Martin.

"I'm pregnant."

Martin pulled back slightly. He stiffened. His eyes went to his own lap, and then to the carpet, and then across the carpet to the bottom row of a bookshelf.

"Yeah. I know," said Erin. "That was kind of my reaction."

"And you're telling me this because...?"

"Because...as far as I can tell...it would be you...the person who made me pregnant. You would be...that person."

"Me? I don't think that's possible."

"I know. But the thing is...well, that's what I wanted to ask you. Like that time in September, after the thing with your company and Simon and all that? You came over. Are you sure you used a condom?"

"Yes. Of course, I did."

"Both times?"

"Both times?" said Martin, looking at her. And then he remembered. The condom. There had been a condom malfunction. One of the condoms had ended up in an odd place. But he'd been pretty sure it was on, when it needed to be on.

"Is it possible...?" she continued.

And there was another time—which Erin probably didn't know about—when a condom had simply *vanished.*

Martin's face gave him away. "I guess it's *possible...*" he admitted.

"And the other thing is," said Erin, "there wasn't anyone else during that time."

"Are you sure?"

"Yes."

"But you guys used to cruise the Jack London? You mean, you never...?"

"No," she said. "I mean, that was kind of...what happened with you, with *us*...that wasn't...I don't usually do that.... There wasn't anyone else. It would be you.... I mean, we could always do a test or whatever...."

Martin looked at her.

"Seriously. I would tell you if there were other possibilities. But there aren't."

"You never met any other guys at the Jack London?"

"Not that I had sex with."

"Okay," said Martin, nodding and looking away.

Erin looked into her lap again.

"And you're definitely pregnant?" said Martin.

"Yes. I went to the doctor."

"Okay..." said Martin. "And so...if that's true...what were you thinking you wanted to do?"

"Well, that's the thing.... First, before I did anything, I wanted to tell you. And discuss it with you. Like, what are your thoughts?"

"My *thoughts*...?" said Martin. He almost laughed. Then, when he tried to express his thoughts, he found he didn't have any.

"I know," said Erin. "It's super weird."

"It is," said Martin. "It's super weird."

"I've been crying a lot," said Erin. "I don't usually do that."

"No, you don't...."

"Not because I'm sad," she explained. "More like...I guess, lots of strange things happen when you're pregnant. That's what my sister says."

"So your sister knows you're pregnant?"

She nodded.

"No wonder she was so nice," said Martin.

"I'm sorry to dump this on you. I didn't know how else...."

"No, no, that's all right. Don't worry about that."

The two of them sat there. Martin found his mind had scrambled. He couldn't organize anything in his brain. He again looked at the carpet and the same spot on the bookshelf.

"And so what are you proposing?" he said.

"I'm not proposing anything. I just want you to know. And for us to think about it. Or whatever."

"Okay."

"So yeah," said Erin. "That's it."

"So you're just putting it out there," said Martin.

Erin nodded that she was.

"Okay…" said Martin. "Well, first of all, on my end, I might need a little time to process this."

"Yes. Yes, of course. Absolutely," Erin said, nodding. "Do you have any questions?"

"Questions?" Martin repeated. "Not that I can think of… not right at the moment."

"I know we've never talked about anything like this," said Erin.

"Maybe we should have."

"We can talk now," she said.

"I don't know that I can do that," said Martin. "I think I might need to just…let it sink in first."

"Sure. Yeah. Let it sink in. Take some time. But it can't be too long. Because…you know…."

"Yes, of course," said Martin.

"I'm glad you're not…I'm glad we agree."

"Me too," said Martin. "It's good we agree. We'll think about it. Have you thought about it?"

"I have been thinking about it," said Erin. "I wasn't sure at first if I was pregnant. But once I knew for sure, then I started thinking about it."

"Okay, and now I'll think about it too," said Martin.

They both nodded, without looking at each other.

"And just so I know," said Martin. "You're like...you're open to different options...? In terms of...?"

Erin thought for a moment. "Yes. I would say that. I haven't made any definite decisions. That's why I wanted to check in with you."

"Right," said Martin.

"And you?" asked Erin. "Are you open to...different possibilities?"

Martin nodded. "Yeah. I guess so. I mean, I'll just need a little time, is all. I'm sorry if that sounds...."

"No. Not at all. I want you to think about it."

"Yes, yes. I will."

"And then we'll talk. Maybe in a couple days?"

"A couple days," said Martin. He nodded more. "Yes. A couple days. That sounds like a good plan. Let's do that."

"Okay then," said Erin. They both stood up. They smiled awkwardly at each other. Then Martin followed Erin back downstairs.

43

"SERIOUSLY," SAID ROB. "When you think about it, why else are we here? This is why we exist. To bang out some kids. I mean, what else are you gonna do with your life that makes any difference?"

Martin sipped his beer.

They were at the Arena Bar, watching an NBA game. It was the Sunday after Thanksgiving. Rob had just spent his first night back in his house, sequestered and isolated in the basement, but still within the walls of his home. He was extremely relieved and very happy.

Martin was also in a good mood. But his was more of a gallows cheerfulness. His life was focusing down to a single irrevocable point, and he was giddy with the weight of it. At noon the next day he was having lunch with Erin.

"Yeah, but everyone in the manosphere tells you not to get married," said Martin.

"Who says you gotta get married?"

"Well, *you* got married."

"Personally," said Rob, "I never listened to the manosphere that much. The important thing about that stuff is to break you out of your bubble thinking. Plenty of people in the manosphere get married. And have kids. *Middle Aged Dad*. You still read him?"

"Every day."

"So what does he say?"

"He likes being married. And having kids."

"And anyway, why not get married?" said Rob. "You got the cash. What do you care?"

"And she does work at a bank," reasoned Martin.

"That's right. She works at a bank."

"And her family..." mused Martin. "I wasn't sure at first. But her sister's married to a smart guy. He's doing pretty well."

"That's a good sign. Family stability."

"I just didn't think it would happen like this."

"Yeah, well, nature doesn't give a shit about you. Nature just wants more babies. The sex is good, right?"

"Yeah," said Martin, staring at the TV. "Unusually so."

"So there you go. There's something special there...."

"But maybe it's just an act," said Martin. "She's getting desperate and I'm an easy mark."

"Could be. It happens."

"She's thirty-four," said Martin. "She's hitting the wall."

"Yup. Hitting the wall."

"But then, so am I."

"Yup," said Rob. "You're getting older too."

Martin sipped his beer. On the TV, a Captain Obvious spot ran. He couldn't hear the sound, but the ad was effective nonetheless. Hotels.com, a nothing website driven deep into the American consciousness by a dorky dude in an oversized captain's uniform. Martin bit into a stale pretzel. "Do women ever really love you?" he asked Rob, as he chewed.

"Who knows? It seems like they do. They try to. But they love the kids. There's no question about that. They definitely love the kids."

"They love the kids more than they love you," said Martin.

"Yeah, probably. But what are you going to do? It's the natural order. You love the mom, the mom loves the kids, and everyone's more or less happy. Also, you keep the cave fully stocked."

Martin's eyes absorbed the light of the multiple televisions. "Jesus," he murmured. "How are you supposed to make a decision like this? This is the rest of my life."

"Yeah," said Rob. "It's almost better when you're forced into it."

"I kinda am being forced into it."

"Nah, this isn't a force. I've seen a force. This is pretty non-forced."

"My whole life will be different."

"How do you like your life now?"

"It's not bad," said Martin. He thought for a moment. "I'm basically a gay man. Just me, no dependents, lots of disposable income. Look at these shoes." He stuck out one foot to reveal flashy new sneakers. "A hundred and forty bucks."

"Well, you won't be buying shit like that anymore."

"I guess not," said Martin, looking down at his shoe.

"Yeah," said Rob, grinning. "Get a dog, get a cat...."

"No more trips..." said Martin.

Rob looked at him. "Really? You go on a lot of trips?"

"No," said Martin.

They both watched the TV. One of the NBA players was shooting free throws.

"So if we actually go through with this," Martin said, "what does she do about her job?"

"Whattaya mean?"

"Like she has the kid, and then what? Does she still work at the bank?"

"They have laws for that," said Rob. "She'll still get paid. She'll get maternity leave. They got that stuff all figured out. It's a good deal actually."

"And then when she goes back to work...do I take over with the kid?"

"You can if you want. But she might want to stay home for a year or two. That's probably the best way. Sadie didn't want to stay home at first. But that changed pretty quick."

"Yeah, but you could afford it."

"I couldn't afford it then!" said Rob. "I had to hustle my ass. Nobody can afford kids, if they think about it. That's why you don't think about it. I didn't know what was gonna happen. I figured, I got a good woman here...might as well take my shot...." Rob swallowed. He might have teared up for a minute. He took a swig of beer. Martin averted his eyes. He stared at the pretzels on the bar and then ate one of them.

"You like it though, overall?"

"I'd say I like, it, yes," said Rob. "Overall...."

the red pill

It got to be eleven. Martin had nursed two beers and didn't want to have another. He wanted to keep his head clear for his lunch with Erin tomorrow.

Martin had thought they might be at the bar for hours. Hashing things out. Weighing the pros and cons. But after half a basketball game there seemed nothing left to say, and they paid their bill. Martin followed Rob out to the parking lot. The two of them walked to Rob's oversized pickup. Martin watched as Rob climbed in, shut the door, and lowered his window in the dark.

"Hope that helped in some way," said Rob.

"Yeah, thanks."

"Good luck tomorrow."

"I'll let you know how it goes."

Rob started his engine and drove away. Martin walked to his Audi. He got in and sat for a moment, in the mostly empty parking lot. The night was cold, and the thick northern cloud cover was having its usual smothering effect. No stars, no sky, total darkness. He started his car and was reassured by the lights of the dashboard and the sound of the heater coming on. He looked up into the rearview mirror. "Do women ever really love you?" he murmured silently to himself. Then he shifted into reverse and backed out of his spot. It appeared he was going to find out.

about the author

Blake Nelson is the author of many acclaimed novels for both adults and young adults. His works include the classic coming-of-age novel *Girl* and the young adult thriller *Paranoid Park*, which was later made into an award-winning film by Gus Van Sant.